I think your debut novel is as good as some of the big name writers that are available today. I like that all the characters and their personalities are well written. Have you thought about who should play them in the movie? The plot moved along and you didn't over describe details. Some authors wear you out with the descriptions. It was nice how you wrapped it up.

Sue A.

This book wakes you up to the fact that we have Terrorist in our own country living among us. Scary, but thrilling. Reading this book will open your eyes.

Linda M.

I had one MAJOR problem with your book; I didn't want to stop reading even to make something to eat! It's very good, compelling and with an excellent juxtaposition of the exciting and mundane.

Lynn

I am really impressed with your creativity and imagination. You made a ride to the bar exciting.

Freddy

DEADLY PLANS

By
Rob Davis

Evershine Press, Inc.

Published by Evershine Press, Inc.
1971 W Lumsden Rd #209
Brandon, FL 33511

ISBN 978-0-9975108-0-5
eBook ISBN 978-0-9975108-1-2

First Edition:
First Mass Market edition:

Printed in the United States of America

Dedication

Deadly Plans is dedicated to my understanding wife, some dear friends, the Tampa Bay Business Owners organization, and especially my publisher and editor. Without help and inspiration from all of them, I could not have expressed any of the God given talent I have for writing. Thank you!

Chapter One

At a remote location in Afghanistan, Almir Najya meets with his father Armo to discuss an email he received from one of his comrades. Almir and his father both received higher education schooling in the United States and learned to speak fluent English during that time.

"I have seen a video of how efficient this bomb is." Almir says. "We need this weapon in our plans. It covers only a small area, but does so very effectively. I will order one hundred and distribute to our allies."

"I trust you will make it clear what will happen to him if our weapons are not received."

"Yes father. I will."

Rising from his chair and closing his office door, Mark Goodman the CEO of Silvan Enterprises in Fort Lauderdale Florida, takes a deep breath before sitting down at his desk. Opening the email from Almir Najya with the subject line 'Order', he reads the following:

'We order one hundred of your chemical bombs. One million dollars will be wired into your Bahamas account within 24 hours of receiving routing information. The remainder will be wired upon delivery.

Address the order to Alan Young, care of Heathrow Airport, London, England. Someone with that identity will receive it.

We expect our order to ship within 72 hours and for you to confirm the arrival date at Heathrow with an email message upon shipping. We will send Mr. Young to retrieve our package quickly.

If you fail to deliver our order as contracted, death will follow!

The last line of this email makes Mark's heart skip a beat. His mind begins racing with thoughts. *There's no turning back now.* Hesitating for a moment, he dials a number and a voice answers two rings later.

"Yes?"

"This is Mark."

"Did you receive an order?"

"Yes, from Mister Almir Najya. I just read the email. The order has to ship in 3 days to someone named Alan Young, care of the Heathrow Airport in London. I'll have them wire the money to our account at the Bahamas National Bank. You have the account information, can you verify the funds?"

"I'll check on it. Mark, you understand that nothing can go wrong. It is too late to back out now. I hope your people don't screw this up. Your neck is the one on the line here, and these people are not forgiving. We must deliver the product to them. Are you sure you can handle things from Fort Lauderdale without going to Jamaica again?"

"I have a man there I trust completely to watch over everything. There will be no screw-ups. Only a few key people on my staff know parts of what we're doing and they can all be trusted. Most of the people in the Jamaica plant only work on pieces and don't know how everything will go together. Only a small assembly team has any inkling, but even they don't really know anything with the cover story I planted; besides all they care about is that we're paying them very well. We're paying a bonus so to speak, above their usual wages."

"Just make sure this goes without a hitch. Keep me informed. Let me know as soon as the order is ready for shipment. Have you checked your office for bugs?"

"Yes, it was done two days ago. Do you think I should

have everything checked here, again?"

"Yes, immediately."

"Okay, I will." Hanging up, Mark closes his eyes and says a silent prayer.

Wednesday evening Max Merchado makes his usual call from Fort Lauderdale, Florida to his best friend Sam Stormen.

"Hey Sam, how are things in chilly Denver, Colorado? Is anything new going on this week?"

"Nah, just the same ole same ole. How has your week been Max?"

"Great! It looks like I'm on target to be salesman of the month again for Silvan Enterprises."

"Again! Are you going to give anyone else a chance?"

"Yeah, I know what you mean... hehe

"How's Peggy doing?"

"She's great as always. It's been over a month now since I've played a prank on her though. I was thinking maybe it's time for another one."

"Oh no Max! Almost all your pranks on her get you in trouble."

"I know, but she's fun to watch when I pull pranks on her. The problem is I never know how she'll take it, sometimes she thinks it's funny too, then other times she gets mad, and sometimes she gets really angry and leaves me for a while. I just never know until I prank her how she'll take it."

"What are you planning this time?"

"Well, I was thinking since she does her laundry on Thursday mornings I can get her then. It was funny the other day when a bird flew at her and scared her. I'm thinking about taking that rubber chicken I have and put it on the fan blades in the laundry room. Then when she turns on the light, the fan comes on and the chicken will go flying. What do you think?

"I think you should be nice and stop doing pranks on her. It seems like she is getting tired of being the target of your antics Max."

"I don't know. Maybe, I just like having fun with her."

"I think that's the problem Max. I don't think it's fun for her always being the one you pick on."

"Maybe you're right. I think I'll do this one and then quit and find someone else to prank. Maybe I can get someone at work. It's always more fun when you're here instead of across country. Maybe I'm bored these days, but I'm still King of the Pranks."

"Okay Max, just don't be surprised when I tell you I told you so. Peggy is a great girl and loves you a lot, but I know she's getting tired of the pranks."

"I love her too. I don't know how I got a knockout like her."

"She is a keeper Max. I wish I had a relationship like that. Things have been tense here with Jessica."

"I'm sorry buddy, I hope you can work things out.

"I've tried Max. You know what a fiery redhead she can be. One-minute things are good, and then they aren't. It's difficult trying to talk to her once her feathers are ruffled. Lately, they seem to be ruffled a lot. It almost makes me wonder if I really want to stay here, I mean..."

"Why, what do you mean? I thought you loved it there. You jumped at the job a couple years ago because you wanted to live in the mountains, and then you met Jessica and it seemed like love at first sight."

"I meant to say I'm not sure whether to stay with her. Anyway, that was then. I still love the area, but my job isn't very exciting. I think the best thing about being here is that I really enjoy the exercise I get. These mountains are great for hiking and walking. I can do so many outdoor activities here. I've also been doing really well with my Judo. My reflexes have improved greatly. I never realized what good exercise Judo can be. You know I'm working towards my brown belt?"

"That's great Sam. You must really enjoy the Judo lessons then. I'm sorry you're not happy with your job or your relationship with Jessica. Pity, with the picture you sent me of her, I could see she is pretty hot! Just don't tell Peggy I said that."

"Ha-ha. Don't worry Max, your secret is safe with me. You're right though, Jessica is pretty hot. With her flaming red hair and a voluptuous body, she takes my breath away. Then I notice those beautiful dark eyes of hers and I can almost get lost in them forever."

"I hope you can work things out soon. Do you have any idea of what the problem is?

No, not really. With her classes at the U, she needs a lot of time to study. She also spends time with her mother. By the time we get together, I never know what has her upset, me or something else."

"That's too bad Sam. I wish there was something I could do for you man."

"That's okay Max. Well I need to get going here. I guess I'll talk to you next Wednesday. Try to think about not doing any more pranks on Peggy. If you do decide to do it, don't forget to let me know what happens."

Okay, I'll talk to you next week. Take care Sam. Goodbye."

Two days later, Max Merchado begins his Friday morning in late March driving along Davie Boulevard in Fort Lauderdale. His bright red Corvette shines from recent detailing. Looking at his slim Jaeger-LeCoultre watch, he notes it's a quarter to nine. Ever since he saw the expensive watch on a successful acquaintance, he's wanted to have one for himself. His success at Silvan Enterprises allows him to afford this luxury.

With the top down on his Corvette, his black hair waves slightly from the moist air flowing over the windshield. Arriving at Silvan Enterprises, he whips into his reserved parking space. While putting the top up he thinks about his Wednesday night phone call to his best friend Sam Stormen and the prank he did to Peggy. Max and Sam chat virtually every Wednesday, ever since Sam moved away to Colorado for a new job when they graduated from Technical School.

Walking under the canopy at the rear of the building, Max feels a twinge of guilt come over him. Deep down he knew Peggy would be upset by his prank but he did it anyhow. He still smiles a little remembering the prank. He watched Peggy carry her basket of clothes into the laundry room and turn on the light. He saw the fan begin to spin and the chicken plop down on her face. Screaming, she dropped the basket and ran out of the room. Peggy left an hour later taking her laundry with her to stay with her mother in Boca Raton. Peggy once again failed to see the humor in his antics.

"She'll come back." Max whispers to himself flashing his ID to the guard. "She always comes back. That's why I love her." He waves as Jack Glenn approaches him.

"Did you close that Cosmos account yet?"

"As good as done, Jack." Max says giving a thumb's up sign.

"Nice suit, Max." Jack says looking at Max's dark gray pinstriped suit.

"It's my lucky closing suit. How are your prospects doing?"

"I've got a couple hot ones. I'm going to beat you in sales this year!"

"I doubt it, but good luck Jack!"

In his office, the prepared sales contracts for Cosmos Industries for the purchase of five new helicopters are on Max's desk. It's near the end of the month, and Max knows that no other sales people have turned in a meaningful contract. Max makes it a habit to flirt with Beth the financial secretary every chance he gets and she keeps him up to date on who sold what.

Next to the contracts for his meeting sits the Friday copy of the Silvan newsletter, the US version. Thumbing through the pages, he sees a posting for an electronics technician job coming available next month due to a retirement. Max remembers Sam is no longer thrilled with the mountains.

"Great! I think Sam will be happy back here in Lauderdale." Max says to himself. Picking up the phone, he dials Sam to ask him to apply for the job and speaks as soon as Sam answers his phone.

"Hey Sam, what's up man?"

"Hey there Max. How are you doing?"

"Doing great. A little hectic. I played the prank I told you about Wednesday on Peggy."

"I'm sure you did." Sam says laughing. "Is she still speaking to you?"

"That would be a no. She packed her things and left for Boca again. She is really mad this time. You're right; I need to consider not pranking her anymore."

"I'm sorry Max. I hope you two get back on track soon."

"Are things better with Jessica?

"Not much. Jessica has been spending a lot of time at

the library studying lately, and when we do get together, we seem to argue a lot. You know how red heads are, but she's cute. Why are you calling me on a Friday morning?"

"I'm sorry about Jessica Sam. Hey, I'm calling you because there's a job opening coming up for an electronics technician here at Silvan Enterprises next month. You should email Mark your résumé. I can speak to him about hiring you for the position, but HR has strict requirements and will need the résumé for their files when Mark gives you the job."

"Okay, Max, I'll send it even though I'm not sure I'm ready to leave Denver right now. I have a perfectly good job here and I have a lovely but volatile girlfriend. My life is very interesting. Seriously though, I need to try to work things out with Jessica, Max. I'm planning to have a picnic with her tomorrow so we can see where we stand and I can decide whether I really want to stay with her."

"You know you want to come back here, Sam. Please send your résumé to Mark ASAP, before someone else gets the job."

"You're not breaking our pact to not prank each other are you?" Sam asks knowing Max has a wild imagination at times. This could be something Max just dreamed up.

"No way! This isn't a joke, Sam."

"Okay Max, I had to ask. This is crazy; I just updated my résumé this week. The workload here has dropped drastically. Text me his email address and I'll send it right away!"

"Great! I'll let Mark know to look for it. You'll be a shoe-in my man!"

"We'll see. I do kind of miss the old town." Sam didn't say it, but he misses his friend Max too.

"Really, it's as good as done. He might not get back to you until Monday, but I know he'll hire you once he can look at your résumé and he has my recommendation."

"Whoa! Pretty sure of yourself there Max."

"Hey, number one salesman for the last two years! Mark wants to keep me happy." Max says bragging a little.

"Okay, Max. We'll see what happens."

"Great! Well I have to go; I have to meet a client for lunch soon. Let's get this done!"

"Right, I'll talk to you later."

"Enjoy the journey!" Max is hardly able to contain his elation. He misses his friend and is sure Mark will give the job to Sam.

Max still has time to scan through the Jamaican newsletter before preparing for his lunch date with Manny Cosmos.

Last year Silvan Enterprises acquired a Jamaican company that manufactures batteries of various sizes and small electronics. Max spent a month in Kingston checking out the sales personnel, observing the operation, reviewing sales techniques, and doing some sales training for his boss, CEO Mark Goodman. Max loved his time in Jamaica, the people he worked with, and especially his new friend Byron. He looks forward to returning to Jamaica soon. Ever since then, he's made an effort to read the Jamaica version of the newsletter every Friday via the internet.

Logging on to the Jamaican newsletter's website and scanning the newsletter, something catches his eye, an article titled the 'Orange Puff Cloud'. *What a silly* title? Max thinks and reads more. The article states: *The Jamaica plant will be producing a new deadly chemical bomb in addition to their normal productions. Silvan Enterprises will be using a massive amount of the orange toxic waste sludge that Jamaica has trouble disposing of from the aluminum industry in Jamaica.*

"A chemical bomb!" Max screams, shouting to no one. *I*

have to talk to Mark about this! Max storms out of his office and hustles to see Mark, as his anger grows. Blinded by rage he is boiling when he stomps into Mark's office. Max's face is flush and he fails to wait for Mark to acknowledge his presence before he starts yelling because he is so mad. "This is outrageous!" Max says startling his boss.

"What are you talking about Max?" Mark says jumping up quickly from behind his desk.

"This Jamaica thing! How could you! Are we really making chemical weapons?"

Chapter Two

"Oh! That." Mark says shrugging his shoulders. "It's nothing, Max. Umm, our financials have been weak lately. We have to do things we don't want to in order to keep the company alive." Mark knows Max is his best salesman, and tends to tolerate more from Max than from most of his employees.

Flapping his hands as if it helps him think, Max yells, "That doesn't make any sense, not with all the sales I bring in! Even if that's the case, and we need to expand our product lines, why should that include making chemical weapons? There's a reason we don't make them here, right?" Max knows the US will never allow them to produce this kind of weapon in the states.

"We have to do something Max, and this is a no-brainer."

"Then you approve of this!"

"We have orders for the product and it's very profitable. This is just to get us over this financial problem Max, and it's in Jamaica, not in the US. We have to cover a lot of extra expenses from last year with the acquisition of the Jamaica Company. The stockholders want us to show more profit. The chemical bomb is almost as easy to produce as the batteries. This will also use up a lot of that bauxite sludge Jamaica wants to get rid of. We help our bottom line, and we help the Jamaican government. They are actually paying us to take some of that orange stuff off their hands so it's a win, win. This will greatly help our bottom line, Max."

"A win, win! How in the world can producing chemical weapons that kill people be a win by any means! I don't approve of this! Our customers for these products will be terrorists, not governments! And what about all of our government contracts? What's going to happen when it comes out we're making weapons of mass destruction that can be used against our soldiers? We have never made products that start wars or kill indiscriminately! We shouldn't base everything on our bottom line! We need to find another way!" Max pauses for a moment but Mark says nothing.

"I have more to say on this, but I can't right now! I have to meet Mister Cosmos for lunch. He's ordering five helicopters. I've got to go, but when I get back with the signed contracts, I'm coming back here and we'll sit down and figure out another option."

"No Max, it's done! The first shipment has already been produced! It'll ship on Monday."

"You can always scrap it!"

"No! I can't Max! Besides this topic is not open to discussion so like it or not, it's happening; now please go and get to your appointment!"

"I'll be back later!" Max shouts turning around storming out of Mark's office.

Watching Max stomp out of his office Mark sits down at his desk stunned. *Max never should have found the article about the chemical weapon in the Jamaican newsletter. How in the world did this happen? Thank God, he hasn't seen the video.*

Picking up the phone, Mark dials in a panic. "Max was just here. He knows about the article in the Jamaican newsletter. He was here screaming about how we can't do this. I threw him out of my office. I can't guarantee he won't cause a problem. (pause...) Okay, I'll be right over."

Walking to his office Max is still fuming from his failed attempt at reason with Mark. Sitting at his desk, he takes several deep breaths to calm his emotions. He can't believe the way Mark spoke to him and dismissed his concerns so nonchalantly. *I know I can get through to him. This isn't like Mark. I can't understand why he is being so unreasonable. This can't be about the company's bottom line, which means there's more to it. I need to get him to tell me what it is. Oh no, what if Manny or my other clients get wind of this, I can lose a lot of my contracts.* This revelation causes Max to take another deep breath to calm down.

Sitting quietly with his eyes closed trying to focus on his breathing, his meditation has worked and Max is finally feeling a little better. He decides he can fix this later with Mark and gets back to business by picking up the phone and calling Manny Cosmos. Breathing deeply, it still takes everything in him to force himself to be cheery and positive when a secretary answers the phone.

"Good morning, Mr. Cosmos' office, how can I help you?"

"Hello Donna, this is Max Merchado. Is Mister Cosmos in?"

"Oh, hello Max. Just a moment, I'll get him for you." She says flirtingly. She'd never be so familiar, except that Max always flirts with her as part of his game. He knows that by getting the secretaries to like him and on his side, his life becomes much easier. It helps that he genuinely likes people so his manner doesn't feel like an act. He does this with nearly everyone.

"Hello, Max." Manny says coming on the line. "We're scheduled for lunch at one o'clock at Steak 954 by the beach, no?"

"Yes, Mister Cosmos. I'll pick you up about fifteen minutes before. I have the contracts all prepared for you. We can sign them over lunch."

"Good deal, Max. I will see you then."

"Thank you." Max says ringing off.

Leaning back in his chair, Max tries not to think about the Jamaica situation. He must remain calm for his meeting with Manny, and convinces himself he can get Mark to listen to reason later.

Retrieving a box of Godiva chocolates from his desk drawer, he leaves his office. On his way out of Silvan Enterprises, he barely notices each hallway's different brightly colored walls, denoting he is nearing the exit. The cheery feeling of the building with all of the brightly colored hallways helps him get into a good mood.

Sliding into the seat of his car, he places the attaché and chocolates on the passenger side. Turning the key in the ignition the car roars to life. Seeing no signs of rain in the blue sky, he puts the top down again. The sun and fresh air work to improve his mood as he drives to Cosmos Industries.

Max enters Manny's building walking to the receptionist desk. "Hello again Donna." He says slipping her the box of chocolate.

"Thank you Max, you shouldn't have." Smiling she stuffs the box into a desk drawer. "I'll let Mister Cosmos know you're here."

Max shyly sits on the corner of her desk while waiting for Manny to come out. "So what are your plans for the weekend Donna?"

"Oh not much, how about you Max? Are you and Peggy planning anything interesting?"

"Always Donna, and as soon as the little woman fills me in on what that is, I'll let you know?"

"Oh Max, you are too much."

Max stands as a side door opens and Manny enters the waiting area.

"Max you devil, are you buttering up my secretary again?"

"Only a little Manny, only a little" Max turns his head and winks at Donna. Manny believes Max is his usual jovial self.

"Well let's go so you can buy me lunch, because I'm afraid if we stay here much longer, you'll be feeding Donna instead of me."

"Never!" Max says indignantly. "I'm feeding Donna for dinner later." Max smiles big causing everyone to do the same. This routine plays out every time Max comes to Manny's office.

"That about raps it up. As soon as you have the shipment ready to go, we'll get things rolling on our end."

"You're sure Silvan's name will be kept out of the press?" Mark asks his government contact.

"I can't promise that. That will depend on several factors beyond our control."

"What do you mean, 'things beyond your control'? That's not what we discussed."

"Calm down Mark. We won't leave you or your company hanging. It's just that we can't control how England handles the situation on their end, and then there's the press. However it plays out, we will do whatever we need to so Silvan's reputation won't be harmed."

"I hope so. I think that's what freaked me out the most when Max flipped out. We could lose a lot of customers and government contracts."

"Your contracts and business will be fine. Silvan doesn't produce products for the open market. Only governments or qualified suppliers can order the military equipment you make. There aren't many places to buy equipment like that. True, bad press wouldn't be good, but it won't hurt your sales. We are monitoring things closely and can redirect any unwanted press that may result."

"Yeah, you're right. Max finding out freaked me out. I really believed this whole thing would happen unnoticed. I was more worried about the safety factors of these groups having my contact info that I didn't think about our customers. I was more worried about terrorists coming after me or the company."

"Yes, that should be your main concern. We promised to protect you and the company through this however; you still have to be careful. I am still not pleased that the article in the newsletter was found so easily. You should be grateful Max came to you instead of going to the press or something."

"Oh my God, it never occurred to me that Max would do anything like that. Maybe I shouldn't have dismissed him the way I did. How do you suggest I handle him so we can get him on board? He is so patriotic, there's no telling what he might do."

"This is just great, of all the people to learn of this now! Okay, tell me more about him and let's come up with a plan to deal with him before he can go off halfcocked."

"Well Max, I guess it's time to think about heading out."

"Really? What time is it?"

"It's nearly three Max. I'd love to stay for a few more drinks but then I can't have Donna leaving for the day just as I get back from lunch. It doesn't look good." Manny says winking.

"I guess you're right Manny. You have a reputation to uphold. Whereas me..."

Laughing Manny has a hard time containing himself because Max is always poking some sort of fun. "Max you

are a funny guy." He says getting up to leave the restaurant.

"We thank you for the order, Manny." Max says as he
and Manny Cosmos wait for the valet to bring the car.

"Your copters have the best specifications of all the ones
we looked at." Manny replies.

"Yes, they are state-of-the-art units."

Max feels good about the afternoon. Now he just needs his
luck to hold trying to get this situation resolved with Mark
after he drops off Manny and gets back to the office.

As Manny gets out of the Corvette, Max waves goodbye.

"I love your car, Max. Thanks for lunch."

"It was my pleasure my friend. Call me if there is anything else I can do for you... anything at all."

"Thank you, Max. I will call if we need anything."

Driving back to the office, Max decides to leave the top
up on his Vet. The afternoon sky looks dark with clouds
and before long, the sky bursts forth with a torrent of rain
and lightning as expected. "Glad I left the top up."

The change in weather causes a slight change in Max's
mood making him think about his life at Silvan Enterprises. Aside from this issue with Mark, he is extremely
happy with his job. He makes a small fortune selling helicopters and other related equipment. His job is a whirlwind
for him. He doesn't quite understand why he is so successful but he enjoys every minute of it.

"Life is good!" Max says aloud pulling into his reserved
parking spot remembering it was nearly a year ago, that
Mark gave him the coveted spot. Max loves his reserved
covered parking spot near the rear entrance of the building.
He feels honored to have it. He smiles grabbing his attaché
and locking his car. He likes that he is able go from his car
into the building without getting a drop of rain on him. The

reserved parking spaces are only for the top executives and the top two salespersons. With Max being part of that exclusive group, he feels more like an executive of the company than a salesman.

Inside the building, he heads directly to the financial section in order to register his sale and turn in the substantial deposit check Manny Cosmos gave him. He wants to get the ball rolling so the company can begin the production, and of course pay his commission. Stopping in front of the financial secretary's desk, he speaks in his sexiest voice.

"Hello, Miss Avery." He says looking down at her ample chest.

"Stop staring!" She says with a smile. "What *company* business can I handle for you today Mister Merchado?"

"It's just another signed order for you my dear." Smiling he looks into her face while he opens his attaché to retrieve the signed contract and deposit check.

"Not bad." Miss Avery remarks looking at the check.

Max bows to her and smiles before turning away. With all the paperwork properly filed and noted, Max rushes back towards Mark's office instead of staying to flirt with the secretary. He is forming an outline in his mind of what to say to Mark.

Perhaps talking about the agony and disfigurement chemical weapons cause for the victims will help sway Mark. He knows Mark is a caring person based on the many company donations he makes to charities, especially those involving kids; he's also portrayed a highly developed sense of patriotism. Max is determined to convince Mark to stop any production of a deadly chemical weapon. He has to give it one last shot even though Mark says he will not discuss it further.

Max enters Mark's office heavily engrossed in his

thoughts and walks all the way to the desk before realizing Mark is gone. He mutters words under his breath and walks around Mark's desk to leave him a note. Before he starts to write a note, something catches his eye. Looking down a small silver thumb drive is lying on the floor under the edge of Mark's desk. *Mark probably knocked it off his desk or dropped it, maybe when I startled him this morning.*

Reaching down and picking up the disc, Max starts to place it on Mark's desk, but stops. There are three black X's written on each side of the thumb drive. Triple X means pornography to Max. *Why does Mark have pornography in his office? I can't just leave such an item on the desk in the open where anyone can happen to see it. That's not a good idea. I don't want to open a desk drawer to stash it. Someone might see me in Mark's desk and get the wrong impression.* For a moment, Max doesn't know what to do with the drive. *I'll be back later to see Mark so I'll just give it to him then.* He decides dropping the drive in his pocket on his way out and walking back to his own office.

Slipping into his office, he has missed calls because the light on his phone is blinking. Pressing the play button, he listens to them. The only one of immediate interest is from Peggy.

"Hi Max, I'm staying at mom's. I still have a pink spot on my face near my eye where that rubber chicken hit me. I'm going to be here a few days. After all, mom's place is almost as close to my job as yours is. I also want to spend some time with mom. She says I can stay here forever. Are you sorry for what you did? I'm not coming back until you promise you will stop playing your little pranks on me. Do you hear me Max? Call me when you think you can behave yourself. Do you miss me yet?" End of message.

Of course, I miss you. He can tell from her voice that she misses him too. He sighs as he erases her message. *Take care of business.*

"Hello Joy, this is Max Merchado calling. May I speak with Mister Bracken?"

"Hello, Max. I'll buzz him now."

The afternoon goes by swiftly having returned so late from lunch. It's late in the day when Max prepares to check back with Mark. Just as he starts to leave his office, his phone rings.

"Max, Manny here. We used the wrong image for the logos. Our publicity department said we also have to change the wording for the print under the logo. Can we make the changes now?"

"Of course. Give me the details and I will take care of it."

"Wonderful, I can email most of the information to you, but here's what we want..."

Writing down the changes needed, Max knows it's necessary to send the changes in as soon as possible to prevent delays. By the time Max finishes, it's well after five o'clock and too late to be able to see Mark as he'll be gone by now. *Maybe I'll give him a call at home later. If I can get him to have drinks with me, I might be able to get him to listen. Yes, I think that'll work. He won't be expecting me to continue our conversation. At least, not at first.* Max starts for home.

Heading home to his cozy frame house Max is happy the rain is ending. Approaching his house on Clifton Street, he sees his empty carport. "She'll come back. She always comes back."

In spite of his wealth, Max chooses to live in an older wood frame house in a well-established section of South Fort Lauderdale. He likes the nine-foot high ceilings and the comfortable feeling of a big house. A few years ago, he bought the repossessed house cheap. It was in need of a lot of repairs including a new roof, termite treating, adding central air, plumbing and wiring needs and restoring the beautiful wood floors. He spent a ton of money, but now it suits him perfectly. Max could easily afford a nice condo or a mansion on the water, but that isn't who he is. This older refurbished house feels like home to him. They don't build houses like these anymore and he considers himself lucky to have been able to acquire this house.

Pulling into his three-stall carport, he feels lonely since Peggy's pink truck isn't here. Max always enjoys spending weekends with his girlfriend. Knowing he will be alone this weekend, he tries not to feel lonely, but to no avail.

Getting out of his car and walking to the side door, he presses the code into the keypad on the door and walks inside upon hearing the click signifying it unlocked. In the kitchen, he retrieves a bottle of Michelob from the refrigerator and after twisting the cap off takes a large slurp of beer. Walking to the living room, he reaches for the remote and clicks on the big screen TV, flipping the channel to his favorite news station. A woman is talking about the weather as he takes off his tie before walking into his bedroom and taking off his suit jacket. He feels an unfamiliar weight in the right coat pocket. "What the..." He says reaching in and finding the thumb drive he took from Mark's office.

"Good grief, I completely forgot about this." He mumbles aloud. Staring at the small drive for a moment it bothers him that his boss would bring pornography to work. *I'll have to ask him about this later when I call him for drinks. There's no reason for me to sit in an empty house anyway. Hmm, maybe I should give this little thing a glance since Peggy isn't here. Then I'll really rib him later for bring it to the office.*

Hitting the power on button on his laptop computer, he walks across the room to his closet and hangs up his jacket before going back to his desk. Sitting in his desk chair, he thinks, "I'm going to rib the heck out of the boss-man about this!" He chuckles.

It's probably best that Peggy isn't here. He plugs the thumb drive into the USB slot. *Let's look at this baby!*

Max picks a file at random to open since there are a lot of files and none have erotic names on them. "Oh my God!" he exclaims. "This is so much worse than porn!"

Chapter Three

Max doesn't expect what he finds looking at a list of terrorist groups with names, phone numbers and email addresses. He feels his world suddenly turning upside down.

"Holy cow!" Max gasps realizing his friend and boss Mark Goodman may be a traitor! Leaning back in his chair, blowing the wind out of his lungs he wonders what to do next.

Opening another file, a video starts playing graphically showing the killing power of a weapon called the Orange Cloud. Max watches the entire video in horror. A man with a cloth over his face explains how the cloud chemically reacts to whatever it touches killing it. He notices his hand trembles slightly as he opens another file.

Thinking this can't possibly get any worse, he finds an order for one hundred bombs from what looks like a known terrorist group. A chill runs up his spine. *Is this the order Mark said will ship on Monday?* He's always regarded Mark as a close friend and not just his boss. He considered Mark to be loyal American citizen, and a jovial person for a CEO, honest and upright. Now, he just doesn't know. What Max is seeing now isn't the man he's come to know. Max is having a difficult time trying to regain his composure. *That's it! I'm calling him now! He needs to explain himself!* Max's hand shakes dialing the phone.

"Hello Max." Mark says seeing the caller ID on his phone.

"Yes, Mark... I, I found this thumb drive on the floor of your office when I came back to talk to you. It has some really bad stuff ..."

Mark interrupts. "You, have what! Did you look at the files?"

"Yes. It's like… treasonous stuff. Is this your stuff?"

"Max, this is bigger than just Silvan Enterprises or me. No one is to know about this. People could get hurt. We'll be right over to get it and explain…"

"How can you…" Max starts saying, but suddenly ends the call as fear hits him. He can feel the hair on the back of his neck bristle up warning him he is in danger. *My boss is selling weapons to our enemies! Why didn't Mark say 'I,' will be right over? Why did he say 'we,' will be right over? What am I going to do now?*

Mark dials Max's phone immediately as he rushes to his car. It rings unanswered. He closes his eyes for a second shaking his head before starting his car heading for Max's house. As he drives, he dials his contact.

"I think we have a problem." Mark reluctantly says.

"This can't get screwed up, Mark. Is it with that fellow Max that you mentioned?"

"Yes, he has my disk and looked at the files. I'm worried; he suddenly hung up on me and now won't answer my calls. I didn't dare explain about the disk over my phone."

"How in the world did this happen? That disk should never be seen by anyone else! I thought you were going to talk to him like we discussed."

"I know, I was. He was gone by the time I got back to the office. I never imagined he would find my disk. I thought I'd call him tomorrow and we'd get together away from anyone overhearing."

"How did he find that disk? Why wasn't it with you?"

"I thought I had it. Max said he found it on the floor of my office. It must have fallen when I tried to put it in my pocket. Max came in shouting and startled me just at that moment. He must have come back to my office after I left and found the disk. I didn't know the disk was missing until he called me just now."

"Bah! That never should have happened! You must find Max and silence him! We cannot have anything go wrong. What are you doing to find him?"

"I'm on my way to his house now to talk to him and get him to understand."

"Will you be able to get through to him, or will he be a problem?"

"I'm not sure. He is extremely patriotic. It may be difficult to convince him. It may be best for you to send someone to his house just in case. They can meet me there."

"Fine! I'm sending a couple guys to make sure this is handled one way or the other."

Gulp. "Okay. I'll be in touch once we have Max."

Max's phone rings. According to the caller ID, it's Mark. He doesn't answer and hurriedly shuts down his laptop taking the thumb drive out. Pocketing the drive, he goes to his closet and digs out a travel bag. Max feels sweat forming on his body as he hastily stuffs his laptop and clothes into the bag.

"Mark can be here in ten minutes. I gotta get out of here!" Starting to panic, Max finishes packing and rushes out of the house.

Arriving at Max's house, Mark rushes to the door and starts pounding. "Max! Open up! It's Mark! Max! I need to talk to you! Come on Max, let me in!" *Damn, I hope he didn't run off. I don't need this right now!* Looking around, he notices Max's car is gone.

Ringing. "Did you talk to him?"

"No! He's gone! He ran off."

"Are you sure?"

"Well, he's not here and he saw the video so yeah I think he's scared and ran."

"You've got to find him! Do you hear me? We have a timetable to meet and can't afford problems now!"

"I know. I know. Your guys just got here. I hate to do it, but I need to break in and try to find that disk and see where he might have gone and I need to get in before his girlfriend gets home. I don't know how long we have before she gets back. I also need you to put a trace on his phone and his girlfriends' phone. We need to know who he might tell so we can contain this."

"Okay, but what else are you going to do?"

"I'm going to call Fred Holland, he's the police captain; he can issue an APB for Max as a possible robbery suspect. There are a couple things your resources can do to help, too."

"Alright, I want him found and fast!"

Roaring away from his house onto the Federal Highway, Max heads south. Spotting an ATM along the road he stops, withdrawing the maximum allowed. Stopping at another bank, he takes a cash withdrawal on his credit card. He's afraid he may need lots of cash before this problem is over. Continuing driving around aimlessly, his heart is beating heavily as he tries to decide what to do. Feeling sweat forming all over his body he turns the air conditioner on high.

Even more panic sets in remembering Mark has good friends on the Fort Lauderdale police force. *What if Mark calls Captain Holland to put out an APB on me?*

Seeing a Wal-Mart off to his right and the local BCT bus approaching the bus stop next to the store, Max comes up with a plan. Winding his way into the parking lot, he parks his Vet close to the bus stop. Grabbing his bag and hustling across the parking lot, he jumps onto the bus just before it begins pulling away from the curb. Paying the bus driver and staggering backwards, he chooses a seat near the rear door as the bus is rocking and moving forward.

Twenty other people are on the bus as best as Max can tell without drawing too much attention to himself. Cautiously looking around he's trying to see if he can recognize anyone. A moment later, his cell phone rings, causing him to jump up a little from his seat. The caller ID shows it's Mark calling again. As paranoia sets in it dawns on him, he can be tracked through his cell phone. Pressing the power off button, he removes the battery. Looking for he doesn't know what, Max keeps an eye out watching the people on the bus and the people outside the bus. He's trying to see if the bus is being followed, all the while watching buildings and signs floating by as he looks out the windows. Suddenly, a sleazy motel with a half-lit vacancy sign appears. Grabbing his bag and pulling the cord, he gets off. When the bus stops and the doors open, Max runs off.

Walking along the sidewalk a bit, he darts across the street when traffic permits and into the empty office of Griffin's Rooms Motel. An older man with ruffled gray hair comes from behind an employee only door when he rings the bell.

"I'd like a room." Max says.

"Twenty dollars a night."

Handing the man a twenty, Max waits while the man flips open a registration book and hands Max a pen. Max signs the book as "John Nott". The clerk frowns at the signature and shrugs his shoulders handing Max an old well-worn key.

"Number four." The clerk says pointing to his left.

Nodding to the man, Max takes the key and backs out of the office. Hustling along the walkway, looking for room number four, he finds a door with an upside down number four hanging on it. Cautiously opening the door and fumbling along the wall, he flips on a light switch. A single dim lamp comes on across the room on a dresser. Taking a moment to look around the room it proves to be empty except for a night table, a single bed, a TV set and the lamp on the dresser. Closing the door, he edges his way toward the bathroom to peek in. No one is there. Letting out a puff of air Max tries to relax.

No one will find me here. He thinks to himself flopping down on the bed. His normal world has been shattered. Closing his eyes trying to figure out what to do next consumes him. He looks at his Jaeger-LeCoultre watch. It's nearly nine o'clock at night. *I think it might be worth it to risk making one more call. If I'm lucky, I can get hold of Sam to come help me.* With a shaky hand, he dials.

The crisp air feels good on Sam Stormen's face as he walks out of Riff's Urban Fare café and into the Pearl Street Mall in Boulder, Colorado. The mall is less than ten minutes from his work in Denver and Sam likes the charm of the open-air mall, which he's never found anywhere else. The late spring temperature is down into the fifties now after dinner. It's a beautiful evening, cool but not cold. Looking around the open-air mall, Sam enjoys everything he sees. The sky has no clouds or haze as it begins turning into an incredibly beautiful dark blue. With a clear view of the mountains, he stretches his limbs before walking across the street. The pedestrian street is crowded with mostly tourists and students from the University of Colorado or CU-Boulder.

His girlfriend Jessica, a student at CU, is spending time with her mother this evening causing Sam to dine alone. Jessica is a typical redhead with flaming red hair however;

her eyes are her best asset. Sam knows those eyes some-times emit sparks and fire when she is mad. She doesn't live with Sam because of their strained relationship caus-ing him to think about breaking up with her often because of her temper tantrums.

Dining out isn't as much fun as it is when Jessica is with him. He never enjoys eating alone. When he has to dine alone like tonight, he usually starts conversations with people at surrounding tables. This evening he struck up a conversation with a young couple eating dinner at the table next to his.

As he ate, he heard a couple talk about a band, the Danglebatts who were playing a concert in town tonight. Sam once thought about playing in a band himself. He plays guitar and sings at a local jam session in his church's fellowship hall on Sunday nights. He likes performing old Country Western music. He once thought he might like to be a rock and roll star in a band. *After all, those guys get all the women they want, right? They travel all over the world and enjoy playing music they love. It seems like a rock star is living the dream.*

Sam believes he's stuck in Denver at a somewhat boring job although it pays fair, yet he thinks of himself as a slightly boring person anyway.

He only has one girlfriend because he can only handle one woman at a time. He just isn't the type of man to play the field although he sometimes wishes he were. Jessica is an exciting, yet challenging woman for Sam. She studies anthropology and Sam knows virtually nothing about an-thropology so he can't connect with her on that.

Thursday night she said she wanted to spend some time with her mother again on Friday night. Lately he feels like she seems to spend more time with her mother than she does with him.

Walking along he enjoys all of the goings on along the Pearl Street Mall. Although this is a great place to spend alone time, he has something to mull over in his brain for a while. His best friend Max mentioned a job opening that would require moving back to Fort Lauderdale, which means he has a decision to make.

Relaxing as he stops along the sidewalk here and there gives him an opportunity to watch the street performers. Many of the students from the University perform in the late afternoon in front of stores or on the grassy knolls of the mall. Some students do it just for fun; others solicit donations for their singing, dancing, or crazy outfits. Sam always gives a few dollars to some of the performers to help them with their expenses. It's cheap entertainment for him, and thousands of people each year. It's just a comfortable place to hang out. *Life is good!*

Being a guitarist himself, Sam stops to hear a guitarist play a song and watch the chords the man is playing on his guitar along with a few other listeners. He hears a riff he doesn't recognize while listening and wants to ask the man about it when the song is over.

Standing there peacefully, listening and enjoying the guitarist, his leisurely evening is interrupted by his cell phone. Stepping away from the music, he answers the call. According to the caller ID, it's his friend Max. Staring at his phone a moment, he finds it strange for Max to call him on a Friday evening. Especially so being he just talked to Max earlier in the day. Now Max is calling him for the second time today.

Hitting the connect button he starts to say hello. Max starts talking immediately before Sam can say a word. His voice sounds strained and a little shaky, very unusual for Max the confident one.

"Sam, is that you?"

"Yes. Max why are you…"

"Thank God! Listen, I need your help! You must come to Fort Lauderdale. I need to stop this abomination! It's wrong, just wrong! He's selling chemical weapons to our enemies! My boss is a traitor! No joke!" Max's voice trails off. He sounds like he's losing his composure. Just as Sam is about to ask what the problem is, Max continues. "You'll never get to the airport in time tonight, so please catch the first flight from Denver tomorrow! Bring your passport. I'll meet you at the airport if I can or I'll call you. I'm sure they're trying to locate my phone and it may be bugged! I have to ring off. No joke Sam. Please, please come help!"

Before Sam can say anything or ask about the sudden panic Max hangs up. Sam stands staring at his phone as if it will explain what just happened. The tone of Max's voice had been shaky. Max actually sounded scared.

Max disconnects his call and quickly shuts off his phone. Restlessly he checks the bedding and sheets for bedbugs as best he can in the dim light before plopping down to rest. A moment later, he gets up again, grabs the only flimsy chair and props it against the doorknob. He stretches out on the bed, closes his eyes, and tries thinking of a plan for tomorrow. "God help me!" He says to himself and tries to sleep. He knows he will have to be alert tomorrow.

"Have you heard anything yet?"

"No. We got into Max's house. The drive isn't here; he must have taken it with him."

"Any clues where he went?"

"No. We tore the place apart trying to find anything that would tell us where to look. Even his girlfriend hasn't come home yet. I wondered if she was with him, but there was a message on his answering machine stating she's at her mother's because of a fight they had. Did you get anything off the trace on his phone?"

"Yeah, he just called a number within the hour located in Denver, Colorado. We tried to get a trace on his location but he wasn't on long enough in order to triangulate the call. Do you have any idea who this person is in Denver he called?"

"Yes. His best friend lives there. He just emailed me his resume today. I need to call him. If I can talk to him I can probably get him to listen to reason."

"Okay, well if his phone becomes active again, I'll let you know."

Sam can't believe what Max just said as he stares at his phone. *Max actually sounds scared.*

Max is a happy-go-lucky person. Nothing ever seems to rattle him. Even that time at the County Fair when Max decided to try bungee jumping he wasn't remotely scared. It takes guts to bungee jump no matter how brave you are. Max is the one person who always takes risks fearlessly so this shakiness in his voice now worries me.

Dialing Max's phone back Sam wants to get some answers, but the call goes right to voice mail. Dialing two more times, the calls continue going directly to voicemail.

He wants me to fly to Fort Lauderdale on the spur of the moment because he thinks his boss is a traitor. I wonder if this is one of his pranks. We promised each other years ago that we would never pull pranks on each other. We have remained true to that pact ever since. If Max is breaking the rules now he is doing a good acting job. Standing in the mall for a while thinking, Sam realizes he has no choice, he has to fly to Fort Lauderdale.

Walking to his old Cherokee SUV parked at the end of the mall, his quiet evening has ended leaving him feeling sad. He really doesn't want to leave. It's an unusually active night so he has to push his way through the crowds to his SUV.

Walking away from the happy crowd, his focus switches to the reason he's cutting his evening short. *What's going on?* Clicking the key fob of his SUV, he hears the familiar chirp and the flashing lights indicate the alarm shut off. Getting into his SUV, his girlfriend Jessica also enters his thoughts. *Jess and I are supposed to meet for a lunch tomorrow. Now I have to cancel on her. I was really looking forward to seeing her so we could work out our issues and get back on track. Oh well, I'm sure our issues aren't as bad as what Max is dealing with so I have no choice. I can't abandon him, especially since he's never needed help before. He called me because he trusts me and I know he would drop everything to come if I needed help.*

I just hate canceling on Jess because I was planning a picnic at Estes Park on Fall River Road where we went on one of our hikes. We'd found a small shady place to stop and picnicked by the Fall River. I like that quiet relaxing place in the mountains. We go there to enjoy the quiet. The only noises come from the whistling of the pines and the rushing of the water in the river. Occasionally we could hear birds chirping. It's a great escape from the hustle-bustle of the city, and the perfect place to connect and have a serious discussion about our relationship. Without the usual distractions, I was sure we could get back on track.

I'm afraid though that she'll get angry when I call to cancel. Well there's no sense stalling, I have to let her know and convince her how important this trip is. She's at her mother's house, so I should just do it. If I don't and I stand her up, the consequences might be even worse!

Closing the door, he starts the engine. Taking a deep breath, he dials Jessica. Her voice sounds different when she answers.

"Hello, Sam." Her voice seems distant to him, like she's talking to a stranger.

"Hi Jessica. Listen, about tomorrow…"

She interrupts, "Sam, wait a moment… I've been meaning to tell you something. I'm seeing someone else."

"What! I thought you're with your mother tonight!"

"No, I'm sorry, Sam. I'm with Harry. I started seeing Harry last week. He's an anthropology student like me studying ancient cultures. We just hit it off. I don't understand your electronic stuff anyway. Harry and I study together and things. It just happened, you know. I'm sorry."

"Great! I was calling to tell you I have to go to Fort Lauderdale tomorrow. Have a good time with what's his name!" Disengaging the call Sam sits thinking about what just happened. In just a few minutes, his whole world has changed. A knot forms in his stomach as he's shifting his SUV into gear heading to his apartment. *Damn, the stress must be getting to me. Now I have a knot forming in my stomach. I sure hope this doesn't mean I'm going to start having nightmares again. I really hate having those weird frightening dreams. Come on Sam, a knot in your stomach could just be indigestion. Don't go adding to your troubles, we don't need those dreams again!*

Thoughts of all the crazy pranks Max did from time to time begin flooding Sam's mind. *I hope this isn't just an elaborate hoax and Max will call back later laughing. I don't think so. The panic in Max's voice seemed genuine. I have to believe it isn't a practical joke. He was panicky. I have to check it out.*

I need to call Ed and request a few days off. What the heck, I need a vacation anyhow! Maybe I can tour Silvan Enterprises and see if I like the place. Sam's company The Store

Tech in Denver manufactures surveillance and data storage equipment for use in stores, warehouses, and multi-million dollar estates.

A year ago, Ed Blackstone took over the manager job at Store Tech. Ed is a friendly boss, and gives all his technicians his cell phone number. He says he wants everyone to be able to reach him in case of an emergency. To Sam, this is an emergency. *I hope his phone is on.*

"Hello." The local news is blaring from a TV. A second later the sound is muted.

"Hello Ed, this is Sam Stormen. I hate to bother you on a Friday night, but I have a problem."

"What's the matter?"

"I have a friend who needs my help. I need to go to Fort Lauderdale like right away!"

"You mean right now?"

"Yes! I'm leaving in the morning. My friend is desperate. He needs me there to help him with some problem. He's in a real jam."

"How long will you be gone?"

"I'm guessing not more than a week. I need a little vacation anyway and I figure nothing should take longer than a week to resolve. What do you think?"

"Take your time, Sam. Our schedule is very light for the next month or so. Is there anything I can do to help?"

"No, just let me use up some of my vacation time. I will get back as soon as I can."

"Okay, I'll tell personnel on Monday. Good luck Sam."

"Thanks, Ed."

Chapter Four

Sam's mind is flipping back and forth worrying about Max and being annoyed that Max might be joking. *I don't really believe Max would pull a joke like this. I'm just upset and stressed. It's Jessica I'm upset with not Max. True Max is a big prankster and one should always be on guard around him, but he's never turned his pranks on me. This situation with Jessica really caught me off guard. We've had issues, but this… Besides, if Max broke our pact and this turns out to be a joke, I'll just take a few days to relax in Fort Lauderdale at Max's expense. It will teach him a lesson. He'll have to pay all my expenses for making me fly to Florida. If it isn't a joke, then maybe I can actually help Max fix whatever it is. I'm ready for some time off anyhow, especially now that Jessica has dumped me. I can't believe she wasn't honest with me, and she's been seeing someone else. She really isn't the girl I thought she was.*

Parking near the outside stairs, Sam climbs up to his third story apartment. Although his apartment is in a decent area of North Denver, the building is old and in need of repairs and comes with no special amenities.

Entering the apartment, and shucking his coat, he kicks off his shoes and sits down on the swivel chair at his small desk, hits power switch on his laptop, and waits for it to come alive.

Quickly he begins looking for a cheap fare to Fort Lauderdale. It doesn't take long to discover there are no cheap fares to Fort Lauderdale. "Wow!" He says seeing the ticket prices. He needed to book his trip well in advance instead of last minute in order to get a decent rate. All he can do now is check for the earliest flight to Fort Lauderdale in the morning with a return for a week later. The cheapest round trip ticket on American Airlines leaving at

6:20 a.m., Saturday morning available, is in first class.

Max will pay for this if he's spoofing me! And maybe even if he isn't!

With his ticket purchased, realization starts kicking in as he sits staring at his computer screen. The reality of what Max said continues to sink in the more he thinks about it. He lived with Max for nearly a year at the University in Gainesville. Then later in Fort Lauderdale, they dated together, drank beer and got drunk together, and always watched each other's back. Sam knows Max wouldn't be joking about this! Even though things don't make sense, somehow he knows Max really is in trouble. An eerie feeling about the trip is starting to take hold.

Knowing he is worrying too much, about what lay ahead, he digs out a small leather bag from the back of his bedroom closet preparing to start packing. *Let me put the TV on; it's too quiet and I need something to focus on for a bit.*

Let's see, what should I pack for this trip? I won't need much for clothing for only a week in Fort Lauderdale. Weather won't be an issue so let me grab some casual shirts and shorts. I'll need underwear, shaving stuff, deodorant and sandals. Oh, I'd better not forget my cell phone charger. I really wish Max would call saying this is just a joke. Sure, I'll be upset with him at first, but maybe I can cancel that expensive plane ticket!

Jessica is history and that means I really have no romantic ties to Denver anymore. I'm actually starting to feel good about it considering how unexpected it was. Maybe I wasn't as serious as I thought about Jessica. She certainly isn't someone I'd want to be with all my life anyway. Well, no big loss.

Damn, I nearly forgot. Max told me to bring my passport. I wonder why? Maybe this is Max's way of a surprise vacation after we fix his problem, because I don't need a passport in Fort Lauderdale. Unless it has something to do with the trouble he is in, but what? Why would he need to leave the country?

My passport! What did I do with my passport? Opening the top drawer of a two-drawer filing cabinet, he looks for a file folder in the back and finds it with a tab labeled "Passport".

Oh yeah, I remember doing that now. Getting my passport was a big hassle. I had to scrounge up my birth certificate and a bunch of other ID cards and stuff in order to get it. What a pain, I never want to go through all that again.

I'd better double check and make sure I have everything before I close my bag. Well, all that's left to do now is wait for morning. Since I'm ready to go, I better try to relax for a bit. I'm not sure why, but this trip has me a bit nervous. Let me grab a book and try reading a while. Maybe that will relax me.

Damn, this isn't working. I can't seem to focus, Sam slams the book down dismayed. Looking around at other options, he reaches for the remote and begins clicking through news stations on TV. Most of the news seems of little interest so he to switches to an education channel.

A story is running about a large metal shredding factory in Ohio. Seeing the announcer standing in front of a row of shredders, Sam suddenly realizes just how big these shredders really are. It's actually quite frightening.

"Here we see some metal scraps, two metal chairs and a metal drum as they go down the conveyor belt ready to be shredded into manageable scrap metal pieces." The announcer's voice says.

Watching how the shredder devours everything, Sam is impressed. The shredder readily accepts the metal drum as it easily begins squeezing, crunching and shredding it.

"These big shredders are extremely dangerous. Several times a year someone loses a finger, a hand, and even an arm to these types of shredders if they aren't extremely careful. There is only one case we know of where a man actually was pulled into a giant shredder and killed."

"This particular factory in Ohio has a perfect safety record though. No one has ever lost as much as a finger here. The management takes extra care to train all their employees who work around these shredders."

Sam finds this program somewhat interesting. When the program ends, he's once again flipping channels trying to find something else of interest to watch. The problem is as much as he tries, he can't turn his brain off. He keeps thinking about what Max is doing and what sort of trouble he might be in that he requires Sam's help.

Max's desperate words continue haunting him. "Sam, please, please come help!" *This is so unlike Max. Even if a prank had gone bad, Max wouldn't be acting like this. He sounded like someone whose life is in danger, but everyone loves Max. No one would ever want to harm him. He's fun loving, kind and generous to a fault, so why did he sound so desperate?*

Get a grip Sam. You're worrying too much about this call. It's probably nothing. Max is likely blowing something out of proportion and all will be resolved by the time you arrive. Maybe he's stressed because Peggy left him. I don't know. Whatever, I'll go and get a quick vacation out of this trip and check out the new job. I just need to relax, but why does the sound of his voice have me so uneasy...

Okay, let me go take a shower to relax. Shutting off the TV, he begins stripping down. *Why do people kill friends over the smallest things? Like in that article I read a while ago about a man stabbing his friend to death during a quarrel. They were fighting over a quarter they found lying in the street! Oh, come on Sam! Now you're pulling stuff out of thin air. This is something simple and Max is fine! I hope.*

Stepping out of the bathroom after taking his shower and brushing his teeth, he hears the tail end of a message on his answering machine.

"... how we can find him."

Sam sets his alarm clock to wake him at 4:00 AM and starts to check his messages quickly hoping Max tried calling him back, and becomes aware how much he really wants to talk to Max before he goes to bed if he can. *That's it! I'm calling him. I need to know what's going on.* Sam drops everything and calls Max. *Damn, voicemail!* "Max, this is Sam. I'm calling because I was hoping I could reach you. I'm worried. Well, uh, I booked my flight and I guess I'll see you tomorrow. Please, call me back if you can."

Sitting on the bed, Sam goes back to checking messages, finding a call from an unfamiliar caller with the same area code as Max, Fort Lauderdale. *Maybe this is Max. Maybe his phone died and he used someone else's.*

"Sam, this is Mark, Max's boss... Max has gone berserk and is hiding out somewhere. He could be in a lot of danger! He may try to contact you so please help me find him before he does something we will all regret. Call me if you hear from him or know how we can find him."

OMG! That's weird. Why is Mark calling me? Does this mean Max is hiding from Mark? This doesn't make sense. Max is close friends with Mark, so why... Wait, Max called his boss a traitor. Now Mark says Max could be in a lot of danger. This means Max really is in trouble.

Putting the phone down, Sam crawls into bed with an uneasy feeling. *Since this isn't a prank, what in the world kind of trouble is Max in! I better try to get a good night's sleep before the morning drive to the airport. What could be so bad for Max to call me so scared? What could have happened to cause Max to be in danger? Why is his boss involved in Max's problem and why is he calling me? I only met Mark that one time last year. How does Mark have my number anyhow? Oh yeah, he probably got it off the résumé I sent him.*

Scrunching up into a comfortable position under his nice warm blanket Sam attempts to doze off to sleep, the last thing he remembers before nodding off is the knot in his stomach tightening. Sam has a history of not being able to handle stress well, but his friend needs him.

Falling into a fitful sleep, he starts dreaming. Sam wakes up suddenly. His head aches and throbs terribly! He can feel a cold concrete floor under his butt. His back is hunched against a cold concrete wall. *How can this be?* Sam knows his apartment doesn't have any bare concrete floor or walls. Looking around a chill runs through his body. He seems to be in a metal recycling plant of some sort. He can see bins full of various shapes of scrap metal and suddenly hears the whirring drone of a machine. Looking up, he sees the pockmarked face of an unshaven man staring at him! This man is obviously angry and pointing a cold black barrel of his gun at Sam's face!

"Ah, you awake now." The gunman grumbles staring at Sam with dark eyes.

"They told me to get rid of him. He knows Mark is a traitor! He also kicked my dog and she died!" An old brown and white mongrel is lying near the man. It isn't breathing.

"I hate him!" The man says. "If you try to save him, I shoot you! He gonna die a bad death!"

A short distance away, Sam realizes the whirring is coming from a large metal shredder. Max is hogtied with rope and wiggling around on the conveyer belt as it slowly carries him closer and closer to the whirring and ripping blades! Max's black hair is ruffled and his frightened brown eyes are looking at the pock-faced man and Sam.

"It's not my fault! It's not my fault!" Max keeps yelling.

"You pay now!" The pock-faced man roars at Max. "You die!" He shouts making a grunting sound as Max comes closer and closer to the ripping blades of the shredder.

Sam watches as Max wiggles and twists but isn't able to get off the conveyor belt. Watching in horror, Sam sees Max's legs enter the shredder, hearing Max scream in agony as the shredder chops away. Sam can do nothing. He wants to go pull Max off the belt but his legs won't work. Max goes silent as the shredder rips through the rest of his body. A moment later, all Sam hears is the whirring drone of the shredder motor again. The pock-faced man grunts his approval.

"You killed my friend!" Sam screams.

"You next! You friend of his. You know too much! I just shoot you. I have no more rope!"

Suddenly, Sam sits bolt upright in his bed waking up with a start. Looking around wildly, it takes a few seconds before he realizes he's just had a bad dream. Even seeing that he is safe in his own bedroom does little to ease his tension. *That's the worst nightmare I've ever had!* He feels cold sweat on his face. Exhaling a deep breath, he tries to calm himself down. *I guess I shouldn't have watched that story about the metal shredders in Ohio!*

Realizing his imagination has once again gone wild, he can't go back to sleep. Carrying the alarm clock and a blanket into the living room, he hopes changing locations will help. Stretching out on the couch, he turns on the TV, and switches to a cartoon station. Somehow, he feels safer with the TV spouting nonsensical gibberish.

You know, before I had this dream, I knew I was dreading this trip, but now I know I have to help Max! I don't know what I can do to help in this situation; I don't have any abilities in this area. Max must have a plan knowing this. He's smart; I have to trust that he can guide me to helping him get out of whatever this is.

The trouble Max is in can't be near as bad as what happened to him in my dream. Starting to dose off to sleep again, Sam's mind adds, *or could it? God I hope not!*

Chapter Five

Max tosses and turns throughout the night in his sleazy motel room until nearly seven o'clock in the morning. A sense of fear rises up as he prepares to head out into public. He peeks through the window before cautiously opening his door and stepping outside to head out to find a place for breakfast.

Finding a small café, Max sits down at a table near the front door and notices one of the waitresses staring at him after he orders. *I wonder why she's watching me. I don't want to leave because I'm really hungry, so I'll have to take a chance.*

The waitress heads his way and Max tenses up ready to rush out if necessary.

"Aren't you Max?"

"Who wants to know?"

"Kidder as usual. Don't you remember me from Marcy's Restaurant?"

"Um... Oh yeah, Nancy is it?"

"You do remember! I moved to this side of town and took a job here. Are you still going with Peggy?"

"We're separated right now."

"Hey, let me give you my number. Maybe you can call me some time."

"Okay."

Walking out of the diner after breakfast, Max looks for a bus stand. He walks for several blocks and finally finds a bench to wait for the BCT to come. A short time later, a bus arrives and Max gets onboard. He knows where he wants to go but doesn't want to ask the driver how to get there directly and asks for a place nearby instead just in case. Knowing an APB may be out on him, it's only a matter of

time before the cops start looking into public transporta‐
tion.

Max pays his fare and rides to the bus station. He switches to a bus going to the beach. By eleven in the morn‐ ing, he steps off the bus and walks two blocks to the Elbo Room. *Sam will have to meet me here.*

Mark glances at his watch after hearing his phone ringing. It's seven in the morning and his phone shows it's his con‐ tact calling. He exhales loudly and answers the phone.

"Any luck locating Max yet?"

"No."

"What did you find out about that number he called?"

"Max called his best friend in Denver. Knowing how close they are, I think he is coming here to meet him. I called him last night to see if I could get through to him but got his voicemail. I left a message saying I needed his help because Max is in trouble but he hasn't returned my call."

"Is that the same guy you gave me information on?"

"Yes, did you find anything?"

"Yes. There's an airline charge on his credit card. He's probably heading here."

"Has there been any more activity on his phone? Max may call him when he arrives at the airport."

"Only a local call. What are your plans if he doesn't call Max when he arrives?"

"I'm going to stake out Max's house. Since they weren't on long enough for the call to be traced, they probably didn't have enough time to arrange details on a place to meet up. Even if Max doesn't come back here, I'm hoping Sam will, so I can get to him before Max does."

"Okay. Whatever you do, be discrete. We don't want the media to get hold of this."

"Yes sir. We'll handle it quietly. We'll follow him. He can

lead us to Max."

"Make it happen!"

Sleeping restlessly until morning, without any more terrible dreams, Sam awakes to the sound of the alarm clock buzzing in his ear. Staring bleary eyed at the dial its 4:01 a.m. and he switches the alarm off. The image of Max screaming and being shredded still haunts his memory. Somewhere in the night, he must have hit the mute button on the TV. Trying to wake fully, he keeps rubbing his eyes. Now that he can see somewhat, blue Smurfs are prancing on the screen. He struggles to get up feeling a little stiff from all the tossing and turning on the couch.

The Saturday morning weather placed a light blanket of snow on Sam's SUV. Punching the key fob, he opens the door, slings his bag inside, and reaches in the back to grab a scrapper to clear the snow off the windshield. Sliding the key into the ignition his old SUV chortles to life in the cold morning air.

Traffic is heavy driving to the airport, especially for so early in the morning on a Saturday. Fortunately, Sam can see the roads are all free of any ice. Focusing on driving, he's forgotten how worried he is until he turns on to the final road to the Denver airport as reality comes back to him.

Heading for the airport lobby, he needs to look around a few seconds to locate the ticket counters. The area is busy with many lines of people waiting to check luggage or get their tickets. He only has about an hour until flight time since the trip to the airport took much longer than he anticipated due to the traffic. Sam hustles through the lobby to the row of check-in counters. To his amazement there are only two people waiting in the American Airlines line.

Looking at the large clock, ten minutes has passed before he is finally standing at the counter as a short heavyset man wearing the airlines uniform greets him.

"Just the one bag to check." The man asks.

"No, I'll carry it on. You should have an e-ticket for me, Sam Stormen."

The attendant clicks the keyboard then shakes his head frowning. "I'm sorry sir; I don't see you in my computer. Do you have a confirmation number?"

"Yes, I do." Reaching in his pocket, Sam finds a crumpled piece of envelope with the confirmation number, and hands it to the attendant.

"Ah, here you are! I was spelling your name wrong." A moment later, the clerk hands Sam a small folder. Noting the time, Sam needs to get through security and hopes the lines won't be long because he is running late.

Lucking out at security, he makes it through quicker than he feared. Heading to Gate 49 he notices he is hungry as he begins passing a snack bar. Checking his watch, he considers whether to stop. *If I go check in first, and then come back to get something the line might be long. It's probably better to do it now and then check in because I really need to eat something before the flight takes off.*

Gazing through the steamy glass display Sam sees several things looking like fried eggs on toasted muffins sitting on a grease-stained sheet of paper.

"What can I get for you?" The girl asks.

"I'd like one of those." He says to the girl pointing.

"Anything to drink with that?"

"No thanks."

"Thank you." He says taking the egg muffin from the girl. After paying, he hurries to his gate to check in.

The lounge area for Gate 49 is full. Sam sees an open seat

next to an older man with a short white beard reading the Denver Post Sam asks, "Is this seat taken?"

The man shakes his head no and Sam removes his coat and sits down next to the man.

"Business or pleasure?" The man asks.

"I'm not really sure. I'm hoping it's for pleasure, and you?"

"I'm returning home from a business convention. Smiling politely at one another it's easy to tell the conversation has concluded. For the remainder of the short wait Sam is content to people watch.

With flight time nearing, people start gathering in line by the gate attendant.

The attendant soon announces, "All first class passengers may now board. Please have your boarding pass available."

Getting up, Sam walks toward the woman to board the plane. Handing her his boarding pass she checks it, before smiling saying, "Welcome aboard". Then she ushers him to enter the gangplank for the plane.

Inside the plane, a stewardess escorts Sam to the window seat in row 3A. Plopping down in the extra wide soft seat he notes all the legroom he has. The stewardess places his bag in the overhead compartment for him. *This is why people pay extra for first class!*

Settling in his seat, no one else has arrived for the seat next to him yet so he just watches other passengers boarding the plane. Just as the doors are preparing to close, the final passengers' board, and a man plops down in the seat next to Sam.

Sam can't help eyeing his first-class seatmate with a twinge of disgust. The man has multi-toned brown hair, denim pants, a nose ring, four earrings on his left ear, and

an eyebrow stud. He is also wearing a blue and gold de-
signer shirt open at the top revealing a massive gold chain
around his neck.

Sam can't understand why people mutilate their bodies
that way. His first impression of the man is that of a rich
drug dealer. He's perhaps ten years older than Sam, and
just as the man starts to say something to Sam, the speaker
comes on.

The routine safety speech isn't impressive and the jet
engines start to whir as the stewardess talks. Displays
swing down and snap on to show a safety video as the plane
backs out of the terminal to taxi toward the runway.

As the video ends, the stewardess makes a final an-
nouncement. "We will arrive in Fort Lauderdale at approx-
imately 2:20 PM local time. The chances of rain are sixty
percent for the Fort Lauderdale area. Please remember
East coast time is two hours later than Denver time..." She
continues talking after the video screens swing back away.
She hopes we will all have an enjoyable trip blah, blah,
blah.

"Hello mate." Sam's seatmate says cheerfully. He has a
hint of an Australian accent in his voice.

"Hi, you look kind of different." Sam says before he realizes the words that just left his mouth as he starts ad-
justing his watch forward two hours.

"That's a bold thing to say. In what way do I look different? I look the same as always." Smiling at Sam the man
says, "I'm Chet, Chet Hatter. Ever hear of me?"

"No, I guess not, sorry." Sam is glad this man wasn't
offended by his comment. He didn't mean to be offensive, it
just blurted out.

"Ever hear of the 'Danglebatts'?" He asks.

"No. Is that a band?"

"Yes! We've just had a concert here in Denver stadium

last night. I think there were over fifty thousand people there. I'm the lead guitarist for the "Danglebatts". I'm Chet."

"Oh yeah, the Danglebatts. Where's the rest of the... ah, 'Danglebatts'?"

"My mates were too sick to fly out this morning. We all partied after the concert into the wee hours. I drank a bit. My mates drank too much. They may have been doing some weed, too. They have no wives to think about at home. I have a wife. I want to get back, you know."

"Do you do rock and roll or rap or what?"

"Oh, we mostly do hard rock. I do a lead riff for a couple minutes sometimes. The audience goes wild."

"I play guitar too, but I just play rhythm - no lead." Sam says.

"What kind of music do you like?"

"Mostly Country Western and some rock and roll, but I like just about any kind of music, even hard rock."

"Cool!" Chet says. "We should jam together some time. Have you ever played in a band?"

"I always wanted to but no. I jam with some guys on Sunday nights at my church recreation hall in Denver. I bet it's fun traveling all over the world and playing music you love. It seems like a great way to..."

"Ah, it's not as great as you think, mate." Chet interrupts him. "It was great for a while, but I get tired of eating out all the time. The partying gets old after a while, too. Some towns I just go back to the hotel because I don't want to party anymore and I don't know where else to go in a strange city. Now that I'm married, I have to avoid temptations. You know what I mean?"

"I can only imagine what that would be like, but what about being in the limelight? Isn't it great to be living the life of a star? You get to play for thousands of people. You make a ton of money. Don't you have fans that adore you, too?"

"Yeah, but sometimes it's hard to make it to my room alone because of all the groupies. The lifestyle makes it hard to settle down and have a normal life. This was my farewell performance in Denver. I have a concert in Fort Lauderdale next month, then that's it for me. No more on the road for me. I'm going to be a disc jockey for a local radio station in Fort Lauderdale when I get home. My motto is 'let Chet Hatter spin your platter!' Not bad, huh?"

"Wow! You're giving up the band for the home life." Sam notices the flight attendants strap themselves into their seats and feels the acceleration as the plane begins speeding down the runway. Sam doesn't care for flying if he can help it. Someone told him once that the take-off is the most dangerous part of an airplane flight. If you lose power, you have no lift, so you just crash and burn! Ever since then he prays for a safe take-off. His tight grip on the armrests seems to help the plane take off safely.

Sam leans back in his seat wondering what he is getting into. He closes his eyes as the plane climbs higher above the mountains until Chet interrupts his thoughts again.

"Hey, you can lighten up on the armrests now." Chet says smiling at him.

"Oh, yeah, it's a habit of mine when we take off." Sam says releasing his death grip on the armrests. Trying to relax he brings his hands together.

"Are you married?" Chet asks.

"No, never have been."

"Well someday, if you're lucky, you will meet miss wonderful. I did. I got the strangest feeling the first time I touched her hand. I just knew she was the one for me. In a few months, we're having our first kid. I want to be there when that happens."

"Ah, that makes sense now. I just broke up with my girl, but she never gave me any strange feeling. You're a fortunate man."

"I know. I think I'll take a little nap now if you don't mind. I didn't get much sleep last night."

"Nice talking to you," Sam says. "I might do the same."

Chet doesn't fit the visual image Sam saw based on his appearance. He feels bad now about his first impression of Chet. *I guess you can't judge a book. Chet is an interesting and likeable person in spite of having so many pierces and earrings.*

Chet puts his ear buds in and listens to his MP3 player. Tilting his seat back, he gets lost in his music quickly as he dozes off to sleep.

Sam mumbles a silent prayer, still wondering what lies in store for him when he gets to Fort Lauderdale. He can't help his apprehension about what to expect when he lands. He wants to take a nap but remains wide-awake.

The long flight time gives Sam a lot of time to think. In all the time he's known Max, he's never felt like Max was afraid of anything. Recalling Max bungee jumping, he was fearless! Yet the haunting words Max said over the phone reminds him Max has to be in serious trouble. *Why does Max think his boss is a traitor? Why did Mark call me about Max? Why didn't Max just go to the police for whatever it is? Why did Mark also say Max could be in serious trouble?* Sam remembers meeting Mark on his last trip to Fort Lauderdale. *What kind of problem could occur that Mark is involved in that's causing Max not to trust him?* Maybe one of Max's pranks got him in trouble. As the plane cruises along, Sam remembers some of the pranks Max did in the past and chuckles to himself. Max's list of pranks is long. This is why Max's problem might be a problem of his own creation. Sometimes what Max finds funny, isn't to his victims.

The stewardess announces the pending arrival in Fort Lauderdale, interrupting his thoughts. Sam taps Chet on his shoulder to wake him. He waves at Sam and continues listening to his MP3 player putting the seat upright.

Sam feels the strong slowdown as the flaps on the wings extend for landing. It is 2:10 p.m.

Chet asks, "Are you expecting to meet someone at the airport?"

"Yes I am," Sam says. "I'm a little worried about him, though."

"Why?"

"I think he is in some kind of trouble. Although he wasn't very clear about what the trouble was."

"Well, if I can be of any help… Here, let me give you my card." Taking out a gold case from his pocket, Chet pulls a bright blue and gold "Danglebatts" business card out. Before handing Sam the card, he scribbles on the back of the card with a gold pen.

"I wrote my cell phone number on the back. The number on the front is for our agent. Give me a call if you need help or want to jam a bit." Chet says handing Sam the card.

"The guys talked me into one more gig with the band here in Fort Lauderdale before I drop out completely. They haven't found a replacement lead player they like yet. After that, I'll be semi-retired here in sunny Fort Lauderdale most of the time."

"Hey, thanks. I might call you if I get freed up." Sam says. Not having a business card of his own, he tears off a piece of the ticket folder and writes his name and cell phone number on it. "Here's mine. Call me if you ever get to Denver again. Maybe we could jam there, too."

"I don't think I will get back to Denver, mate, but I'll

keep your number.

A moment later the tires shriek as the plane touches down. Easing his grip on the armrests Sam waits for the plane to taxi to a stop at the terminal and is relieved when the jet engines shut down and the exit door opens.

Chet smiles, "See you soon Sam. I hope you will call me. Nice meeting you, I hope your friend is okay."

"Will do Chet. I'll give you a call before I head home if not before." Sam watches Chet leave as he retrieves his bag from the overhead compartment.

Speed walking towards the airport terminal Sam is looking around for Max trying to find a man five-foot ten, with jet-black hair, a rounded face wearing impeccable clothes. Good at spotting people Sam doesn't see Max anywhere.

"Where are you Max?" He mumbles hoofing past a few slower walking people. "Where are you, you rascal?"

Suddenly he remembers Max say he might just call if he can't meet him at the airport. Sam dials Max's number. Max's voice mail picks up and beeps.

"Hey Max, I thought you'd be here at the airport." Sam says and hangs up. *Why didn't Max answer? Did he really have his phone shut off to avoid someone locating him? How will I find Max now?* Believing he has no option, Sam leaves and heads for the rental cars area.

Off and on for the whole flight time from Colorado, I tried convincing myself this is just a bad joke and Max would be here at the airport to greet me.

Sam heads towards the baggage claim area still looking for Max. Max always enjoyed performing playful pranks on people, but said the challenge is to never get caught. Sam now wonders if Max was caught, maybe caught in something very bad!

Chapter Six

Snapping back to reality reaching the baggage claim area on his way to car rentals, Max still isn't anywhere in sight. Trying Max's phone again, the voice mail answers.

Since Sam already has his bag, he heads for the car rentals. Surprisingly he locates a car rental specializing in vintage cars instead of late model ones like Hertz or Alamo. Thinking about it quickly he opts to check out the deals here.

Approaching the 'Vintage Car Rental Agency' counter, a woman wearing a light gray company suit with gold buttons and a large gold 'V' embroidered across the left pocket greets him as he walks to her counter. "Can I interest you in a Vintage rental car today?" She says in a cheery voice.

"Yes. What kind of cars do you have?" Sam asks smiling at her.

"We specialize in classic specialty vehicles. We are able to offer better daily rates for these types of car to our customers."

"How late are the models?"

"We have some only five years old. But I think the best ones are the older ones."

"For example?"

"Well, I personally like the older Mustangs. We have a 1990 black V-8 Mustang in stock. It has been maintained perfectly and…"

"That sounds like exactly what I want." He interrupts.

"Really? You like the old muscle cars?"

"Yes I do!"

"Me too! I'm Danielle by the way." She says offering her hand to Sam.

"Sam." He says shaking her hand. "It's my pleasure to meet you Danielle. Let's do it. I love old muscle cars."

Handing him a form, Sam takes a pen from his shirt pocket and it snags on Chet's business card. The card falls onto the counter right side up showing the distinctive Danglebatts logo.

"You know the Danglebatts?" Danielle says with a surprised tone.

"Well, I met Chet Hatter on the plane and we talked. He gave me his..."

"Oh my God! He's the coolest guy! You met Chet Hatter! I went to the Danglebatts concert here last year. You know he can jam out a crazy melody for like five minutes! He's the best guitarist! You know him?"

"Just a friend." Sam says with a grin even though he thinks he'll never see Chet again. Yet Danielle's enthusiasm is intoxicating he says casually, "We're going to be jamming together. We promised to get together in the next week or two."

"Really? I can't believe he was on the plane with you? Oh yes, there he is, I see him! Hey Chet!" Her voice grows louder as she shouts at Chet walking by with a steward rolling his luggage alongside of him. "I love your music!"

Chet smiles and waves at her, then recognizes Sam. Turning toward them he says, "Hey Sam, give me a call and we'll jam." Then continues to walk toward the taxi stand.

Sam couldn't have paid Chet to say anything better to make points with Danielle! She went pale and speechless. If it hadn't been for Max's problem Sam probably could have had a great weekend with Danielle. For now, he just waves and smiles back at Chet.

"Thanks, I'll call you next week." Sam manages to say stuffing Chet's card back in his shirt pocket and starts filling in the rental form.

"That was awesome!" Danielle says. "He wants to jam with you!"

"I know. It'll be fun. I hope he has a spare guitar because I don't have one with me."

"I have one," Danielle says. "I have a Martin D something. My brother gave it to me when he went in the Army. I sing better than I play, though."

"Maybe I could take you for a ride some time." Sam says flirting.

"Maybe you could." She says coyly jotting something on a scrap of paper. He figures it's her phone number when she hands it to him. "I get off at 5:30. Maybe you'll call me."

"Maybe I will." Sam smiles at her and stuffs the note in his pocket.

After filling out the forms, he asks a question about a couple lines he'd left blank on the form. Giving Sam a broad smile showing her perfect teeth, she leans over the counter to explain. Sam asks several questions.

Sam likes the thought of getting an older car so the old Ford Mustang seems to be just fine. In between doing the paperwork and looking at Danielle, he looked around occasionally for Max, but Max still hasn't shown up.

By 3 o'clock, Sam is walking outside and gets into the small mini-van to take him to the car lot. Along the way, he takes out Danielle's note to open the folded paper. Smiling, he can see she has drawn a neat large heart and inside it, she wrote her name and her phone number. *So maybe if Max's trouble is nothing, I might end up with a gorgeous date! Might even see Chet and jam for a while.*

The van pulls to a stop right next to the Mustang. *This old car looks gorgeous, unlike what I expected. Maybe I should go back and change it to a less noticeable car. This one shines as if it's just been painted and detailed. The black paint is lustrous on this Mustang and I love the detailing with the gold pinstripes on the sides. This car is impressive and aggressive. I really wanted a less conspicuous car. Shiny cars tend to attract attention and I don't want to attract attention today. Although it looks so good and I do like this kind of muscle car, I think I'll go with this Mustang after all.* Opening the door, he tosses his bag inside and slides into the driver's seat. The inside is plush black and white leather seats, a black dash, and black floor mats. There is a skeleton head for a gearshift knob.

I think driving an older car is more appropriate for this situation for some reason. I'm hoping this old Mustang won't have a factory installed LoJac in it. In addition to meeting the delightful Danielle, the LoJac is my excuse for not renting a shiny new car in case it's trackable.

The feeling inside this Mustang is quite different from my old SUV. For one, I definitely sit a lot lower to the ground in this Mustang, in spite of the low to the ground feeling. I love old muscle cars!

Sticking the key in the ignition and cranking up the engine, big V-8 engine gives a distinctive roar coming to life. The air conditioner comes on a second later. Taking a deep breath, he closes his eyes for a moment. With some apprehension, he slips the gearshift into drive and leaves the parking lot. Driving out of the airport area towards Max's house in South Fort Lauderdale is a beautiful ride. He has no idea of how to contact Max though. *Maybe I should go to Max's house. Maybe I can find a clue about where Max is there.*

Growing up in Fort Lauderdale, Sam knows many of the older sections of the city and a few of the newer ones. He knows they often have winding roads and they have names rather than numbers. Nowadays, with the population growth and many new sections of town, one almost needs to have a GPS or a good map to find someone here.

Max bought his house soon after he hired on at Silvan Enterprises and Sam spent time at Max's house last year on vacation, so finding the place will be easy. He knows it's in the middle of a beautiful older section in south Fort Lauderdale. In general, old money owns most of the houses around Max's house. The houses tend to be more elegant and well maintained. Even though he is hurrying to get to Max, he decides to get off the main thoroughfare onto the back streets.

To a certain extent, Sam ignores the majestic coconut palm trees, lush greenery, and pampered streets along the way to the house. Just thinking about finding Max captures all of his thoughts! His senses are giving him a creepy feeling, as if someone were following him! Possibly, they followed him the entire way from the airport. *It doesn't look like anyone is following me. It's just a feeling I have. Damn it Max! Why weren't you at the airport to meet me?*

It's nearly three thirty on a sunny afternoon by the time Sam approaches 812 Clifton Street. Max's house is on one of the oldest streets in Fort Lauderdale. As Sam turns off the main road onto Clifton Street, the road of old brick stones is straight ahead. *This road is too bumpy for driving along at any high rate of speed; I'll have to slow down to a crawl.*

Max's old house, sits in the distance looking inviting and comfortable for an old home. The elegant frame house in the middle of the block is stark white like many of the other homes on Clifton Street. Driving closer, Max's carport is empty. The bright red Corvette isn't there. His girlfriend Peggy's pink pickup truck isn't there either. "She's probably still at her mother's."

Parking along the curb next to the front of the house, he shuts down the engine and steps out. Blue jays and sparrows are chirping in the trees around the house and a gentle breeze is sweeping across him as he heads for the front steps of the house. Everything on Clifton Street seems cheery and normal. A squirrel in the front yard dashes off to a tree as he approaches.

Across the street, a man is sitting in a black car with the engine running and his face turned away from Sam. It looks like the man is wearing a suit but his dark car windows are up and it looks like the man is studying a map or something, which is easy to understand in this area. *Maybe he's lost, or maybe he is watching me! It's odd someone would be just sitting in a car on Clifton Street in the middle of the day.* Sam tries unsuccessfully to shrug off an uneasy feeling.

Even in the bright sunlight of the afternoon, it's clear lights are glowing behind the semi-opaque blue curtains in Max's house. The air conditioner is humming outside, keeping the inside of the house cool. Stepping up the stairs to the front of the house, he knocks on the door, and rings the doorbell. Max always keeps the curtains drawn so Sam can't see inside. As expected, there is no response. Max added a combination lock on his front and side doors because he doesn't like having to fiddle with a key to unlock his doors. Sam remembers the old numbers he used from his last visit, but the lock doesn't open. He knows Max keeps an emergency key hidden outside the house just in case of a power outage or other emergency. Max told Sam to use the key if he ever needs to get in, or if he's forgotten the combination.

Stepping down from the front of the house, he walks around to the side. He finds a small fake rock under a sage bush on the side of the house and retrieves the key. With apprehension, he walks back up the front stairs and cautiously puts the key in the lock. After jiggling the slightly corroded key and turning it, the door unlocks. His muscles tense and his body is on alert as he slowly eases the door open and looks inside.

Max's normally neat home is a shambles! What Sam sees stops his breath for a second. Every light in the house is on. The big blue couch in the living room lays on its back, and the end tables and a footrest are tipped over. Papers are scattered all over the floor. On the left side of the living room, books are strewn about from the bookshelves, and the door to Max's bedroom/office is open. Even his lounge chair is on its side and the stuff in the living room closet is laying all over the floor. Oddly enough, the table lamps, spread out on the floor, aren't broken. This seems strange. It's obvious someone has rifled through everything all through Max's house, however they were careful not to break anything.

Cautiously walking across the living room and into Max's bedroom the desk and filing cabinet drawers are all open or on the floor. Stepping back into the hallway, suddenly the hair on the back of his neck bristles. He realizes the rear door to the house is wide open! Picking up a baseball bat lying on the floor next to the hall closet, his body already on alert grows tenser. He feels his muscles tighten up as they do during one of his Judo matches. Adrenalin kicks in as he finishes scouting around the house. Cautiously he checks out all four bedrooms, both bathrooms, the laundry room, and all the closets. Every area is empty; no one else is in the house. Turning off lights in each room he looks through the house for clues to where Max may have gone and finds it's not an easy job with the condition of the place. Sitting on one edge of Max's overturned couch he's wondering what to do next.

Obviously, somebody has been here before me and rifled through just about everything. Max's laptop is missing from his office desk. Even the connecting wires are strewn about as if someone took them in a hurry. They weren't worrying about neatness. Max will be really upset if he sees this!

If! Am I really thinking Max will never see his house again? What's happened here? Sam is now more concerned than ever for his friend. He's feeling creepy about his surroundings. Wondering what to do, he sits on the end of the overturned couch, bewildered. His phone rings and he jumps up. Relieved, the caller ID shows it's Max calling. Answering he sets the baseball bat down against the side of the couch.

"Hello!" He shouts into his phone.

"I can't stay on the phone long. Did you make it to Fort Lauderdale yet and do you have a car?" Max asks.

"Yes of course to both. You didn't meet me at the airport. What happened? What is going on? Where are you?"

"Don't say where it is," Max blurts. "But meet me in an hour at the place we went on our last double date together. If you don't show, I'll assume they got to you and I will move somewhere else. Do some evasive maneuvers on the way in case someone follows you! Oh, and turn off your cell phone now! Please hurry!"

That's all Max says and hangs up, leaving Sam standing in the living room dumbfounded. He's still hoping there is some simple confusion or misunderstanding at play, but that thought is slipping away quickly. Looking around Max's house and the tone of Max's voice, he knows this is no game or misunderstanding.

Sam needs to think back a moment in order to remember where the four of them had gone when they went on their last double date together. It was just before they graduated from Tech school. That was nearly three years ago.

Let's see, I kind of remember a great looking Cuban girl named Eliza that Max was dating. My date was a Southern brunette named Charlotte. We all had a terrific time together on that date. We tipped many brews on that double date at the…Elbo Room! That's it! The Elbo Room! I remember now, it's a friendly little bar and it's right on the beach road.

Thousands of college students spend spring break in Fort Lauderdale and the Elbo Room Bar is a famous watering hole for them. It became famous because of an old movie called 'Where the Boys Are.' We liked the bar because it's next to the beach. Even with the doors open, a gentle breeze always keeps the place comfortable in the warm weather.

When we left the bar late that night, we were feeling happy and a little tipsy and didn't want the night to end. We left the Elbo Room, crossed the street and walked down to the shoreline. I took my shoes and socks off and strolled along the shoreline in my bare feet. Charlotte and the others also took off their shoes, eventually. I remember feeling the cool sand between my toes and listening to the waves slapping on my feet at the shore. After a long walk along the beach, we found some unused canvas cabanas near the water's edge. Charlotte and I paired off into a nice cozy cabana and Max and Eliza went into another one. The moon was full and shined in on us as we laid down in the cabana and listened to the gentle splashing of the waves on the shore. We stayed there until the wee hours of the morning before we all headed back to our cars. That was a happy time.

I have to get to the Elbo Room on the East side of town and I have to do it in less than an hour. I also need to make sure no one follows me!

Chapter Seven

Mark dials his contact again.

"Did Max show at the airport?"

"No. I had one of your guys watch the incoming flights from Denver. He saw Sam when he got in and he was looking around like he was looking for Max, but Max wasn't there. Eventually he headed to baggage and rented a car."

"Where is Sam now?"

"He's at Max's house. I was going to talk to him here but if he gets spooked he won't take us to Max."

"He just received a call from Max. We intercepted the call from the tap on his line, but we still can't get a GPS location on him."

"Did you hear anything useful?"

"Well, sort of. He wants Sam to meet him somewhere they went many years ago. I have no idea where that is because he didn't say. He mentioned it was a place they'd gone to on a double date. He gave Sam an hour to get there or he'll leave."

"Okay, I called Ann to come and act like a worried friend. She'll be here in a couple minutes. I'll get her to drive him to Max and I'll follow her."

"Ann, is she the one who set up the foreign account? We're getting too many people knowing about our plans. This whole thing may go south, Mark. We never should have put that article in the Jamaica newsletter either!"

"We had to tell the Jamaican crew something. They think we're selling to our allies. I know Max is very patriotic, but it never occurred to me that he would read the Jamaican newsletter. Hell, I'm surprised any of my employees read our newsletters. And now all he sees is that we're selling weapons to a terrorist group and he wants to stop us."

"I hope you can stop him before he can do that."

"It shouldn't be a problem now. Sam will lead us to Max. I know I can handle Max when I see him."

"Keep me informed."

"Ann."

"Hey, Mark." Ann says answering her phone.

"How soon will you be here because Sam is getting ready to leave? He has to meet Max in an hour."

"I'm just a block away."

"Great! I'm glad you got here so fast. Thank you for doing this for me."

"No problem. What do you need?"

"Max's best friend, Sam is inside. He just flew in to help Max. Max is in some trouble and we're all trying to help him, but Max is confused and isn't trusting anyone. He went into hiding last night."

"Oh my! That's horrible! I don't know Max that well, but he seems okay. What do you need from me? How can I help?"

"Right now, Max only trusts his friend Sam. I need to make sure Max gets the help he needs. He is extremely valuable to the company, as you know with his high sales volume. He might lose a few of his sales if he can't get his problem resolved quickly. I know I can help him but I need to find him."

"Okay, tell me what to do boss."

"I believe Sam is getting ready to leave to go meet Max. Max just called a few minutes ago. Sam has to get there in an hour or Max is going to leave. I'd like you to knock on the door and tell him you are a close friend of Max's and that you are trying to help him. Offer to drive Sam to Max. Say whatever you have to, to get Sam to believe you aren't a threat. In other words, I need you to flirt with him. It's imperative that I locate Max."

"That's not my style, but in this case I'll do it. I don't want to be the reason you can't get Max help. It must be something bad if he went into hiding."

"Thanks Ann, I know I'm asking a lot and I'll make this up to you. This problem Max has affects the company so I really need to help him get it resolved."

"No problem. I'm pulling in now."

The rear door of Max's house poses only a small problem. It was literally pried open with a crowbar. There is splintered wood on both the jamb and the deadbolt area from the door being busted open from outside. Sam grabs a chair from the dining area to prop against the rear doorknob to secure the area. *That should hold it.* He stands admiring his work for a moment.

Without warning, the doorbell rings startling him. Frantic pounding on the front door makes Sam's body go back into full alert. Walking back toward the front door, he grabs the baseball bat leaning against the overturned couch. With a firm grip on the bat, he approaches the front door, ready as he cautiously turns the doorknob.

Opening the door, a petite young blonde woman is standing there looking at him anxiously, which dazzles him for a second as he locks onto her blazing steel gray eyes. She's wearing a tan business suit and matching shoes.

"Are you Sam?" She asks.

Easing his grip a little on the bat, he answers, "Yes". Pausing a second he adds. "And... ah, who might you be?"

"Thank God!" She says leaping forward catching Sam off guard, giving him a hug of desperation she quickly steps back staring at him for a few seconds.

"Um... I'm Max's friend, Ann." She says finally.

Noticing she is still touching his waist with her hands,

for some foolish reason, Chet's words came into his head. "Someday, if you're lucky, you will meet miss wonderful."

"Max." Sam mumbles stunned for a second until she begins talking again.

"Hasn't, um… hasn't he ever mentioned me?" She seems to be momentarily at a loss for words. "Anyway, he needs our help!"

"What the heck's going on? The house is a mess and where is Max?" He asks her dropping the bat and holding her arms with his hands. It is like an electric feeling unfamiliar to him. A moment later, she draws her arms away.

Looking into his eyes for a second, she appears puzzled before turning away. Seeing the car across the street she says, "We need to get away from here now! Will you take me to him? I can explain a little along the way. We have less than an hour to find him!"

"Um… Okay, Ann. Let's go!"

"We can take my car." She says stepping outside as Sam steps out closing the door. Pressing a button on the combo lock to engage the lock, a little motor whirs informing him the lock engaged. Checking it anyway, he wants to be sure the door actually locked.

Ann's car is a nice new white sedan with dark tinted windows, as if it just came out of a show room. Her car is much newer and nicer than the old Mustang. Maybe it will even be more comfortable, but Sam isn't concerned with comfort right now.

"I'd rather take mine. It's not as fancy, but my clothes and stuff are there, and it's fast." The excuse sounds good to him, because he doesn't want to go in her car. He knows someone may be able to follow her car. However, what concerns him much more is that she knows he only has an hour to get to Max!

Looking a little worried at what he said she agrees to go

in his car. Helping Ann into the black Mustang, gives him an opportunity to casually check out the street for anyone watching him. Getting into the car beside Ann, even with all the stress he's had, at that moment he can't help but to glance at her and admire her beauty as she sits next to him. Her mini skirt rose well above her knees when she sat down in the low car. She looks gorgeous sitting there in the Mustang in her business suit; with her fingernails painted a tan shade matching her clothes and her shoes. Her facial complexion looks flawless. She's wearing dark red lipstick, and of course those steel gray eyes! Sam is beginning to feel that under different circumstances he might want to know her a lot better.

In a true spy tradition, he purposely drives towards West Fort Lauderdale, away from where he really needs to go while questioning Ann more about Max but she doesn't offer much information.

"I know he's in some kind of trouble. I... I don't know exactly what it is. I know the boss wants to see him... before Max does anything crazy. I mean we need to convince him to talk to Mark. I just want to help out."

"You know, I didn't know Max had a friend as beautiful as you!" Sam blurts out without thinking. He immediately feels like a jerk.

"Oh, thanks." She says turning her face away from him as if embarrassed by his words.

"Sorry, I usually don't make bold statements like that. I'm just not thinking too clearly right now. My best friend is apparently in trouble over something, and I don't know what it is. Anyhow, do you know if... Did he pull a prank on someone? Maybe he got in trouble for it. You know, he is a big time prankster!"

"He is? No, I don't think this is a prank." She replies

facing forward again. "I'm not sure exactly what the trouble is. That's why I want to see him and convince him to talk to Mark. I know Mark wants very much to talk to him. Mark can explain everything."

"Well, let's see what happens. This whole thing is a mystery to me, too."

Driving along, his feelings are convincing him more and more she isn't telling him all she knows. *Something in her voice doesn't seem convincing. Plus, why did she seem surprised that I said Max is a prankster? True, it's not common knowledge. Only the people closest to him know he is a prankster. That means she can't be that close to him. She isn't his girlfriend. He isn't the kind of guy to fool around on Peggy, so what is her relationship to Max. She sounds like she is doing something she really doesn't want to do. Nearly every question I ask her she seems in a big hurry to get to Max. She keeps repeating that she just wants to help Max, and that Max needs to talk to Mark.*

She also said we only have an hour to find Max. How could she know that? There is only one way she could know about the one-hour limit and that is if she knew what Max said in the call!

Glancing at his rear view mirror, a black sedan seems to be keeping pace with him! Just like the black sedan across the street from Max's house. A little panic is beginning to set in now because he has a possible bad person in the car with him with another possible bad person following him. Remembering an evasive move he read about in a mystery book a long time ago, he needs to act.

The traffic is thick at this time of the day. Moving to the inside lane he waits and a few seconds later the black sedan moves to the inside lane also. He needs to find a gap in the right lane's cars to coincide with a right side road. A lot of cars are in the right lane. It's a perfect setup for his plan.

A few blocks later, a side street lines up just right with a gap in the right lane traffic. Gunning the engine and crossing in front of the other cars Sam makes a right turn from the left lane onto a side street. The lead car in the right lane just misses hitting him and blasts his horn. The black sedan following Sam in the inside lane can't follow without hitting another car. It worked! He is sure he is able to ditch the follower.

"My God! What did you do that for?" Ann shrieks staring at him with both her hands clutched to her chest. Her breathing sounds so labored and intense he thinks for a moment she might throw up in the car.

"Someone was following us. I had to lose the tail."

"Oh." She says quietly and begins looking at her lap. She seems to be even more worried than before. "You knew someone was following us?"

"Yes! I saw that same black sedan parked across from Max's house. I believe he was following us. What do you think?"

"Maybe it's Mark. Maybe he just wants to talk to Max."

"Maybe he wants to do more than talk." Sam notices Ann shrug her shoulders.

Sam drives around another few blocks zigzagging through back roads. As much as he hates to do it, it's time to ditch the blonde beauty. Suddenly pulling to the side of the road, he stops. He doesn't want to ditch her. He has to ditch her!

"Okay, get out!" He says looking straight ahead.

"What are you saying?"

"I'm sorry. I want you to get out, now."

"But what about Max?"

"He wants me to come alone. He will call you if he needs you. Now please get out and call a friend to come get you."

"I thought you were my friend!" Reluctantly she undoes

her seatbelt and opens the door to get out.

"I'm sorry Ann. Really sorry..." He says sincerely trying to apologize. Somehow, he is extremely attracted to this woman he knows nothing about. How can such a lovely woman be the enemy? *She must be one of them. Go figure!*

"Good luck, Sam!" She says sounding sincere, until the door slams shut.

Taking a quick glance at the pouting woman, he speeds off before he changes his mind. With a few more twists and turns, he's back on Sterling Road heading east this time toward the beach now that no one is following him.

"We lost him!" Mark says to his contact.

"You what! How did that happen?"

"He tricked me! He made some wild move in traffic and I couldn't follow him. He's long gone now. Hold on I've got another call." Mark says and flashes to the other call.

"Mark, Sam made me get out of his car. I'm standing here alone! I need someone to pick me up." Ann says.

"Get a street name for me. I'll come get you. Let me finish my other call." Mark flashes back to his contact.

"Um... Sam has ditched Ann, too. She's stranded along a road somewhere. I've got to go get her."

"This is bad Mark! Max and Sam will have to stay somewhere or go somewhere. They will have to use a credit card sometime. They can't keep paying cash too long. We'll have to wait and see."

Sam thinks about the situation driving along. *There really had to be a bug on Max's phone! Ann heard (or someone told her) about Max's brief call to me and she wanted me to lead them to Max. Holy cow! I feel like I'm in an espionage plot of some sort. This whole scene is crazy. Max really is in trouble and someone may really be out to kill him! Now*

I'm in it too! Ann will tell her cohorts all she's learned from our brief encounter. Jeez, I can't help feeling that Ann is a nice person, though. Someone I want to know better...

When I touched her arms at Max's house, I experienced such an unfamiliar feeling like an electric shock. I promise I will make this up to Ann later if she really is a friend of Max's.

Having ditched his tail, Sam accepts someone really is after Max. *If they've tapped Max's phone, there must be powerful people determined to get to Max!*

The voice mail from Mark came back to his memory. "Sam, this is Mark, Max has gone berserk and is hiding out somewhere. I am not a traitor!" Roaring along he races the main thoroughfare heading east because he still has a long way to go to reach the Elbo Room and Max. By now, he only has another twenty minutes or so to get to Max. If he doesn't get there in time, Max will leave. The knot in Sam's stomach tightens as he drives on toward the beach and the Elbo Room.

The Mustang finally reaches the coast and rumbles north along the A1A beach road passing the Bahia Mar Marina. Rolling along the beach is more developed than he remembers. In the past, he never paid any attention to the buildings along this area of the beach road. Now he is concentrating on remembering just where he has to go.

It's a warm day and the beachgoers are out in force. Sam is getting distracted glancing around with all the girls walking along the beach road passing by parked cars, wearing next to nothing. The warm friendly atmosphere makes him homesick for the city. He isn't sure exactly how to find the cozy little bar. As the Mustang rumbles along, the sky is changing from a bright blue to light gray and cloudy. "The chances of rain are sixty percent for the Fort Lauderdale area." He remembers the flight attendant on the plane saying. He knows rain is a typical forecast for this time of the year.

A few hundred feet ahead, he finally spots the Elbo Room. After stopping for a red light, and turning left onto Las Olas Boulevard, he passes right by the place. The Mustang loafs along the road for a couple blocks. Ahead is an office building with a decent sized parking lot. Swinging the Mustang into the parking lot and parking it just over two blocks from the beach road, he's sure it won't be spotted.

Walking down Las Olas Boulevard, and looking back toward the car, a low fence surrounds most of the lot helping to hide the car from the main drag. It will be hard to spot there, even if someone is looking for it.

The sky is turning grayer. A blanket of darkening clouds now covers the once bright sky as he walks along the boulevard. His nose catches a hint of ocean mist in the air. The walking feels good since he's spent a good part of the sitting due to traveling. Approaching the front of the Elbo Room, he hopes Max is still inside. Stepping inside he whispers to himself, "It's show time!"

Chapter Eight

Max is sitting in the back corner of the Elbo Room under the dimmest of light. His brown leather bag sits on a chair at his side. He is wearing tan slacks and a flowery Hawaii type shirt open at the top, but he looks depressed. He stares at a nearly empty Coors beer bottle on the table. His brown eyes are sunken in a bit and his black hair is unusually messy. He feels a slight hunger pang as he sips on his bottle of beer.

Checking his watch, it's been nearly an hour since he made his call to Sam. He looks around the practically empty bar. Perhaps this is normal at half passed four on a Saturday afternoon. It's too early for dinner and too late for lunch. Near the front of the bar, a man and a woman sit at a table sipping on orange colored drinks. *They must be taking a break from the beach since they're in skimpy bathing suits.*

Max sips the last of his beer and sets the bottle on the table. He feels his unshaven face with both hands.

"A little early for drinking." Sam says teasingly as he reaches the table startling Max. Looking up from the table Max breaks into a smile.

"You're here! You remembered!" Max's eyes light up as he gets up from his seat.

"Of course I remembered. You think I would..." Max jumps forward giving Sam a strong bear hug preventing him from finishing his sentence. It's Sam's second unexpected hug today. He actually enjoys both hugs, for different reasons. He's relieved that Max is still alive and hasn't been tortured or killed or something.

Max and Sam never hug. They joyfully shake hands or pat each other on the back. For some reason, hugging just isn't the manly thing for Max to do. Thus, it makes things even more absurd for Sam. Max backs off a few seconds later embarrassed having hugged Sam.

"Hey. I think that's our first hug. We should do that every five years or so."

"Yeah okay, so I overreacted," Max admits. "It's probably from the beer."

"It's okay, Max. I'm here now. I'm thinking this isn't just a big joke. So what's going on?" Sam asks speaking in a low voice.

"Really!" Max says with a hurt look on his face. "You thought this is a big joke! You thought I broke our pact!" Max looks shocked for a moment. Sam believes he might stamp his foot for emphasis.

"Let me show you," Max says recovering quickly. "I have this thing I shouldn't have!" He reaches in his pocket, brings out a small silver thumb drive, and waves it at Sam.

"Yeah, I know what that is. It's a thumb drive. I use them all the time to back up some files at work and home."

"It's only a sixteen gigabyte drive, but those sixteen billion bytes are damning! I know Mark wants this back at any cost. I believe he will even kill me to get it!" Max's voice is a little shaky as he sets the thumb drive on the table. Picking up his laptop from the chair next to him, he sets it on the table next to the thumb drive.

Max continues, "I hope you weren't followed and that you really did lose anyone tailing you because now Mark will have to make you disappear, too!"

Raising his eyebrows, Sam says. "You're kidding, right?"

Max shakes his head no. Looking at the cell phone on Sam's side, he grimaces. "You know they can track where you are and find us if you have your phone on. I only turned mine on down the street to call you and then I shut it off again and..."

"Relax Max. I turned it off right after you called me. When I was still at your house."

"You were at my house? That was a risky thing to do! What were you thinking! You know they think you are in on this thing. You could have been held for ransom - for the return of this disk!"

"Well, I didn't know what else to do. I tried calling you..."

"Gee, I should have told you not to go to my house." Max says turning sideways to think, seeming to be almost in tears. "I hate this!" Regaining control, he asks, "Was anyone there? What did you see?"

"Matter of fact it shocked me. What I saw I mean. Someone pried open your back door with a crowbar to get in. They totally messed up the doorframe. Your house is a mess. Someone's rifled through everything in your house. Things are thrown about and your furniture is over-turned. It's just awful. Who are 'They'?"

"Wow!" Max exclaims. 'They're traitors, Sam. My boss, Mark is a traitor! I can't believe it! I thought he was my best friend other than you, of course. I hate what I found out! I think there are others involved, too. I'm glad I left when I did. No telling what they'd do with me if they'd caught me! Thank goodness I was able to call you, because I know too much now."

"Traitors... your boss? Why are you calling him a traitor? I only met him the one time, but he seems like a nice guy."

"No, he's not! I have the proof right here!" Max picks up the thumb drive again waving it in the air. It takes Max a couple shaky attempts to stick the USB in the socket on the side of the laptop.

"I need to show you what's going on. Boy, you think you know someone, and then this happens! You know con men can act like your best friend and then they take you for everything! In case something happens to me and you can get away with this thumb drive, take it to the authorities wherever you are! I should have done that yesterday, but Mark is my... well he was my friend. I know he is friends with the local police. His high school friend is a Captain in the Fort Lauderdale police force. I think maybe the cops are looking for me, too?"

"Wow Max, this is all hard to take in. It's hard to believe what you're saying. I think you should go to the police or someone, anyhow. Maybe you are right. By the way, do you know a blonde woman named Ann?"

"Ann? The only woman I know named Ann is from the accounting department. She's a blonde, and a good looker, maybe twenty-five years old or so. She doesn't seem very interested in men, though. I think she had a bad experience with a guy, or maybe she's gay. I tried to date her with no luck. She gave me a very polite turndown, though. I know another guy who tried to date her, also with no luck. I doubt she knows anything about this. Why do you ask? What's her last name?"

"I don't know her last name, but she is a beauty! She showed up at your house and tried to act as if she knew you and wanted to help. She has gorgeous gray eyes and..."

"Oh my God! Miss gray eyes! That's her! Ann from accounting is a blonde bomb with gray eyes! You're saying she was at my house? She must be one of 'them' too! You didn't bring her with you did you?" Max acts panicky again.

"Does it look like I did?" Sam waves his hands around the bar. "No! I ditched her. Something she said bothered me. She knew I had less than an hour to find you. She must have been listening to our phone conversation somehow. I guess they really have tapped your phone, whoever 'they' are. She wanted us to go in her car. I thought if someone followed us, I would need to make evasive maneuvers and there is no way I could do that with her driving. She was reluctant that I didn't want to use her car, but seemed desperate to have me take her along. I admit I liked looking at her and it influenced my decision. I took her along even though I knew I shouldn't have done it. You never mentioned anyone named Ann, which should have been a clue. I don't think Peggy would approve of you having Ann as your friend, either. Well anyway, I saw we were being followed."

"You were followed!"

"Yes. A black sedan followed us. I swerved through some heavy traffic. I tried a trick move and it worked. I lost the tail. Ann looked shocked I did that. Then as I was driving around some side streets, I realized it's stupid to bring her with me, so I ditched her."

"That's good! That's very good!" Max said raising a hand to his face. "I guess she must know about this thing, too." He pointed to the thumb drive again. "She must be in on this with Mark. You did good to ditch her, Sam!"

"She didn't seem to know much of anything about your situation. She just wanted to convince you to talk to Mark."

"I bet!" Max blurts. "Lead Mark right to me so he can..."

"Hey, what's on that disk thingy that's so damning?"

"You'll see! Come on this side so you can see the screen. Hey look outside; it looks like a storm is rolling in."

"Oh yeah, it was getting dark out there when I got here. I can feel the air has changed though. I guess I got so caught up in our conversation I didn't notice. Okay, make room and let's see what you've got here." Settling into a chair on the same side of the small table as Max, Sam can't wait to see what has Max so upset that he believes his boss Mark will kill him to get that thumb drive back! Even though he's hungry, Sam knows the knot in his stomach isn't a hunger pang!

"Before you start, let's order something to eat," Sam says. "I'm starving. I haven't eaten anything since early this morning.

"Go ahead." Max frowns.

"Hey miss!" Sam waves at the waitress.

A young ash blonde woman in her twenties comes over to their table. Leaning over the table and smiling she takes their order, Max checks out her black short-shorts and red and black bikini top.

"What can I get you?" She asks.

Sam smiles back at her and notices she has a tattoo on her upper left chest area of a black, teeth-bearing bat hanging from a horizontal golden guitar.

"Are you a 'Danglebatts' fan?" Sam asks remembering the logo on Chet's business card.

"Yes I am! They're the best! I went to their concert here last year. I have all their albums. They're coming back again. I want to show them my tattoo!"

"I'm sure Chet and the gang will love seeing it." Sam says knowing it will get a rise from her.

"You know Chet, Chet Hatter? He lives right here in Fort Lauderdale somewhere. How do you know Chet?"

"He's just a casual acquaintance. We jam together some time."

"OMG! You gotta take me when you do that!"

"What's your name?" Sam asks.

"Like Chet-ah... I call myself Chet-ah for Chet Hatter! Let me give you my number." She says.

Sam glances at Max for a second. Max closes his eyes and slowly turns his head back and forth in disbelief.

"Sure. Could you bring us a couple of roast beef specials and two Coors? You can give me your name and number then."

"Deal! Oh, what's your name handsome?"

"I'm Sam and my friend here is Max. I love your outfit too!"

"Thank you Sam." She smiles.

Max and Sam watch her as she turns around bounces away with the order. When she's out of earshot, Max gives Sam an evil eye look. "I can't believe it! What are you doing? With all my troubles, you're hitting on this girl! And... what about Jessica back in Denver?"

"Jessica is history. She broke up with me last night. I wanted to split with her anyway. We were starting to bore each other."

"Sorry about that Sam. Okay, so who the heck are the Danglebatts, Sam? Somehow I don't think you realize the gravity of this situation." Max says visibly annoyed being Sam isn't as nervous and edgy as he is. However, behind Sam's masked expression, he is just as nervous as Max.

"I apologize." Sam says sincerely. "Don't tell Chetah but I just met Chet Hatter on my flight from Denver. I had to book a first class ticket in order to get here today and that's how I met him. He was my seatmate. We had a good chat. He plays lead guitar for the Danglebatts band. He gave me his business card with their logo on it. It's just like the tattoo on Chetah. You see why I couldn't resist asking her about it?"

"This is insane! Sam, you need to concentrate on this problem at hand. You need to see this stuff!"

"I'll try not to get distracted again. I'm sorry. Now please show me what this is all about."

Closing his eyes Max sighs and begins telling his tale, almost in a whisper.

"The Jamaican bulletin is quite different from the bulletin Silvan Enterprises prints for the US." Max says. Continuing, he informs Sam about why he went to see his boss

Friday morning, ending with how he found the thumb drive and why he accidentally took it home with him.

"Silvan Enterprises in Jamaica is producing a new chemical weapon! That's bad enough."

Sam asks, "Silvan Enterprises is making a chemical weapon? Isn't that illegal in the states?"

"Yes, I think so." Max blurts. "Apparently the Jamaican government and Mark are less concerned about manufacturing and selling deadly chemical weaponry. As I said, the bulletin said Silvan Enterprises developed a deadly chemical warfare device called the 'Deadly Orange Cloud'. They called it the 'Deadly Orange Cloud' because the main ingredient is the toxic orange mud from the 'Bauxite Lakes' in Jamaica. It's a small device, but it can distribute a massive deadly 'orange cloud' into the air over a large group of people, soldiers, or any living things. Whatever it touches, it kills! When I confronted Mark about why he would authorize making the bomb, Mark told me not to mention it in the US!"

"Mark told you that?"

"Yes, and there's more! He told me it's an attempt to help keep Silvan Enterprises solvent in our tough economic time! Heck, I know we're very solvent! With all the sales I brought in last year plus all the others, our company is rolling in dough. My sales alone were millions of dollars. Unless someone is embezzling money, there is no way we're hurting financially. Anyway, let me show you why I'm hiding out and what's on this thing."

"Hey, maybe someone is stealing from the company."

"If that were the case Mark would report it to the authorities. An investigation would be launched, new temporary or permanent procedures would be installed, and the persons would be caught. You can't embezzle that kind of money without leaving a trail. Besides, you don't decide to develop and produce chemical weapons because your company was a victim of embezzlement."

"You're right. I wasn't thinking that far, sorry."

Opening the first file, a boilerplate brochure appears. It explains how easy it is to disburse the Cloud into a group of soldiers or a crowd of people. The next file is a list of organizations, names, email addresses, and phone numbers.

Most of the names are hard for Sam to pronounce. "This file is a list of terrorist organizations with last known email addresses and phone numbers. This next one has the Jamaican Bulletin article in it."

"Look at this, this file has information about various terrorist militants all over the world with whom Mark has apparently sent an e-brochure and invitations for ordering the new 'Orange Cloud' weapon! Then there's this, it's a video clip that shows how easily the 'Orange Cloud' kills some sheep. Let me run this video. This is a really scary thing! Put on these ear buds and listen to how it kills!" Max says handing Sam ear buds.

Both men wear an ear bud in their ears as the video starts playing. Watching in amazement as the video comes to life on the laptop screen; they couldn't peel their eyes away from the screen.

The title appears and reads "Demonstration for the Orange Cloud."

"Hello." A man says wrapped in a poncho with a bandana across his face. "We're a part of the hidden society. We want to show you the power of our new bomb. It has deadly powers beyond what you may think for such a small bomb. It's easy and safe to store, and it's highly effective at killing. The effects have a half hour life so within a short time the area is safe again. Additionally it's nearly undetectable until used because it contains no detectable metals."

The man holds up a small black container about four inches long and two inches in diameter. It looks like a large black ostrich egg. Then the masked man begins explaining how to detonate the Cloud. The narrator explains. "The main ingredient in this bomb is toxic orange sludge." The man says as the camera swings down onto a tray of orange goop.

"Jamaica has tons of this, and by concentrating the toxins from the sludge we're able to speed up the killing power a thousand fold when mixed with some other compounds. That is why we make the bombs here in Jamaica. This weapon is easily carried or transported and kills everything within a hundred meter area when ignited. Nearly any kind of triggering device can be used to detonate it once you are a safe distance away.

The scene cuts to a group of sheep peacefully grazing in a field. He sets off a bomb in the area and quickly an orange cloud forms over the small group of sheep.

One by one, the sheep seem to writhe in pain and sink down and die. They tip over one at a time jerking their legs for a few seconds and then are quiet. The whole process takes less than a minute and all the sheep are dead! The narrator waves at the sheep. "See how easy it is to kill?"

Chapter Nine

Let's get a quick recap of this new weapon. It's small and easy to carry; it contains no detectable metal parts, is highly efficient and uses any triggering device of your choice. Place your order 'today' by emailing us." The man continues after giving the price per bomb in US dollars as the ordering email address banner comes on the screen.

"Incredible, huh. Now, look at this." Max says closing the video and opening another file.

"Here." Max scrolls down the order to show where a man named Almir Najya ordered one hundred of the Orange Clouds to be shipped to London, England.

"Almir Najya is a terrorist!" Max shouts in a whisper. "I always regarded Mark as a fairly close friend and not just my boss. I thought he was honest and upright. Yet after seeing all the shocking things on this thumb drive, I called him to see if he had really authorized selling chemical weapons to a terrorist group. "Now you see why I say Mark is a terrorist? He told me he is doing this because the company needs money, but this proves that's a lie."

"But he can make lots of money selling these bombs."

"True, but they can make trillions without making bombs from what I see."

"You've lost me Max. I'm not following you."

Max waves a hand clamming up as Chet-ah approaches with their sandwiches and beers. Leaning across the table again, she sets down the food and drinks, before reaching into her cleavage and retrieving two slips of paper. After handing the bill to Max, she turns towards Sam and smiles brightly handing him a small piece of paper. The bill is just over twenty dollars. Taking a wad of bills from his pocket and peeling off two twenties, Max hands Sam the money and bill to give to Chet-ah.

"Keep the change!" Sam says handing her the money.

"Really? You guys are the greatest!" She says, giving Sam a little hug and a big smile. She bounces up and down a few times before turning and walking away.

Max is annoyed as he and Sam watch Chet-ah walk out of sight and into the kitchen. Shaking his head as Chet-ah disappears out of hearing range Max says.

"You're awfully generous with my money!"

"I thought she deserved a big tip. Anyway, what happened then?"

"Oh, forget it!" Max says. "By the way, Sam you gave that girl almost a hundred percent tip, using my money!"

"I wanted her to be happy!" Sam says hunching his shoulders at Max again.

"She would have been happy with a fiver!"

"Yes, but then she'd have to bring back change. I want her to leave us alone so I can hear what you have to say. So it makes sense to me."

"Oh, never mind!" Max says frowning for a few seconds. "Okay, the video says they've found a way to concentrate the toxins in the sludge a hundred fold. I started thinking about that after I got over my initial shock. Sure, the sludge is toxic because it's polluted from the chemicals used in the aluminum mining, but it doesn't kill on contact as this video shows. It takes a long time for the toxins to build up in your system in order to kill. Mark also says we're helping the Jamaican government to get rid of this stuff and that the government is going to pay Mark to take it."

"Yeah, so?" *I think Max has lost it!*

"So, if it is that easy to get rid of tons of sludge the country would have done so already. These bombs are only the size of an ostrich egg, which means they aren't going to get rid of a massive quantity of sludge in the bombs. They could easily just take the small amount they need for the bombs.

Are you following me now?"

"No Max, I'm sorry. I get what you are saying about Mark handling all this sludge and that he only needs a tiny bit for the egg thingy. Then he's stuck with large amounts of this stuff. So why would a government sell it knowing Mark can't get rid of it either, but then you've lost me again."

"You're almost there Sam. As I see it, the only reason the government would give this stuff to us is if they know it can be disposed of without illegal dumping or any other use like bombs where the country could be held responsible. This tells me, Mark has found a way to cleanse the sludge of the toxins and the left over portion has to be the concentrated chemicals removed from the mud. It explains why the bombs are so potent and why the government is willing to give Mark the sludge. Therefore, if Mark has a process that can remove the toxins from soils, he can make money from every country that has contaminated ground soil. The problem I still have is Mark must have either made the government think he is able to neutralize the toxins he removes or that he will give them back to Jamaica in extremely small quantities."

"Why would the country want it back?"

"Because Sam, they have to know what happens to the toxins so they won't be held responsible for illegal use. It seems to me they would require government officials to oversee the process. This means Mark wouldn't be buying the sludge, it's more likely he's being paid for the cleanup and removal of the toxins. A process like that would make untold amounts of money around the globe. Think of all the places that have mining operations that pollute the soil, or nuclear plants and oil and gas stations and refineries. Having a process like that is priceless so there would be no need to make bombs for cash flow."

"I think I see what you mean, so why would he?"

"Exactly! That's the question. I just don't have an answer. Maybe I'm off track on this decontamination process, but these documents prove I'm not crazy about him making and selling chemical weapons. The proof is all right here."

"And you called him after seeing this stuff!" Sam looks at Max in amazement. "Why didn't you go to the police or someone?"

"Looking back, I think calling Mark was a big mistake! I called as soon as I saw the video without thinking. I was in shock like you. Plus, Mark is my friend. I wanted him to explain why."

"At first, he was cheery. Then he realized I have his thumb drive and that I looked at his files. His tone changed immediately from the carefree person I know to a clipped cold voice of a maniac! He told me this is bigger than just Silvan Enterprises. He told me the order has to stay top secret. No one is to know about it. He seemed anxious to retrieve this thumb drive saying many people will be hurt if I didn't cooperate. Then he says, 'We'll be right over to get it'! When he said that, I felt a chill go up my spine. I panicked. Suddenly I felt my life was in danger. I mean, this is major stuff, my boss selling weapons to one of our enemies! Besides why didn't Mark say 'I' would be right over? Why did he say 'We' would be right over? At that time, I knew there were others, perhaps powerful others involved in this. I didn't want to hear his explanation. I hung up on him and took the thumb drive and my laptop; I stuck some clothes in a bag, and left the house. I drove around for a while trying to think about what to do next."

"You mentioned embezzlement too. Maybe Mark or someone has drained the till and the company really is going broke. Why didn't you just go to the police or someone? Why did you end up here?"

Max's face momentarily flushes red, and he shouts, "My God, you still don't get it! Mark has powerful friends. Even in the police force. Believe me Sam; I really didn't know what to do! Now I've pulled you into this mess! Now both our lives are in danger!"

"Hello." Mark answers his cell phone.

"He's apparently parked somewhere near the beach along Las Olas Boulevard."

"Are you sure? He was west-bound before I lost him."

"Absolutely. The car is stopped."

"Why did it take so long to get this information? I could have been there already."

"The car rental place refused to just hand over the GPS codes for the car so we could track him. I had to pull some strings. Is there any place near there that they may have gone to on a date?"

"Las Olas and the beach… I don't know, there could be a lot of places. That area is all hotels, restaurants and clubs. I'd have to drive along the boulevard to see if I can spot them. Do you have anyone near there?"

"No. I'll send a man there to check it out right away."

"I'll head there too. Let's hope they'll still be in the area. They may have ditched the vehicle and gone elsewhere by now."

"Call me if you find them. Bye."

"I can see now why you sounded so panicky when you called Max. I've never seen you like this before. It all seems so unlikely Mark would do this, yet the evidence is right here."

"You can imagine how shocked I am too; he's like my best friend other than you, but he knows the police Captain Fred Holland. He could have me arrested and then I don't know what would happen, so I ended up in a run-down motel called Griffin's Rooms last night. The attendant took cash with no questions asked. I was able to register with a fictitious name and hide out for the night."

"You, Max Merchado, slept in a dive last night!"

"What else could I do? Most hotels require you to provide ID, so it was my only option!

This morning I got on a BCT bus again and rode around to Las Olas Boulevard, and walked to the Elbo Room. That's how I got here. I don't think Mark or anyone else knows where I am now. My only traceable actions are my phone calls to you. I knew you would remember where we took our last dates and no one else would know that."

"You're right there. I had to stop and think a bit myself. That was a while ago."

Pressing the power off button on the laptop Max says, "I only turn this thing on when I need to. I forgot to bring the charger with me." Finishing his sandwich Max says, "You know I spent a month down there in Jamaica. I like to keep track of what goes on. That's what started this whole mess, but I'm glad I found this disk. We can stop Mark and his illegal shipment! It looks like Mark is willing to produce and sell that weapon to whoever pays the price. Even to radicals and enemies! So you see Mark lied to me saying he has an order from one of our allies!"

"I'm still in shock over your news Max. I never in a million years imagined anything like this."

"I know, right. I searched that name, Almir Najya. He is a leader in a terrorist organization in Afghanistan. An article on him also says there is currently a small cell believed to be operating in London, England. The order is supposed to ship from Kingston, Jamaica directly to the London airport. Once I saw the invoice for the chemical weapons and who it's for, I have to believe Mark is a traitor!" Max hushes up as he sees the waitress walking toward them again.

"You need anything else?" Chet-ah asks.

"No thanks Chet-ah." Sam says. "I'll call you if I get to jam with Chet some time."

"Call me anytime!" Chet-ah says flashing a big smile at Sam before turning around to leave.

Being so engrossed in Max's tale Sam didn't bother to watch Chet-ah walk away, and instead urges Max to continue. "What now, Max?"

"I think selling weapons to our enemies has to be illegal, doesn't it?"

"I think so, Max." Sam says nodding his head in agreement again. "As far as I know, selling weapons to our enemies has to be illegal or at least unethical. This is incredible news. Your boss definitely sounds like a traitor!"

"No doubt about it! Now let me explain my plan."

"Plan?" Sam hushes up as Chet-ah comes back again.

He watches her come to him and lean against his leg smiling. "Are you sure you don't need anything?" She asks.

"I'm good for now." Sam says. "I've got your number. I'll call you later." He says grinning at her, and patting her bare leg.

"Okay, Sam." She says smiling again. She continues smiling back at him as she walks away. Sam shakes his head smiling at her.

"We have to go now." Max says and gets up to leave. "Where's your car?"

"It's just a couple blocks west of here." Sam knows he needs to stop fooling around and help his friend. *Max is under a lot of stress and we need to deal with this.* Sam's brain is having a hard time processing things, as he gets up to join Max. So much information has come to him in such a short period, making him feel stunned listening to Max's plan. Try as he might all Sam hears is mumbling. With reality sinking in, he realizes how formidable their situation is. Mark is conspiring with a terrorist group about to ship chemical weapons to one of our enemies.

The gravity of all this hits, just as the sky opens up and begins pouring rain on the roof. A clap of thunder sounds outside causing Sam to jump. He wonders if someone wants to wipe them out. Another loud clap of thunder makes him jump again, as it booms through the rain. Sam is more than concerned. He is scared! He has to try to sort out what Max is saying as he stops at the doorway with Max.

As Max is concluding, Sam tunes back in.

"You see why we have to go to Jamaica and stop that shipment?"

"Jamaica? No, I don't Max. Why do we have to go to Jamaica? Why not just call the authorities?"

"As I told you, that order is probably ready to ship on Monday. This is Saturday, not much time left to stop the shipment. With all the red tape here in the US, they would never get to the shipment in time. We might cause an international incident, if that shipment isn't stopped. You are the only person I know who I can trust. I have a plan. We have to get to Jamaica right away!"

Another clap of thunder comes just as Sam is about to speak, startling him again. The sky is now a very dark gray and the rain pelts hard on the roof of the bar. The whole scene seems like a murder mystery without the dead bodies. At least so far! Sam is hoping against hope that Max's plan will not lead them to being dead bodies!

Even though it's a warm rainy afternoon, Sam feels chilly and has a huge knot in his stomach threatening to squeeze the air from his lungs.

"The police can investigate and stop that shipment.

Why do you want to go down to Jamaica? It sounds like 'they' might really kill you!" Another clap of thunder strikes before Sam can say another word. He is in awe of the storm. The thunder and the rain just add to the feeling of excitement and danger!

"Listen, Sam, please! I don't believe the US will react in time. It's a political thing. It's also a weekend in Jamaica, none of the people I know down there work on a weekend. You know it would create a newsworthy incident if I just blow the whistle here. It's a matter of principle too, Sam. I think together we can stop that shipment and get some people thrown in jail! I cannot stand the thought that Mark and some other people in Silvan are conspiring with enemies of America! And..., I can't do it alone, Sam."

"I don't know, Max... Jamaica?"

"I spent some time working down there last year. I know a police officer Mister Lokie and my friend Byron who I'm certain is not corrupt. Between all of us, we can fix whatever is wrong in Silvan Enterprises. The package is probably ready to ship on Monday. We have to go there and stop that shipment! Are you in or out?"

Max stares at his best friend hating dragging Sam into this horrific situation but he has no choice. He waits what seems like an eternity for Sam to speak.

"Yeah, I guess. I think you're right that calling the authorities won't be good. It's already the end of day on Saturday, so they probably won't be able to get to the shipment before it's too late. I doubt they'll take our word for it and will want to investigate first. By that time, the shipment could be gone. You know how government works, everything takes time, it's time we probably don't have."

"Do you see why I need you?" Max says. "Now we need to get some guns, and disguises, and fly to Jamaica. We need to get to Kingston!"

Chapter Ten

"Hold on there!" Sam says. "You want us to get some guns? You want us to shoot someone?"

"They're just for protection. We might need protection."

"And how are you going to get guns through metal detectors at the airport?"

"You know we can't, silly. We can buy guns when we get to Kingston. I have a wad of cash on me. It'll be easy to get them there." Max says, whispering in Sam's ear.

"Well, I guess, if we have to. I can't think of another option, so... We'd better get going. I have an old Mustang a couple blocks from here. I don't think they can find it. You think we need disguises?" Sam asked getting up to leave.

"Yeah, we need to go incognito. Anyhow, it's time to move out. I don't want to stay anywhere too long and we need to get to an airport. Excellent! The rain is a mere sprinkle now." Peeking out, Max starts down the sidewalk. "We're good. I don't see anyone suspicious. Let's hurry though."

Walking quickly towards the parking lot in the light sprinkle Sam remarks, "Boy that was a quick storm. After being in Denver, I've kinda forgot how Florida weather can be.

"Yep, it may rain buckets but these storms can blow over fast. I especially like how it can pour on one side of the street and not on the other. I'm not real crazy about the lightning though." Max says.

"I know what you mean. Well here we are."

"Where? I don't see anything that looks like a rental."

"It's here, see that Mustang. That's it. What do you think?"

"Wow! This is some car! Look at the rain beading up on it. They must have a lot of wax on this baby."

"I'd have preferred something duller." Sam says. "This looks conspicuous."

"Maybe it's so conspicuous no one will notice it. You know how easy rental cars can be to spot. Nobody would look for a fancy sport car like this."

"Maybe." Sam says unlocking the doors and getting inside the car.

"Let's go to the Miami Airport." Max says. "I already looked up the flights. There is a flight to Jamaica on American Airlines leaving from Miami at 7:25 PM. I didn't want to make a reservation since they might be watching for that."

Sam maneuvers the Mustang out of the parking lot and turns west on Las Olas Boulevard toward I-95. Realizing the danger is real; Sam keeps checking his rear view mirror for anyone tailing him as he eventually drives southward. The traffic is terrible. Cars are cutting in and out of lanes, but the traffic never comes to a complete stop. Sam handles the fast bumper-to-bumper traffic flawlessly all the way to Miami International Airport.

It's almost six o'clock by the time they finally make it to the car rental agency. "I've got to return the car before we fly out. I only rented it for the day with an option to extend since I didn't know what your plans were."

"Okay. Good thinking. I'm not sure how long we'll be."

"Hi." Sam says stepping up to the rental counter. "I rented a car earlier today when my flight got in and I've had an emergency and need to fly home tonight so I need to return the car now since I won't be here tomorrow."

"Sure, no problem sir. I'm sorry your plans have changed. As you know as a Vintage car rental company, we need to ask a few questions to ensure our quality service. Were you happy with the vehicle may I ask?"

"Oh yes. I liked it very much."

"Did the vehicle you rented," The clerk looking at Sam's rental agreement says. "The Mustang was it? Did the Mustang meet or exceed your expectations?"

"It definitely exceeded them."

"How likely would you be willing to rent from us again?"

"A lot. I'm sorry. I know you have to ask all these questions, but I have to catch my flight."

"Sure sir. I understand. Were you able to fill the tank before returning the car?"

"Oh crap! No. It slipped my mind."

"Okay, no problem. If you will sign here and initial here we'll get you on your way."

Grabbing their bags, they hustle to the airport lobby. "See, this is where we could use disguises." Max says walking alongside Sam. "We could be changing our appearance as we walk. I know they have cameras in the lobby. Someone might recognize us there."

"They have cameras in the parking lots too, Max." Sam says. "I really don't think they are looking for us here. How could they know where we are?"

"Maybe you're right. I just hope they don't know we're going to Jamaica. They could have us detained. Maybe even kill or disposed of us, too. Let's hope they don't know we are going to Kingston! I think it's easier to get away with murder down there. What do you think?"

"I think your mind is spinning, making up scenarios because you're scared, but thanks for reminding me about being killed in a foreign country. Do you even know if there still is room on the flight to Jamaica?"

"I think you think too much." Max says.

"Let's see if we can get on this flight."

"I'm almost to the beach." Mark says answering his cell again.

"The car is on the move again. It looks like it's moving south toward Miami. Does he know anyone in Miami?"

"Yes. His parents live there and so does his girlfriend's family."

"It looks like he's headed for the airport."

"Well maybe they're planning to pick up Max's car or switch rentals now that we know the car Sam rented. They could be planning anything at this point. Max is slicker than I anticipated. I never thought he'd be smart enough to elude us this long."

"Uh oh. The tracking on the car just went dead. Hold on, let me make a call."

"Okay."

Pause… "He just returned the car. He told the clerk he had an emergency come up and he needed to fly out right away."

"Did he say where?"

"No, but we have a trace on Max's credit cards already and started one on Sam's this morning. There's no way they can have enough cash on them to buy airline tickets so as soon as they charge the tickets we'll be able to know what they're up to."

"By that time, they could be gone again. Why don't we just get them now?"

"We can't just barge into the airport and apprehend them. That would mean bringing a lot of other people in and making a scene. Our goal here is to stay under the radar."

"That's true. I guess I can take the corporate jet to wherever they're heading. I can get there before they do since they're taking a commercial flight."

"I'll let you know as soon as I get a destination."

"Hey, we're in luck, there's no line at the counter. Let's see if we can get seats because this is the last flight to Jamaica today."

"Can I help you?" An attendant asks.

"I hope so." Max says. "I need two tickets on your flight to Kingston, Jamaica today."

Tapping several keys searching for options the attendant says, "The economy fare is booked sir. The only seats we have left are two seats in first class. Do you want those?"

"Yes please, also can you book a return economy class for next Friday?"

"Do you have any bags to check?"

"No."

"That will be twenty eight hundred and fifty eight dollars. May I have your names and ID's for the tickets please?"

Max's eyes open wide thinking he heard the price wrong. "Um, okay, how much?"

Max hears the clerk repeat the amount. "It is first class sir."

"Wow! Here's my Visa card and passport. Sam, she needs your ID, and give me your passport."

"Here you go, Max."

"Very good, sir." The clerk says to Max tapping the keys entering their info and charging Max's card.

"Your tickets for Kingston, Jamaica will be right up."

A minute later, the clerk hands the tickets to Max, pointing to his right saying, "You guys better hurry!"

Walking swiftly toward the security check, Max and Sam glance around looking for anyone suspicious. All looks normal.

By 6:45, they are at the gate. They still have almost a half an hour until boarding time.

"Your man just purchased two tickets to Jamaica."

"Wow! I can't believe he's actually trying to go there."

"Yes, the plane leaves in less than an hour. You have to go there and stop him!"

"Damn! Max is patriotic to a fault. He's going there to kill this project. I'm heading home now to grab a bag, and then I'll take the corporate jet."

"This shipment has to go through as planned. Do whatever you have to do to stop him, Mark!"

"I'll keep in touch." Mark hangs up and calls his man in Jamaica.

"Mister Lokie?"

"Yes, Mister Goodman. What can I do for you?"

"We have a situation..."

The gate area is crowded and Sam nervously twitches worrying about the bad guys finding him before he gets on the plane. After what seems like an eternity, he finally hears the boarding call.

As Sam is walking to board the plane with Max, a wave of dizziness comes over him. *What am I doing going to Jamaica? What if we die there? I don't even have a will made out. I bequeath all my worldly goods to my mother! I should have written that down somewhere.* Staggering a little, he pauses a few seconds. Max grabs his arm to keep him from tipping over. Finally, they move forward.

"Are you all right?" Max asks as Sam steadies himself.

"Oh, I'll be fine."

Max watches him for a bit to be sure Sam is all right before stepping forward and boarding the plane. After Max goes on board, Sam steps forward to join him.

"May I please see your ticket sir," A neatly dressed female attendant asks Sam.

"Oh, yes." Sam answers handing her his folder. As he walks inside the plane, he sees Max has taken the window seat.

"Um... I wanted the window seat," Sam says, a little annoyed.

"But my ticket says 2A."

"You gave me the wrong pass."

"Well, okay." Max concedes.

Paranoia is taking over Sam as it had Max previously. *I can't believe I'm on a plane heading to Jamaica. I've never been outside the US before and now I'm heading into a dangerous situation. Why was Max able to convince me we could stop Terrorists! Terrorists! I must have been so shocked by Max's news that his plan sounded doable. We'll have terrorists after us. Oh my God, I have a headache.* Staring out the window Sam watches the ground crews work before turning in his seat to watch each passenger come by to see if there is any hint of - he doesn't know what as he looks for someone who seems out of place, maybe a spy. *Why am I watching everyone? You know the bad guy I'm hoping to spot will blend in with everyone else. It's not like they'll be wearing signs that say I'm a bad guy or I'm a terrorist. We probably won't be able to spot the people after us until it's too late. I think that's what I'm afraid of; Max and I are not professionals at this sort of thing. Whatever this 'thing' is.*

"Well, we're on the way! Thanks for coming, Sam. I know we will get this problem solved quickly." Max says oozing confidence again.

"I just hope we get through this problem alive!"

"The crooks will be jailed down in Jamaica, and we'll get Mark and company when we bring back the proof! I know we'll be successful, Sam. Have some faith and just relax. After we land, we should be done with this in a few hours. I have good connections down there. I have my good friends Byron and Mister Lokie there. They will help us, afterward we will party and celebrate!"

"I hope you're right."

"You'll see, Sam. The worst that can happen is if the plane goes down. Mark thinks I am hiding out some place. I know he doesn't think I would actually go to Kingston. The surprise attack is a good offense for us."

For a moment, watching out the window as the ground drops away, Sam watches the sun cast strange looking shadows on the buildings and trees while it slowly sets in the west with sleepy eyes due to the lateness if the day. Even with the adrenalin pumping in his veins, the drone of the jet engines makes him drowsy. Getting up at 4 a.m. Colorado time isn't part of his normal routine, especially on a Saturday morning, so between the tension and a day of travel it's all catching up with him quickly. In spite of his apprehension about the events to come, leaning his seat back, he dozes off into a dead man's sleep.

The drone of the engines is relaxing letting Sam rest in complete comfort dreaming peacefully about a quiet walk along a sandy shore. A loud cracking sound wakes him up and his eyes fly open as a window on the other side of the plane disintegrates! An enormous whoosh of air comes as small objects are flying around the cabin. People are screaming! A woman is shouting, "No! Please God, help us!" Another crack comes from the port side engine and begins making a popping sound before it explodes falling off the wing and sending the plane spinning! The Captain announces, "We're going down! Brace yourselves for impact!" Just as the other engine quits the plane spirals and some people are bouncing around the cabin from the planes sudden nosedive! Bloody faces and arms, clothes and other objects float past him! Screams and blood is everywhere! Panicking, Sam knows this has to be someone shooting them down to save Mark's shipment!

Fumbling desperately trying to unbuckle his seatbelt, Sam believes the safest place on a plane is in the tail section. Sam thrashes around wildly. His seatbelt will not release, and he keeps tugging and tugging at it until he feels Max grip his shoulder shaking him awake.

"What are you doing?" Sam hears Max shouting. "What are you doing with your belt?"

Dazed, Sam wakes up finding he has a death grip on his own pants belt instead of his seatbelt. He's pulled it so tight he is in pain and can barely breathe! Looking around frantically nothing is amiss in the plane, although a few passengers are looking at him strangely.

It was a dream! We're not falling out of the sky! The plane isn't being shot down! Oh my God, it was just a dream! With some effort, he relaxes his belt to its normal notch. He can feel sweat running down his forehead.

"Sam! What's wrong? Talk to me!"

"Uh... Just a bad dream." He manages to say.

"What do you mean a bad dream? You were pulling your belt and thrashing yours arms."

"Sorry Max. I dreamt the plane was being shot down to stop us and we were all about to die."

"Oh, so you still have nightmares when you're stressed. You didn't say anything to me. I didn't realize."

"That's because until this situation arose, I hadn't had any in a really long time."

"Well I'm sorry Sam. Stay awake, we're almost to Kingston."

"Trust me buddy, you have no idea I don't want to sleep

again while this plane is in the air." Sam says watching as Jamaica approaches outside his window.

His nightmare is over, but he knows another nightmare is about to start; only this one is real!

Max knows Jamaica very well from his stay here. He's always been interested in the country. It's a good-sized island about one hundred twenty miles south of Cuba. The population is approaching three million people of various descents. About one third of the people reside in or around Kingston, the capitol of Jamaica, which gained its independence in August of 1962 from the United Kingdom. The primary language is English and Jamaicans drive on the wrong side of the road (the left side), just as the Brits do.

The Jamaican motto is, "Out of Many, One People". Max has always been interested in Jamaica and reads a lot about it.

Except for Sam's nightmare, the flight to Kingston is uneventful. Max peers out the window at the beautiful blue waters on the Southern side of the island as the plane makes a large circle around Kingston. The view is breathtaking to him. He sees an enormous number of trees, houses, and buildings. Kingston looks like a normal city in the United States. A few minutes later, the plane touches down at Norman Manley International Airport on the Southeast edge of Kingston, Jamaica.

"We're here!" Max shouts as the plane comes to a stop.

"Are you sure about this?" Sam asks.

"Yes! The first thing we need to do is get a car."

"What are we going to do?" Sam mutters as they debark from the plane and start walking toward the lobby.

"Let's get to the lobby and rent a car." Max says confidently grabbing his bag. "I have a plan."

Chapter Eleven

"I hope you have a good plan," Sam says. "I still think we should have talked to the authorities. I don't even know why I am here."

"You'll see." Max assures him. "I can't do this without you, Sam. Thanks."

Max hustles through the lobby heading for the baggage claim area with Sam tagging along behind He ignores the cultural drawings along the way that he usually loves and takes the time to admire. Aside from a few decorative displays and shops, the Kingston airport looks like any other airport. Under the circumstances, he's too concerned to be able to enjoy any of the cultural scenery.

In customs, Sam displays his new passport for the first time to a customs official while silently freaking out a little. Instead of enjoying the experience, he is anxious and uneasy. He can't shake the feeling someone is watching them. *I'm in Jamaica surrounded by strangers! What am I doing here?*

Once through customs, Max goes to the car rental area opting for Budget Rental Agency because the cute Jamaican girl behind the counter smiled at him and said hello as he approached her counter.

"Hello beautiful," Max said trying to sound like a tourist. "We need a car."

"Hello! We have cars. My name is Brenda. Your name is?" She asks Max.

"Oh, um, Max Merchado pleased to meet you my dear!" Max says trying to act casual and friendly pretending he is here for sun and fun in a tropical climate. Part of his plan is to blend in with the locals and tourists in case anyone is watching.

"Mister Merchado, do you want a large car or SUV?"

"We only need a small car, Brenda. Please, just call me Max." He says winking at her.

"I'm not supposed to call customers by their first name, sir."

"Oh, then let my friend Sam rent the car. That way we can talk and you can call me Max!"

"Okay." She says, with a small giggle.

Sam can't figure Max out. *Here he has this problem to solve while trying not to be killed and he is flirting, acting like we're on vacation. We don't have time to be fooling.* Frowning at Max, he spouts out.

"Do you have a small car we can rent?" Sam asks the clerk taking over for Brenda.

"Yes sir, we do. We have a Ford Focus. Do you prefer red or blue?"

"Max likes red; you might as well give us the red one."

"It's a convertible, is that okay? Sam nods approval.

"Please fill out these papers and we can get the car for you, sir." He says handing Sam the rental car contract.

Filling out the rental contract, Sam hears Max hitting on Brenda.

"Brenda, have you worked here long?" Max queries leaning over the counter to get closer to her.

"I've worked here for a year now. What brings you to Jamaica Mister Max?"

"We're just vacationing. I think we're having a terrific party tomorrow night. We'll have lots of music, free booze and stuff, and dancing. Would you be interested in coming?"

"I would be if you'll be there."

"Of course I'll be there! My friend Byron will be hosting it. Let me have your phone number and I can call you with details."

Taking out a scrap of paper, Brenda writes her number

on it. Smiling she hands it to Max. "Call me tomorrow," She pauses and says, "Or tonight!"

"Count on it." Max says and turns to Sam. "You got that contract done yet, Sam?"

"Almost, Max." Sam is nearly speechless. With all this dangerous stuff happening, Max is making a date with some girl as if nothing is going on. *However, in some ways we're 'birds of a feather,* he thought to himself remembering Chet-ah.

Ready to leave the car rental and pick up the car, it's time to get going finally.

What a weird situation. Max thinks, *Here we are in a foreign country, trying to save the world, and I'm hitting on some girl at the airport. Things are surely backwards from Friday night when I called Sam because I was panicky. I guess with Sam here I think everything will work out fine. Something about him is calming for me. He's sensible and trust worthy. I don't like how he seems to absorb my stress and panic and still has those terrible nightmares. I really thought he was over them. I feel bad putting this on him, but we'll be done soon and I need him so I can think clearly or we'll never be able to stop that shipment. Dammit, Mark! How could you betray your country like this?*

Brenda's directions were clear and in short order the red Ford Focus convertible is found quickly.

"I should drive," Max says. "I'm used to driving on the left side of the road."

"I was going to suggest that." Sam says in agreement.

Opening the doors of the brand new Focus, they throw their bags in the back and jump in.

"Look at this lovely red car Sam. You know I like red and the black convertible top makes it really cool.

"Yeah, but the interior is backwards, the steering wheel

is on the wrong side of the car." Sam says.

"It has to be cause they drive on the left side of the road here." Max says cranking up the engine. Even though it's been nearly a year since Max left Jamaica, he felt at home driving here again.

Max reaches for the button to put the top down after the engine starts, but Sam stops him.

"No Max, we'll be too conspicuous with the top down."

Max shakes his head but leaves the top up.

The airport is a short distance from downtown Kingston. Max is familiar driving along toward the new Silvan Enterprises, yet he can tell Sam is still feeling uneasy and thinking hard about something.

Sam's mood is deepening into depression. His last nightmare along with the scary evidence Max showed him in the bar left him scared and a little crotchety. He can't enjoy himself and sinks into thought. *Why would anyone want to drive on the left side of the road? It seems so wrong. Actually, this whole trip seems wrong. I have no idea how we are going to stop a shipment from Silvan Enterprises. What is Max thinking? Why am I going along with this? I think I'd run away from this, except people already know I'm involved. I'm afraid leaving Max to fend for himself won't help anything. We're better off sticking together so we can watch each other's back, but I don't like this.*

"I'm glad you let me drive," Max finally says. "It takes some getting used to, you know, driving on the left. I still think we should stop at a gun store and buy a couple of 9 mm pistols!" *What a beautiful country,* Max thinks, driving along.

"Well, it's like this, Max. Are you any good with a gun?"

"No, I don't think so, but what's special about shooting? First you make sure you have bullets in the gun and then you just point at something and pull the trigger, right?"

"It's not that easy, Max. I'm no good at shooting, either." Sam says talking a little louder to overcome all the road noise. "If we actually get into a gun fight we'd lose! We'd more likely end up shooting each other or ourselves. I think we're better off not to have guns at all, Max."

"Maybe. I should ask Mister Lokie if he has some spare guns."

"Who is this Mister Lokie, anyhow? You've mentioned him a couple times." Sam asks.

"He's a local cop, but he moonlights for our company once in a while. You'll like him. He's the one cop I know who is not corrupt. He came to a couple of Byron's parties. He's cool."

"Okay, who is this Byron guy?"

"You'll like Byron. He's a friend I made when I came down here last year. Let me dial him and put him on speaker so you can hear." Max says taking his phone out. "Byron Johnson works at Silvan Enterprises. He's single like us, and he likes to party. We just naturally became great friends and partied during my stay in Jamaica." Max says punching a button on his phone.

"You have Byron on speed dial?"

"Never took it out. I figured I'd be back here someday. I just never thought it would be this soon."

With so much road noise and wind whipping by the car, Max cranks up the volume so they can hear. The familiar ringing comes through the little speaker as Max stops for a traffic light. After a few rings, a husky Jamaican accent answers.

"Hello this is Byron. Can I help you?"

"Yes you can, you old rascal!"

"Is this Max? Max Merchado? Good to hear you my friend!"

Sam can tell by his voice Byron loves hearing from Max and envisions a broad smile on Byron's face.

"Same to you Byron! Listen, I'm here in Kingston, and..."

"You're here!" Byron interrupts. "I'm at home. You must come to the house!"

"Maybe later, I've got you on my speaker phone. I'm here with my friend Sam. You remember me telling you about Sam?"

"Yes, a fine friend he is. Hello Sam! So what brings you two down to Jamaica now, man?"

"We have some business to take care of down here and then we will come over. Do you know of any unusual shipment at the plant?"

"I've got no knowledge about the shipping, man. I work in maintenance. We fix cars and trucks you know. Maybe I can see what I can see. You'll be coming to my place now, yes?"

"Later, yes, but we need to get something done first. I'll call you again." Max says hanging up. Since there's no way anyone could know he's in Jamaica, he chooses to leave his phone powered on instead of turning it off.

"We need to get into the shipping department." Max says. When the light turns green, he presses the accelerator taking off towards Silvan Enterprises. "We need to get inside, damage the shipment and grab a couple of the weapons for proof. I've been thinking and don't think Byron should help. If he gets caught, he'd lose his job."

"Are you nuts?" Sam exclaims. "I thought we were going to the authorities! You're supposed to know some uncorrupted officials here! What do you suppose will happen if we're caught breaking into Silvan Enterprises? We will be rotting in a Jamaica jail, that's what! Or worse! Maybe we'll be shot or killed! I still think we should contact the authorities. Why don't you call that Mister Lokie? Is he on speed dial on your phone? Let's call him!"

Grimacing Max says. "We have to stop that shipment first. The bureaucracy will take too much time. The publicity will be bad for the company especially here in Jamaica. The bad people here will deny they are shipping anything to a terrorist organization. I think most of the employees don't even know about a shipment to an enemy. The authorities would have no reason to search the shipping department. Nothing will happen! It's up to us to save the world and Silvan Enterprises from a disaster! I've been thinking and I know how we can get in the building. They leave the back door by the break room unlocked most of the time. Some people like to go out doors to eat. The trouble is there are usually some people out there. We'll have to wait for the right time to sneak in."

"Sneak in!"

"Yeah, we can do it."

"Okay, but let's think about this first."

"Listen to this. We can create a diversion. Maybe we can get everyone going to the front of the building and then we can sneak in the back." Max says. "I was thinking a diversion, like what we did at the University?"

"You mean The Firecracker Caper!" Sam shouts above the road noise. "The old cigarette and firecracker trick to draw attention to the explosions, then maybe you can get inside unnoticed. All you need is a pack of cigarettes, a lighter, some firecrackers... and a lot of luck!"

"I know. I know. That's perfect!" Max exclaims. "You see, I really need you here! Let's get some excitement in the air! Too bad we won't be able to watch the fun like before!"

"Like we need more excitement? Hey, what do you mean by we? I'm staying outside with the firecrackers, right?"

Shaking his head at Sam for being silly, Max turns off

the main highway changing directions for Byron's house. "Sounds like a plan! My friend Byron smokes. We'll get a pack of cigarettes from him. Maybe he knows where we can buy some firecrackers, too. We'll divert their attention to the front of the building so we can sneak in the rear entrance. The employees out back will probably go inside or go around the building. That will be our chance to get in and take care of business!"

Sam, still thinking, *Even if, uh "we" get in, what will we do? How will we find the package? Will we be able to rip it open as Max wants and steal a couple of the weapons? Will we be able to get back out? If we get inside, I hope Max has all this figured out. I really hope we can do this without being shot. Please god, please don't let us get shot! We're trying to do a good thing here, please.*

Turning down a side street, Max calls Byron again. "Hello, again Max. Did you finish your business?" Byron asks.

"No, not yet. Do you know where we can buy some fireworks? You know, like M-80's or something that makes a lot of noise!"

"Of course, my man! No need to buy any though, I have a stash of old M-80's, myself. You are welcome to have them all. What are you up to?"

"I'll explain all this to you later, Byron. For now just let me use those M-80's and a lighter and a pack of cigarettes. Just be aware it's for a good cause, and keep it secret from everyone."

"Come and get it! This sounds like your firecracker caper, yes? When you are done, I expect all details." Byron said laughingly.

"Sure. A full story will be yours when we complete our mission, my friend! I guess we will be over to see you now. Do you still have some of that special home-made rum?"

"Yes my man, we will have a toast when you get here."
"See you soon." Max says hanging up.

Max really shouldn't have told him he'd reveal the story 'IF' we complete our mission! Sam thought as one side of his brain goes along with Max's crazy idea, only because the plan seems to be so honorable and patriotic. The other side of his brain is saying this is a stupid thing to be doing, and they'll surely be shot dead! "I have a question."

"Okay shoot."

"Byron mentioned the Firecracker caper by name. That tells me he knows about it. You say we should never tell anybody about your pranks because otherwise when things happen, you'll be the first person they suspect. Especially if they know, you're a prankster. You always say the idea is to never get caught and that's why you're the King of pranks. So how does Byron know about it?"

"Well, we became very close when I was here last year. He and I might have pulled a couple pranks together. So yeah, he knows I'm a prankster. Honestly Sam, it wasn't intended, but a little homemade rum and then a little more and a few pranks seemed in order."

"Oh, but you didn't use this particular prank on anyone from Silvan, right? Because then they might..."

"Uh, no, I don't think so..."

"What do you mean you don't think so?"

"No, it's fine Sam. No one at Silvan will know this prank." *I hope! There was a lot of rum flowing back then and I don't really remember, but I don't want Sam to freak out.*

Unlike most of the neighborhood houses in the area that have rectangular holes in the walls where windows should be, Byron's home has glass and screens in the window openings painted in faded purple with yellow trim around the screened windows. The house stands out proudly against the other neighboring houses. The neat grass and flowers around the house means Byron grooms the yard as well.

Max honks the horn and brings the little red Focus to a stop in front of the house. A thin six-foot-five Jamaican man steps outside wearing bright purple shorts and a flowery orange shirt.

Byron greets Max with a huge warm handshake making him feel good. Upon seeing Byron again, Max smiles noticing his giant hands and remembers Byron seems to have an extra-large head for his body also.

"It's so good to see you and your friend. Nice to see the man behind the stories Max tells me about." Byron says smiling at Sam.

"I wouldn't believe all the stuff he told you about me if I were you." Sam says.

Laughing, Byron shakes Sam's hand putting a massive hand on Sam's shoulder. "He says you are the sensible one. You always try to do the right things. You are the thinker. Is this true?"

"Well, sensible most of the time, except tonight, but, Max does seem to step into a pile and come out smelling like a rose!"

"I know!" Byron says laughing a roaring laugh. "Let's go inside. I can tell you of the pranks he did down here." Byron extends his arms around Max and Sam leading them into his humble home.

Chapter Twelve

Walking inside Byron's modestly furnished living room, there is the same old dark wood table sitting in the middle of the living room with three chairs around it that Max remembers. The rest of the room has a couch, and a TV set. Three glasses and a large dark brown bottle are sitting on the table awaiting their arrival.

"Come, my friends, sit. Let us drink a toast to your eminent success!" Bryon says handing glasses to Max and Sam. Clinking glasses they all take a small sip of the rum.

Sam coughs, his throat tries to close in rejection from the rum. Choking and gasping for air he manages to utter, "Holy cow! What proof is this rum?"

"Oh, I think maybe a hundred twenty or so." Bryon says chuckling a little.

"Good grief, we'll be crapped out before we finish this glass." Sam blurts.

Frowning at Sam, Max says, "Don't be a wuss. We used to down this stuff all the time. It cleans out your system! It's good for you!"

"Yeah, but we have a plan, remember?"

"Oh yeah. Byron, you may have to save this hooch for later. Forgive me, I was thinking about our good old times."

"No problem Max." Byron says taking the glasses and pouring the rum back into the big bottle, corking it.

"I saw a hamburger place on the way here. I think I'll go there and get some food. Do you want anything, Byron?"

"No need to go, Max. I have plenty of ackee and saltfish here. It's good Jamaican food, no?"

"Yes, it is. Sam, you'll like it." Max says.

Byron goes to the kitchen to prepare some food, and within a few minutes, the meal is ready. Bringing out some plates, Byron sets the food in the center of the table.

Max quickly loads his plate and watches as Sam takes a small amount of ackee on a fork to sample. Apparently liking the seasonings Byron used, Sam scoops a fair portion onto his plate.

"It kinda tastes like spiced eggs and fish." Sam says smiling.

"You like? For now we drink water." He says handing Max and Sam plastic bottles of water to drink. "Tomorrow we have rum!"

"Maybe we should drink rum now. We'll get so drunk we'll forget about our mission!" Sam says.

Max frowns at Sam once again causing Byron to look puzzled.

"What kind of mission are you going to do?" Byron asks loading his plate.

"It's just a little something we have to do." Max says glaring at Sam. "I will give you all the details when we're done."

Looking out the window Max can see the night sky is bright. A full moon is directly overhead. "We should wait until the night is darker before we go." Max says nibbling on his fish.

"You wait, I will tell story. Did Max tell you about the paper incident?" Byron asks Sam munching on his ackee.

"I don't think he did." Sam says.

"You don't have to tell that!" Max says with a laugh.

"Oh, yes. You know what a commotion you caused!"

"Well, it was fun wasn't it? And I didn't get caught!"

"Yes it was fun for us, but not for the men in the finishing area! Let me tell you what happened, Sam."

With sparkling eyes, Byron says. "Late one night after the finishing area at work shut down and everyone left; Max took a large bag of shredded paper from somewhere and snuck it into the finishing area of the plant. The large vacuum machine is of course idle late at night. They use it to suck up dust when they sand down things. Somehow, he got up to the top of the machine and poured the whole bag of shredded paper into the exhaust tube of the vacuum. It blows the exhaust air up near the top of the ceiling, you know." Byron can barely contain his laughter at this point and Sam has a silly grin on his face imagining what happens next as Byron continues.

"In the morning when they started sanding they turned on the vacuum." Bryon stops talking and laughs a hearty roar of laughter for a moment. "That sander blew little bits of shredded paper all over the whole finishing department!" Byron and Sam begin roaring with laugher and look at Max wearing an innocent smug look on his face.

"They never found out who did it!" Max says grinning.

"No, no one did." Byron states. "There was a labor dispute going on at the time. The company blamed the incident on the labor dispute people. Max says the real test is to never get caught. Is that right, Max?"

"Yes, Byron. You know you gave away our secret prank. Now three people know about it, but I know my friend Sam will never tell!"

Finishing eating they continue chatting for a long time. Byron insists Max and Sam pee on the large oak tree near the side of his house. "Peeing on my oak tree is a tradition. Max and all my friends have peed on my tree. It's good luck, man!" Byron tells Sam.

Talking and drinking water until nearly 11 o'clock at night they managed to kill time until the humid night was dark, or as dark as the sky can be in Jamaica with the moon in the western sky, covered by black clouds.

Keeping to Byron's tradition, Max and Sam pee on the oak tree one more time. Sam thinks its a strange tradition, but what else can he do? Saying good-bye to Byron, they gather the firecrackers, lighters, and a pack of Marlboro cigarettes. Sam can see why Max really likes Byron. As big as he is, Byron is a kind and gentle soul.

Getting in the car, they prepare for their trek to Silvan Enterprises. Max starts the car and insists on putting the top down. "Let's enjoy the journey!"

Once again, fear strikes as Sam wonders if this will be his last goodbye to Byron! Until this point, it's been a fun evening for them causing Sam to forget for a while what they still need to do as Sam starts sticking M-80 fuses through the cigarettes at various points.

The New Silvan Enterprises is located in the Northern area of Kingston. Weaving through the light traffic, they finally approach the entrance of the factory. A makeshift banner printed with 'Silvan Enterprises' hangs across the front of the building. The building entrance has a looping driveway around the front and a split hedge across from it.

Killing the radio as they approach the building and parking the car on the far left side of the front parking lot next to a bush they partially hide the car.

"Let's get started!" Max whispers gathering a handful of M-80's and other stuff before getting out of the car.

Kneeling down at the outskirts of the front parking lot they can feel their hearts beating hard and fast. Sneaking along to the left side of the split hedge near the front of the building Max is about to light up a cigarette when Sam sees headlights coming toward the building.

"Look out!" Sam whispers grabbing Max's arm.

Quickly Max puts the flame out and they slip behind the hedge. The car pulls up in the driveway in front of the main entrance.

The engine shuts off and the lights go out as a tall man in an olive colored uniform wearing a sidearm steps out of the car. Pausing for a moment to put on a military style cap he closes the car door, straightens up and looks around the area.

Max sees the man's face and says, "Funny... he looks like my police friend Mister Lokie. I wonder what he's doing here on a Saturday night."

Walking to the front entrance of the building and disappearing inside the man leaves the car parked in front of the building under a partial covering.

Max whispers. "He must be moonlighting as a security man. They probably change shifts about now."

"Isn't Mister Lokie the man you wanted to contact down here?"

"I'm not positive it's Mister Lokie. It could be another guard that looks a lot like him."

"Why did he leave his car out front?" Sam asks.

"Maybe the guard he relieves will come and use it. Some guys share a car. It looks quiet now. Let's get started!"

"The man has a gun. Are you sure you want to do this?"

"Yes! I'm pretty sure he is Mister Lokie, anyhow. He wouldn't shoot us. I can explain this to him and he will help us. We have to do this!"

Max takes some of the cigarettes and M-80's and sticks a fuse in a cigarette. He lights the cigarette. He can feel the acrid taste of cigarette smoke in his mouth as he lights each one.

"Start placing the crackers. Put them behind the parked cars and the hedges. They'll have to come out to see what's causing all the noise. The cigarettes won't take long to smolder down to the fuse so distribute them quickly."

Racing around behind parked cars, and placing bombs here and there behind the sparse cars and behind the small hedges in the parking lot Max puts his last M-80 next to the hedge where he started. Sam finishes a few seconds later. All the firecrackers were within a two hundred foot radius around the entrance area.

Giving each other a high-five, they sneak around to the back of the building and hide behind a clump of bushes near the rear entrance. A single floodlight is shining down on the two bench tables and a woman sitting at a table eating a sandwich. Taking a drink from a large soda bottle, she picks up a paperback book and begins reading.

Seconds after Max and Sam get to the hedge, the first firecracker blows up. The woman at the table has no reaction; then a second bomb goes off and she still doesn't react. Two more explosions occur and she hurriedly picks up her belongings and rushes back inside the building.

"Now's our chance," Max whispers. "Let's go!"

"I'd prefer it if you go in alone." Sam says.

"Nonsense!" Max whispers. "You came this far, let's finish the job together!"

"Enjoy the journey?" Sam questions.

Max begins sneaking towards the rear door urging Sam to follow. Looking back to Sam, he sees Sam's knees are wobbly and hesitates for a second. Max reaches the rear door and turns the knob. Just as he predicted, the rear door is unlocked and unmanned. Entering the factory without incident Sam nervously follows Max inside.

"Where are we going now?" Sam asks.

"This way, to shipping!" Max whispers rushing along knowing exactly where to go. "We only have a few minutes to get in and out of the shipping department to do our thing."

Inside Silvan Enterprises in Jamaica, Mark is waiting and finally hears the noises outside meant to be a diverse tactic and knows Max well enough that this is his final play to stop the shipment. Entering the 'quiet' room he dials his contact again.

"Hello Mark. Tell me what's happening."

"They're in the building now. They just came in the rear entrance."

"Good. It's about time! Let's put an end to this. Call me when you have control of the situation."

"Yes sir. Mister Lokie is going to get them now. He will bring them to the quiet room so we can handle this without anyone else hearing. I'll call you later."

"Bring good news!"

"I'm sure we'll have good news soon." Mark says and hangs up. *I think I'll have some fun with the boys first.*

Max approaches the shipping department, and it looks empty. "Good! Everyone is outside chasing fireworks." He sees boxes stacked to the ceiling here and there and looks around for the right package. He comes across dozens of legitimate shipping boxes before he spots a large olive tarp covering something. Looking under the tarp, he finds a wooden crate three-foot square marked fragile on its sides sitting on the loading dock ready to ship.

Max looks up at Sam and says, "This is it! It's marked to go to Alan Young care of Heathrow Airport, London. Funny, the return address is wrong. Anyway, we need to open it and bring some of the weapons to show to my police friend." He whispers.

"Are you sure you want to do this?" Sam asks.

"Of course! See if you can find a crowbar or something. We can get one or two of these Cloud things and leave before people come back in. They'll be afraid to ship the package when they see someone has tampered..." Max pauses and freezes hearing footsteps clicking on the concrete floor of the warehouse. Without thinking, Max ducks behind the large crate. Sam does the same.

"Max Merchado! Sam Stormen! You need to come with me!" A man shouts to them.

Peeking around the crate, Max realizes the security man in uniform pointing a big gun directly at him is his friend Mister Lokie. Max's heart is in his throat.

"Please, put your hands up and come this way to the quiet room." The man repeats the gesture with his gun.

"Henry Lokie? You're a fine policeman. Let me explain what we're doing." Max says, reluctantly stepping from behind the shipping crate as Sam raises his hands.

"Please, come this way." Mister Lokie says motioning with his gun toward a door on the other side of the building. "Max! Put your hands up!" He shouts as Max walks toward him. Max reluctantly raises his hands and he and Sam walk to the quiet room.

Max feels sweat forming on his forehead stepping into the room. He's never been in the quiet room and he notices the room is lined with gray padding and gray silencing cones on all the walls. It appears to be a special office used for private conversations. Expecting to see torture apparatuses, Max is glad there isn't any he can see. The room has one large conference table, a credenza with a TV atop it, and some chairs. *If I'm shot in here, no one will even hear the gun shot!*

A man sitting in a swivel chair turns to face them and Max immediately recognizes him. "Mark! What? Why are you here? Why are you selling weapons...?"

"Max, I'm glad we caught you." Mark says raising his hands. "Cuff them Mister Lokie! Why did you think you could break in here unnoticed? We were surprised when you actually came down here to try to ruin our plan."

"You're the one who surprised me!" Max yells gritting his teeth as Mister Lokie clamps cuffs on him.

Sam closes his eyes and bows his head praying silently

as he is also cuffed.

Max, puzzled asks, "How the heck did you get here anyway? There weren't any more flights to Jamaica today, and you weren't on our flight!"

"As you know Max, this is my associate Officer Lokie." Mark says pointing to Mister Lokie.

"He has knowledge of our, shall we say 'clandestine' activities along with a few select employees. Let me tell you about all the trouble you caused, but first, sit, let's talk. Mark gestures to Mr. Lokie to put the gun away.

"Through my friend, police captain Fred Holland in Fort Lauderdale, we were able to get the GPS tracking information in Sam's Mustang he rented once another associate to remain unnamed got a warrant for us."

Both Max and Sam look on in disbelief.

"Yes. I guess you didn't know that Vintage Rental cars have GPS tracking on all their cars. By the time we located the Mustang, you were leaving Las Olas Boulevard. You two must have been together a few minutes before we located the car and we tailed you to the Miami airport. I called Mister Lokie to have him follow you once you landed in Jamaica. We had to let you act out your attempt to squash our shipment so we could legally detain you. This way, it can be said that you tampered with a shipment replacing it with chemical weapons. This means you are an international threat and can be held without due process under the law. Do you understand me Max?"

"I didn't tamper with that shipment! You're the traitor! You can't hold me!" Max yells.

"Yes, Max, I can, or I should say my associates can. What I'm trying to tell you Max, is that we now have enough proof to hold you. We will search your belongings and find the flash drive. We have proof you flew here and broke in and were caught tampering with a shipment. My

US contact can have you declared a threat by Homeland Security, which means they can hold you or send you to Gitmo for detainment. Either way, you will not have your rights to legal counsel and due process because those rights will be stripped. Do you understand Max?"

"You can't do this! I am not a traitor! Sam and I are loyal citizens of the USA!" Fear is starting to envelop him as he looks to Sam and sees tears silently running down Sam's face.

"Okay, enough! Let me explain this to you both. Like you, I am also a loyal citizen and this situation is not what you thought. This whole thing would have been over if I had reached you in Fort Lauderdale. I received a frantic call from Ann, though. Remember the woman you stranded on a side street, Sam? I had to find her and pick her up before I could proceed to you. After I told my associate you had the thumb drive and were heading to Jamaica, we put an emergency plan into action. We didn't want to stop you in the US because it might cause too many questions and we needed you to break in here as you have."

"Who are these associates?" Max demands.

"Don't ask. They want as few people as possible to know about them. Let's just say they are patriots of the US. They decided I must come down here immediately and personally foil your efforts in Jamaica. I am also to retrieve that thumb drive! I used Silvan's private jet to fly here. Actually, I got here about the same time you did since I didn't have to go through normal customs. I had one of the weekend employees pick me up and bring me here. I arrived at Silvan Enterprises a long time before you did. We waited and waited for you to come to the plant and finally you did. By the way, nice trick with the fireworks! You fooled everyone but me. I knew you are not a professional criminal and based upon your rather large ego and personality, I expected you would try to create some sort of diversion. I know your type Max and although you are an excellent salesman, you have a need for the dramatic. It helps that I've heard you are a prankster because that also fits your mo. Anyhow, let me tell you what's happening, then we'll see how you feel about me and this project."

Max still glaring intently at Mark begins thinking. *Why is Mark explaining anything to us? Why does he say he is a loyal American? He caught us, he's informed us he can do whatever he wants with us, so now he should just have us shot and disposed of!*

"We couldn't let you come down here and actually ruin the whole deal, the weapon sale is a setup between a foreign government, who I cannot mention and ours. They will deny any knowledge of what they are doing if asked. Their people are involved also so I will only give you the basics of the deal. Our company appears to have created a chemical weapon for friendly foreign countries."

"Appears!" Max snarls.

"Yes Max, appears! A special group chose our Jamaica Company to advertise the 'Deadly Orange Cloud' discretely to terrorist groups. This was set up in Jamaica as Silvan Enterprises was finalizing the acquisition of this company. We called it the 'Deadly Orange Cloud' and advertised it for sale at an exorbitant price to many different terrorist groups using the internet and other means. We also claimed to be anti-government and ready to make deals with them and that they can easily hide this weapon anywhere and use it against their enemies. Indeed, I attracted interest from several terrorist groups. One man named Almir Najya, perhaps an alias name, placed a discreet order with me for a hundred units to ship to London, England. In return for his interest and of course his money; I agreed to sell these treacherous weapons making it appear to Silvan employees that one of our allies, namely England, bought them. He reluctantly agreed to my terms that I'd manufacture and ship the order discretely and he would pay me in advance. A few days ago, Almir Najya's group wired the money to an offshore account that I had Ann to set up in the Bahamas to pay for the units. Now you know why Ann or Miss Picard is involved. Of course, she doesn't know the reason for the offshore account; she just knows that I needed it. Anyway, I think Almir Najya himself placed the order! It has taken us only a few days to manufacture the weapons. So now we're shipping one hundred units of the 'Orange Cloud' to London on Monday."

"That's incredible! You're selling weapons to our enemies!"

Chapter Thirteen

"It 'appears' that way to you Max, but all is not as it appears." Mark says.

Max can see Mister Lokie still has his hand on his gun ready to draw at a second's notice. This whole calamity is not making sense to him anymore. *Why Mark is taking so much time explaining everything? He can just shoot us and be done with it!*

Mark says, "Let me say that you probably saw a video showing how quickly the 'Deadly Orange Cloud' killed some sheep."

"I saw that! Your weapon killed those sheep!" Max shouts looking ready to attack Mark.

"It's amazing what graphics people can do with video nowadays!" Mark says smiling. He pauses to see if Max reacts to what he just told them. Both Max and Sam look at Mark puzzled and dazed.

"I want you both to know in reality we didn't kill anything or anyone. In fact, the 'Deadly Orange Cloud' weapon is a complete fake!"

"What! I saw the sheep die. It sure looks deadly to me!" Max shouts.

"I'm glad it appeared realistic to you, but again I say it's amazing what graphics people can do nowadays. They call it CGI. The sheep didn't die. It's a fake video. You must not reveal that secret to anyone! The stuff we'll ship is useless as chemical weapons, although the bombs appear to be real. Additionally, the authorities in England will get an anonymous call from somewhere in Jamaica about a dangerous shipment coming their way. They will be on the alert and arrest whomever shows up to claim it. They will confiscate the shipment and England will have good news for its people by capturing the illegal weapons and the militant who comes to pick them up. Perhaps they will catch Almir Najya, I don't know. I understand he is near the top or is the top of that terrorist group. London authorities will tell the press they detected and confiscated weapons and that they are indeed deadly weapons. That should help any other terrorist groups to believe we shipped the real thing to London." Mark relaxes behind the desk seeming to enjoy his talk.

"The press will suspect Silvan Enterprises' branch in Jamaica as the culprit, but they will be unable to prove we shipped the package. The method we are using to ship will make it impossible to prove who sent it. The shipper will pay in cash and be in disguise. The shipping return address is a vacant lot here in Jamaica. Additionally, the Jamaica government is not going to be very cooperative either, against a large and economically good for Jamaica Company. Is this starting to make sense yet?"

Silent, Max and Sam stared dumbfounded at Mark.

"Mister Lokie escorted you here by gun point in case an employee was watching or in the event you tried to escape. Because you broke in it has to look like we really caught you. With the upcoming fallout the company has to show we couldn't have anything to do with the shipment and that our security is top notch.

Relaxing Mister Lokie folds his arms together no longer holding his gun ready to fire at them.

All of the built up tension in Max's muscles seems to relax a bit, too.

Mark continues. "I understand why you tried to stop this shipment. You saw all that stuff on the thumb drive and concluded that I was a bad guy, although I really wish you had let me explain this before you ran off. You know, I thought I put that drive in my pocket when you rushed into my office, Max. I'd never intentionally let the thumb drive get out of my hands. When you came in, I had just removed the drive from my computer. I must have dropped it when I tried to slip it into my pants pocket, and you were arguing about the new chemical weapon."

"I was reluctant to tell the Jamaican employees about the 'Orange Cloud' weapon. We had to tell our production crew something though, to get the supposed weapons built. I commend you both for being so patriotic! However, if Max hadn't been looking at our Jamaica bulletin and hadn't been opposed to the weapon so strongly, this whole episode may never have happened!"

"This whole chain of events was unnecessary!" Sam says giving Max a disgruntled stare. "I hope I don't get stomach ulcers over this!"

"If you just had not looked at the contents of that drive, we would not even be here! It wasn't until you called me, Friday evening Max, that I realized my thumb drive was missing. There is no way I could just tell you what is going on over the phone. After all, I didn't know if someone bugged my phones. I tried to convince you on the phone to return it but you hung up, like we'd suddenly become ene-mies."

Max mutters, "Sorry!"

"I knew you were probably scared and might blow the whistle on us, so as soon as you hung up I went to my car and raced to your house. I have no doubts about you being a loyal American. That made it more compelling to get to you before you did something that might ruin the plan. I wanted to retrieve the thumb drive and give you a reason-able explanation for it as well. However, you had already gone. At that point, I had no choice but to try to retrieve the disk, catch you, and stop you from whatever you were going to do. I talked to my confidential contact, that's when they bugged your cell phone, and we began tracking your cars. That's also why your house was trashed because we were trying to find that drive or were you might have gone."

"Someone did a good job of trashing it!" Sam says as Max frowns and kicks at the floor.

"Sorry about that, Max. We had to do it even though I was sure the thumb drive would not be there it was imperative to try. We couldn't let you get away or blow the whistle to stop the shipment! I had to find you. I had people bug your phone; track your credit cards and your cars. That wasn't easy since you ditched your car and turned off your cell phone. I waited for you to show up somewhere or call someone from your phone and you finally did make a call. That's when I was able to get Sam's phone bugged and we started monitoring your house. We knew Sam would go to your house since you were not at the airport to meet him. Ann from the accounting department is the only other person from Silvan in the US who knows even a little about this so I had her meet you Sam, and try to go with you. Obviously, Ann is no spy, she messed up, and you ditched her. It was a bad idea but I was hoping she could help me keep track of you. I thought she could distract you enough that you would not see me following you.

Nodding at Mark, Sam says, "She is definitely a good distraction!" *Miss Picard.* Sam mentally etched the name in his memory. "If I had not been so worried at that time, she would have distracted me completely!"

"How did she screw up?" Mark asks.

"She said we only had an hour to get to Max..."

"Ah, and there is only one way she could have known that!"

"I wondered how she even knew to come to Max's house for one, and how she knew that."

"That was my goof up. I called her to go to Max's house.

I told her you only had an hour to get to Max. I needed her to get there in a hurry and get you to ride with her. That way I could just follow her. I ended up having to follow you instead."

"Yes, as a good friend as she claimed she didn't know Max is a prankster, so I believed she was one of Max's enemies and I didn't want to ride in her car."

"You found a good way to lose me, too! Then you ditched Ann and for a while we lost track of you."

"From the direction you were heading I thought you were going to west Fort Lauderdale, maybe the Davie area. I continued going that way hoping I would catch sight of you again. Fortunately, the GPS in that Mustang determined where you were heading. My contacts told me you changed directions and determined where you went and parked. It took time for me to find Ann. Then I rushed back toward you. You apparently parked just off Las Olas Boulevard. You guys had left before I got there. A while later they told me you bought plane tickets to Kingston with your credit card, so we knew what you two wanted to do. That's when my confidential contact wanted me to come here to Jamaica immediately to stop you. This shipment is too important not to leave Jamaica as planned. We're hoping other terrorist groups will be watching to see how this shipment goes. If we do it right, maybe they'll think it's just bad luck when the Brits capture the shipment. That's when I drove to the Executive Airport and flew down here in our corporate jet." Making a pleading gesture with his hands Mark says, "I hope I've convinced you, of the importance and facts of this shipment. It must ship as scheduled and be confiscated by the British authorities. I hope they will also capture Almir Najya or someone from his group. Do you understand all this Max?"

"Yes, I'm sorry. When I saw the article and then the

flash drive, I went crazy. I couldn't imagine anything beyond the fact that you were a traitor and that I had to stop this shipment and you."

"Good, I hope you do understand because it's not over yet and I have to cover for your break in. To this end, you guys will have to spend a day or so in jail! We're having you arrested for unauthorized entry to Silvan Enterprises. You can explain that it was a dare, to see if you could get in and out without getting caught. The thumb drive is my only information drive. I don't want to tell my contact it got lost somewhere. They would be very upset. I really need to have my thumb drive back, Max. They are hoping we can entice one more enemy group if I continue the ads. Henry, un-cuff Max." Waiting for Mister Lokie to open the cuffs Mark continues. "Can I have my thumb drive back now? Can I count on you guys to play your parts?"

"Jail time?" Max mumbles shaking his head and retrieving the drive from his pocket and handing it to Mark. "Henry is in on this too?"

Max sees Henry Lokie nod.

"Do we have to go to jail?" He moans.

"Well, you did get caught breaking in to Silvan Enterprises." Mark says. "I'm sure you won't be treated badly. Henry will make sure of that. We'll explain it was a dare, and you are just a couple of pranksters that need to be taught a lesson."

"Mister Lokie, please cuff Max again and call a policeman to help you escort these two to jail. Max, I didn't know you were so patriotic!" Mark said patting Max on the shoulder.

"One more thing, guys. Do I have your word you will not discuss this fake bomb with anyone?" Mark watches as Max and Sam nod in agreement.

"Sam, I commend you for sticking with your friend to

the end, even though it might have been a fatal end! I have looked at your résumé. You should come to work for Silvan Enterprises. You have guts! I think you would fit right in. We need a good electronic technician. We'll talk later!"

The nightmare is almost over. Mister Lokie and a local policeman escort the handcuffed Max and Sam, leading them out of the building in front of all the evening crew of Silvan Enterprises. It's an embarrassing few minutes. Max and Sam hold their hands up to cover their faces being marched out the front door and get into a police car.

Sam feels a great weight fall from his shoulders. The knot in his stomach is going away. Mark, Ann, and Mister Lokie are good people after all! Max is patriotic to a fault! All through this chain of events, he thought at any minute his life could be snuffed out like a bug. Now he finds out some government agency he knows nothing about, is pulling off a great prank. The Deadly Orange Cloud deal is an elaborate set up to catch a terrorist! All seems better.

Sunday afternoon, a guard leads Sam into a private room of the jailhouse where he meets with Mark.

"Hello, Sam."

"Hey Mark. The guard told me we get out tomorrow morning."

"Yes it has been cleared. You guys have been through the mill!"

"Yes sir. It's always exciting being around Max."

"Ten-four on that! Well Sam, I wanted to stop by and talk to you about coming to work for Silvan Enterprises. I know this is an awkward time, but I need to take action soon. Before I get into the job, I want you to know that this little incarceration incident won't leave you with a record.

No formal arrest charges were created and your incarceration will be explained as a cooling off period, kind of like throwing a drunk in the tank overnight to sober up. I just thought it might be important for you to know there won't be a negative record to follow you or Max here or back in the states."

"Thanks, I really appreciate that. It was kind of bothering me that I'd have an arrest record because of this."

"Well, worry no more Sam. Now, let me explain the benefits of coming with us..."

As Sam comes back to his cell, Max asks, "Hey, where did you go to? You're supposed to be in jail like me."

"They took me to an interrogation room." Sam says.

"What! This is supposed to be over!"

"Max! Max! Calm down, I'm just kidding!" Sam can't keep a straight face. "Mark talked to me about coming to work at Silvan Enterprises."

"Oh. Are you sure? Are you keeping anything from me?"

"No Max, it's good. Since we've got some time to kill, let's sit and I'll tell you about it."

"Okay, yeah. So what'd he say?"

"Well, for starters, it's just like you said. You said I'd be a shoe in for the job and you were right."

"See, I told you. So we gotta start finding you a place to live... of course you're welcome to stay at my place until you find something and..."

"Whoa! Slow down! I didn't take it, not yet anyway."

"Why not? Didn't he offer you a decent salary?"

"Actually, the pay he offered is much better than my current job in Denver. The work sounds like it's more interesting too. I was getting bored with what I'm doing so this new job will not only be fun but it will be a step up as well."

"So why didn't you take it?"

"I don't know, Max. All of this came up unexpectedly. A few days ago, I was happy in Denver with my life, my job and my girlfriend, then a few days later everything has changed. I guess I'm not like you. I just need time to process everything and think about things."

"I'm sorry. This is my fault. You dropped everything to come help me when I thought people were trying to kill me."

"It's okay Max. You would have done the same for me. Mark also said, after this shipment is done, if they are able to entice another 'sale' for these weapons, he wants my help working the deal. He said something about needing to use several different people on this last one to handle some of the electronic stuff so that only a couple people would see the final product. Since you and I already know and Mark trusts us, he'd like us working with him"

"Well that's good, I guess. I am glad I was wrong about Mark being a terrorist. I always thought he was a good guy, so it hurt when I discovered the information on that drive."

"He must be glad too because he said we could fly back to Fort Lauderdale in the corporate jet tomorrow when we get out of jail. I declined however."

"What! Are you crazy! The corporate jet is so cool! I love flying on it! Why would you decline?"

"Because Max, first off, you already paid for a return flight on Friday. Plus, I was only able to enjoy this island for a few hours before landing in jail so I'd like to take a couple days' vacation, plus you promised Byron you'd come back to see him and Mark is planning to fly out first thing tomorrow."

"Oh, yeah, right. Good points."

"I told Mark I'll probably accept the job offer and he understands why I'm hesitant. He said I should go ahead and enjoy the next few days, but to just make sure I don't wait too long because he won't be able to hold the position for long. I said I'd get back to him before I head back to Colorado."

"Is that it? Did he say anything else?"

"Yeah, he said he is going to tell the people he works with on this Orange Cloud situation that he has the thumb drive again and that we're not a threat to what they are doing. He will also tell them we're now part of the team and vouch for us that we won't try to stop the shipment or tell anyone about the fake bomb and the plan. As far as our arrest, they'll say the Jamaican authorities are detaining us for unauthorized entrance into Silvan Enterprises because of a prank."

"Well, I guess it hasn't been too bad. With the instructions from Mister Lokie, the guards have all been very good to us and cheerful. It's only been for two nights and the guards have foolishly played poker with us until the wee hours of the night. Life is good!"

Chapter Fourteen

"Well, the two of you are free to go. I hope your stay hasn't been too unpleasant." Mister Lokie says and pats Max's shoulder.

"No sir Mr. Lokie. You and your men have been good to Sam and me. We thank you."

"Silvan has dropped the trespassing charges, so you will not have a record for this incidence."

"Yeah, that's what Mark told us."

"Thank you Mr. Lokie. Max and I appreciate how well your men have taken care of us."

"You are welcome Sam. Now don't let this guy here get you into any more trouble."

"Don't you know it? Thanks again."

"Hey, you're talking about me and I'm standing right here." Max says.

"I'm going to drive you guys back to Silvan Enterprises to your car. Company orders from Mister Goodman."

"It's daytime. Where is your police car?"

"I'm taking time off just to take you to your car, or wherever you want to go."

"We can't beat that."

"No problem, Max. You and Sam get in."

"Oh my!" Mister Lokie exclaims nearing the Ford Focus. "The top is down!"

"Yeah, we left in a hurry, remember. We didn't plan to leave the car, especially with the top down.

"I'm sorry to tell you, but it rained heavy last night. It was a torrential downpour!"

"No!" Max yells as Mister Lokie stops his car alongside the Focus.

"No, no, no!" Max says jumping out of the car and run-ning to the Ford. Bowing his head, he closes his eyes. "There's several inches of rain in here!"

Getting out of his car to look, Mister Lokie lets out a hardy roar of laughter after looking inside the car. "I guess crime does not pay, Max my man."

"Crap!" Sam shouts, looking at the drenched interior. While Mister Lokie laughs Sam whines, "How will I explain this to the rental company?"

"You can open the doors and scoop out what you can." Mister Lokie chuckles.

"Is there someplace we can rent a wet vac?" Sam asks.

Max opens his door and a gush of water dumps out on his feet. Plopping down on the wet driver's seat his face says it all. "Whoa! Cool and refreshing!" He says and in-serts the key in the ignition turning the car over.

"Hey, it started!" Sam says in amazement. "I was afraid it wouldn't."

"Yeah, I know." Max says. "I noticed the dash looked dry and hoped the awning provided partial covering. If so, maybe too much water didn't get in the dash. If I was wrong, the electronics may have been ruined. It looks like everything is okay. The radio and everything seems to be fine."

"We didn't get so lucky with the seats though."

"I know. Screw it! Hop in Sam, we're going to Byron's house!"

Sam looks in the passenger side and there is still over an inch of water on the floorboards. "You're kidding, right?"

"Do I look like I'm kidding? Get in!" Max says.

"Holy cow, that's really cold!" Sam says sitting on the sopping wet seat and gritting his teeth. Cold water starts seeping into the backside of everything he is wearing.

"Refreshing!" Max says putting the Focus into gear. "So

here we are two gladiators who tried to save England, now riding in a water-filled car with sopping wet clothes." Raising his hand, he gives a royal wave to Mister Lokie.

Still laughing, Mister Lokie waves back at him.

Swinging his forefinger forward to the air, Sam says, "Press on, Max! I definitely need some of Byron's rum now!"

"We'll have some of that rum before noon!" Max says as he drives the car out of the parking lot.

"Do you think the warm air and sun will dry the car out? Sam asks worried the rental agency will charge a large fee for the damage when he turns in the car.

"Don't worry Sam, you worry too much. The sun here is strong and the air is very warm. I expect by the end of the day you'll hardly be able to tell the car's been wet."

"Are you sure, we left a trail of water when we pulled out, and now the bumpy roads are causing the excess water to slosh around on the floor boards. Some water is even spitting onto the inside of the windshield, and I don't know where it's coming from."

"Sam, calm yourself before you give yourself an ulcer."

"But they're going to charge me for this damage, and with the air flight from Denver being so pricey because I had to go first class, I'll be paying this trip off for months to come."

"Sam, you know I wouldn't do that to you. You came to help me and I appreciate it. When we turn the car in, I'll have them move the charges over to my credit card. Then when we get back I'll make a phone payment on your card to pay off the air fare, so will you give it a rest and enjoy yourself?"

"I'm sorry Max. I don't mean to be a bummer. You know I don't make as much as you. I try to be cautious though because I don't want to end up with a lot of debt. I always try to pay my card off each month so I'm not carrying a balance and wasting money on finance charges. I just know I can't do that with all these charges on my card so far. I wasn't trying to be a party pooper."

"I know Sam, I know. So let's enjoy our mini vacation as our worries are behind us."

"Sounds good Max. That does sound good. I do have one question though."

"Shoot."

"If I'm correct, we're just around the corner from Bryon's house, but it's only nine-thirty. Isn't it a little early to be showing up unannounced since he'll probably be at work since today is Monday?"

"Nah, this is Byron, we are welcome anytime. Even nine-thirty in the morning and even if he's at work." Chuckling, Max honks the horn pulling into Bryon's drive.

Byron comes out with a big smile on his face. "Good morning my friends."

"Good morning!" Max exclaims getting out of the car.

Byron can't help bending over roaring with laughter seeing how wet their clothes are from sitting in the wet car. "What happened to you? You're all wet."

"Yes, we did this on purpose. Strictly to amuse you my friend, strictly to amuse you. Come look." Max says.

"Oh my, your car is soaked. How did you manage this?"

"It's a long story." Max says. "I hope we're not too early for you?"

"Never, you are welcome anytime."

"Why aren't you working today? I didn't expect to find you here."

"I heard you'd been arrested. I wanted to be here when you got out so I took some time off."

"Yeah, we were, and it's a long story."

"Well, let's get you some towels to try to soak up the excess water. The sun should handle the rest."

"Well, that should do it. I think we did a good job. Now the sun can dry the rest." Byron says to Max.

"I hope so. We've been trying to get the excess water out for a couple hours now and it's getting quite hot out here."

"Well then, while the car is getting some sun, let us go inside in the shade. It's midday; we can have some food and open the rum. You promised to tell me what you two were up to when you were last here."

"That I did, Byron my friend. You'll never believe me though, I warn you. They caught us setting off our prank at Silvan. We were arrested."

"So, you got caught. You told me you never get caught!"

"This is different Byron, we had some bad information. I'm gonna blame it on that."

"What bad information?"

"Let's just say we tried to break in to Silvan and get back out without being caught. Unfortunately we got caught!"

"You flew to Jamaica to do that? Not your best explanation, I think."

"Yeah, I can't really discuss it right now. After the dust settles, I'll give you the details. For now just remember I had bad information, and I can't talk about this now."

"Your 'never get caught' record is broken, man!" Byron says. "It must be something extreme Max."

"Let's just drink and forget about the whole thing. Let's hope the car dries out by tonight." Max says sipping his rum.

"Here's to never getting caught again!" Sam says raising his glass.

"Let me tell you a story about Max when he was here in Jamaica last year Sam. He roped me into one of his pranks and I nearly got caught so I think you will enjoy this one."

Byron grins sitting down at the table.

"You're talking about me and I'm sitting right here guys. Why can't we just drink some rum?" Max says shyly.

"Go on Byron, I'd like to hear this story." Sam says.

"Good, good. Let us eat while I tell you the story." Byron says setting a large pot of chicken and white rice on the table for everyone to snack on. "Oh my, Max I meant to tell you, I have a new woman. Her name is Dana and she will be by after work. We met at the Coconut bar."

"Ah, that's one of our favorite places. Is she the one for you?" Max questions trying to change the subject from himself.

"Maybe. Stranger things have happened lately."

"Hey, how are you doing Sam?" Byron asks.

"Fine, why?"

"You've downed a couple glasses of rum already and we haven't eaten yet. I think you are not used to our rum. You seem to be slowing down a bit and your eyes look heavy. Our rum here is very potent, you know."

"Yes it is. I am feeling very tired though. I haven't been sleeping well lately."

"Aw, I see. Here, you should eat, then lay down on the couch and rest a bit."

"Thanks, I think I will."

I hear party music and a lot of laughter. It sounds like one of Byron's neighbors is having a party. Wait, I know that voice. It sounds like Max. What time is it? It sounds like Max is having a party. Sitting up, Sam looks around to find the noise. It seems like he's only slept for a few minutes, but somehow in that short time Byron and Max have invited the entire police force of Kingston over for rum and snacks.

Max is sitting in a corner with Brenda the rental car

girl, but she looks very unhappy. Max is talking privately with her and Sam can't make out what they were saying, but it sounds bad. Getting up, Sam glides over to interrupt them.

"What's going on?"

"I called Brenda to come to the party, but when she saw the wet car, she called her boss. He says it's ruined. Now he wants to prosecute you. I'm trying to convince her and her boss it was an accident. We didn't mean to leave the car out in the rain with the top down!"

"Is that why all the cops are here?"

"Yes, since the car is in your name, they want to impose the maximum penalty on you."

"They what!" Sam looks confused.

"They want to use a form of punishment torture they call the Jamaican stretch. They use it on criminals instead of jail time. It saves the government a lot of money not having to do trials and house people in jails."

"I don't understand. Even if the car is ruined, the insurance will cover it. That's why we buy it. How can I be tortured or punished or whatever you call it over an accident covered by insurance? Besides, I'm a US citizen."

"That is why there is so much discussion. Although the United States can't tell Jamaica how to handle crimes committed on their soil, the government has close ties and trade with the US and you have ties to Silvan Enterprises, which is vital to the country because of the jobs it produces and the taxes it pays. They do not want Silvan to become angered and move to a different island like Haiti. However, the owner of the rental car company wants to prosecute you. He is also an important person in Jamaica. So there is much discussion."

"What happens if they do prosecute?"

"Many things, they have several options they can do,

but all are bad for you, I'm afraid."

"But this is covered by the insurance. There shouldn't be a discussion."

"Regrettably, the insurance company is owned by the brother-in-law of the car rental company. He says the policy will not cover the damage because it was negligence and not an accident. You should have used your US auto insurance instead of buying the rental insurance."

"That's ridiculous! Why offer it if it won't cover anything."

"We are encouraged to suggest you get it, because it's usually easy money for the insurance company owner. In this situation, he will not pay the damages so my boss is livid." Brenda explains.

"What damages? Why is the car ruined? It got wet, but we dried the seats and the floor. It will be fine."

Max says, "Oh, you don't know. While you were sleeping, it rained again. This time there was no partial covering like at Silvan. At Silvan, the front of the car was covered so only the seats got wet. The dash was protected. This time, it was in the open and now the rain got into the dashboard and many of the electronics got wet."

"It rained again! Why didn't you put the top up?"

"I would have, except Byron and I made a quick run to the store while you were sleeping. We wanted to throw a party later and went for supplies."

"Then why did you call these people knowing the car was rained on again? We would have had time to get it fixed before this turned into a nightmare."

"I…" Max starts to explain before being interrupted.

"There, there he is!" Someone shouts. "Take him into custody now! Get him before he gets away or he can get his embassy involved! We'll deal with them later! Shoot him if necessary!"

146

"Run Sam, run!" Max yells.

"He's running! Shoot him before he gets away! Shoot!"

"Wake up Sam! Wake up!"

Groggy, Sam opens his eyes and sees Max staring down at him, shaking his foot with a puzzled look on his face.

"It's nearly eight o'clock! We need to get ready and go." Max says. "Did you have a nice nap?"

"Whoa! It's nighttime." Sam says rubbing his eyes. "Didn't we get here before noon? Where did all the cops go?"

"Cops? What cops? There's no cops here. Did you have another weird dream?"

"Wow, I guess I did. Thank God, it was just a dream! Have you ever heard of the Jamaican stretch?"

"No, I haven't. Maybe Byron knows what that is. We've been drinking rum since noon and you drank two full glasses. We figured the rum got to you, so we let you sleep it off for a while. I just sat around having a nice chat with Byron. You missed his woman Dana. She just left a few minutes ago."

"Byron wants to have a party, maybe tomorrow night. Anyway, he cooked up another chicken and we ate most of it. I think there is some left. You need to eat! Get some more nourishment in your body. After that we should go to the hotel." Max says.

Dragging his body off the couch, Sam sits down at the table. He can feel his head is still a little dizzy and his legs feel like they have hundred pound weights on them. Rubbing his forehead, he sees Byron sitting across from him at the table.

"Do you know what the Jamaican stretch is?" He asks.

"No man." Byron says smiling broadly at Sam. "What is the Jamaican stretch?"

"I don't know, I'm asking you."

"I don't know either. I've never heard of the Jamaican stretch." Byron says a little confused smiling at Sam.

"So you've never heard of the Jamaican stretch!"

"No. I thought you were telling me a joke." Byron says giving him a puzzled look.

"Maybe you should just eat the chicken Sam." Max says.

"Yes, Max is right. You should eat. After a few times you will handle the rum better, no?"

Just as Byron finishes talking, rain begins pounding on the tin roof of his house.

"No!" Max shouts and runs out the front door to put the top up on the Focus. Byron and Sam hear Max shout over the sound from the tin roof. "Damn rain!"

Sam manages a silly grin dragging a chicken leg from the plate on the table and sinking his teeth into it tasting the spices Byron cooked into it.

"This is great!" He says to Byron between chewing. "Really great. Thank you for everything."

"My pleasure man." Byron says.

Gnawing the last piece of meat off the chicken leg Sam hears Max beep the horn. He quickly rubs his hands on a paper towel and shakes Byron's massive hand before leaving. "Thank you my friend." Sam says staggering out the front door.

The rain is coming down hard by the time Sam gets in the car. The top is up, but the car seat is wet and he is soaked again.

"Whoa!" Sam shouts as the cool night rain seeps into his clothes.

The rain shower is brief and stops by the time they reach the hotel. Walking through the hotel lobby Max and Sam are wet from top to bottom. He and Sam are able to get in the elevator and go to their room unnoticed though. After showering, they sack out for the night. Sam manages

to make it through the night with only a very slight headache.

"Hello."

"Our contact at Heathrow has been reached. Arrangements have been made. They will be watching for the
pickup."

"Okay, good. I'll be happy to have this done. Thanks for
the update. How will we know if we are successful?"

"You will know. As an international incident I expect it
will make the news once the AP wire picks it up."

At an undisclosed building in East London, Almir Nayja
meets with other members of his group. Earlier he received
word from Mark informing him of the flight number and
other details for the shipment arriving today.

"Mabon, you will check again to see if the flight is on
time. Tajo, steal a truck to pick up the shipment at the airport. At Heathrow, you will show this ID for Alan Young to
security and customs. You will go to baggage reclaim to retrieve our package. Mabon will go with you."

"Yes Almir. I shall bring it here."

"Yes, but we must be certain you are not followed first."
Pointing to a map, Almir says, "When you leave customs,
drive the truck to this location. An SUV will be parked here
for you. Our men will follow you from the airport and cause
a traffic jam preventing you from being followed so you can
unload the package and switch vehicles. The SUV is parked
in an area where there are no street cameras or video surveillance so you can make the exchange before coming back
here."

"Get the dolly out of the van to carry the package."

"Okay. We are a few minutes early. The plane is just

landing. It will take a few minutes for the plane to be unloaded and brought to the reclaim area." Mabon says.

"Yes, I agree, but we can't wait too long or we'll get stuck
in long lines."

"Why did Almir only give you a fake ID to retrieve the
package?"

"Originally only one of us was going to pick up the package. I guess later, Almir wanted to make sure I'd have help
in case the package is heavy. We don't want to raise alarms
in customs. You can also help look out for anyone following
us. When we go through customs, I will present my ID and
deal with the customs agent so you won't need to present
ID."

"Then I hope all goes smoothly. I do not like having to
deal with customs agents."

"It will be fine. Let's move faster. I want to get there so
we can be ready to retrieve our package as quickly as possible."

Chapter Fifteen

"It looks like they are here sir, I just saw two Middle Eastern men with a hand truck head to baggage reclaim."

"Good. Send the decoy agents down first to put a barrier between them and the civilians."

"Yes sir. Some civilians have already made it to the area though."

"They will make our people look like travelers. Spread the word that we have civilians in the area and try to keep them farther away from the suspects."

"Yes sir. Radio check, there are civilians in the area. Maintain protocols to avoid unnecessary injury. Suspects are two Middle Eastern men holding a hand truck. We expect they are attempting to retrieve a package from the conveyor belt. Do not apprehend. Once they have the package, we will apprehend them when they go through customs. Maintain radio silence until then."

"Look, a few passengers are starting to come." Mabon says.

"Yes I hear the machine starting for the conveyor belt."

"Good let's get our package and get out of here." Tajo says.

"There it is. It's coming now."

"Yes, help me grab it. It may be heavy." Tajo says reaching for the package as he and Mabon get the crate and strap it onto the hand truck.

"Come on; let's get to customs before the lines are long." Mabon says.

"You take the dolly so I can get my ID and customs forms ready while we walk."

"Good, there is only one person in line. We missed the crowd, but there's a bunch of people coming behind us. I'm glad we won't have to wait long."

"Hello, MI5, Deputy Director's office. How may I direct your call?"

"This is Aaron Hastings calling for the Deputy Director. He's expecting my call."

"Very good sir, he'll be right with you." The receptionist says connecting the call.

"Aaron? Have you spotted them?"

"Yes sir. They have retrieved the package and are heading to customs now."

"Have the BTP (British Transport Police) given you their cooperation?"

"Yes sir, they have. BTP personnel are maintaining a security perimeter while the MI agents you provided are sticking close to the suspects. Both MI5 and BTP personnel will apprehend them in customs. Currently we have an agent in the line pretending to go through the customs procedures and the suspects are next in line behind the agent. We are holding as many civilians back as possible to a safe distance to minimize fallout in case there is a problem with apprehension. It should happen anytime now."

"Where are you?"

"I'm several people back in an opposite line keeping a line of sight."

"Do they suspect anything?"

"No, they seem relaxed. Is the transport van ready?"

"Yes. It's outside waiting."

"Very good. Thank you Deputy Director."

"Go get them Hastings! The Crown will not allow terrorists to conduct activities on our soil."

"Do you have anything to declare?"

"Yes, this crate was shipped to me via British Airways. Here is my ID and a copy of the waybill and customs forms."

"Mister Young, is the value of the contents stated on these documents correct?"

"Yes."

"And the contents are as stated?"

"Yes."

"This says the shipment was prepaid. Is this correct?"

"Yes."

"Based upon this it looks like the tariff you will owe is £455 if the shipment checks out. Please place the package up here. To your knowledge has this package been tampered with?"

"No, it is still sealed. I have not opened it?"

"According to the waybill, the shipment is batteries. Is this correct?"

"Yes, it is."

"Step back please while we open it." Hey Charlie, help me open this crate."

"Sure Carl. Let me grab a crowbar."

"Grab an electric meter too."

Mabon nudges Tajo getting him to speak up. "I was told this shipment had already been cleared by customs on the other end so it wouldn't have to be re-opened on this end. It was checked and approved by customs when it shipped and sealed with their seal."

"Yes, I see their seal sir; however we have orders to open all luggage and packages. Probably somebody shipped something that leaked somewhere. Earlier today, something suspicious was found in the cargo area and since they don't know where it came from everything has to be checked now."

"But you can see nothing is leaking from this package."

"I see that sir, but orders are orders. Is there a reason you don't want us to open this crate?" Carl says as he and Charlie look at the men suspiciously.

"Ah, no. I'm just picking it up for my boss. It's his order and I was told it had already been cleared so all I'd have to do is pay the tariff and go. I was trying to pick it up and get through customs before the lines get long so I could pick up my daughter for dinner.'

"Well, you had to know this could take a while with all the planes coming in all the time."

Tajo just looks at the man saying nothing silently praying now that he is able to get out of here, preferably with his shipment, but this is not what he expects to happen.

Charlie opens the crate and places the voltage meter lead against a battery but can't get a reading from the meter. "There's no reading." Charlie says to Carl.

"Are you sure? Did you put the leads in the right place?"

"Yeah, see."

"Mister Young you and your friend need to step over here." Carl says pointing while pressing the security button on his microphone. Speaking into the microphone, he specifies subjects are being detained at his customs counter with a suspicious package, and back up is needed. The commotion at the customs counter peaks the interest of passengers and others nearby waiting to get through customs. "Charlie, take them to room two until this is resolved."

"What about the crate?"

"No. We can't move it until it's cleared."

"Sirs, you need to go through this door here."

"What? But we haven't done anything. Why are we being detained?"

"Protocol sir. You and your friend need to speak to another customs agent."

"Why? No! I have cooperated and my shipment has the appropriate clearances. This is ridiculous!"

"Sir, I'm not going to ask you again, you need to go through this door." Charlie says as BTP backup appears.

Each of the men approaches the area with their hands on their hips ready to draw their weapons. The number of security personnel moving in toward the customs counter where the commotion is causes a few passengers to pull out their cellular phones and begin recording the situation to show their friends or post on their social media sites later.

Standing still refusing to move, Tajo and Mabon watch as BTP officers appear out of nowhere like cockroaches. Suddenly the area is swarming with officers and they are reluctant to leave their shipment behind until an officer he never sees approach sticks a baton in his back nudging him forward. This unexpected action along with the situation sends Tajo into a reflexive motion. He spins around grabbing the baton from the officer and while spinning him places the baton over the officer's head pinning it against his throat.

"Hands up!" Someone shouts. "Drop the weapon!"

"No! He shouldn't have touched me. Put your weapons down and let my partner and me leave with our shipment or I'll snap his neck."

"We can't do that. Do not make us use force. We will shoot you if we have to."

Mabon positions himself behind Tajo to obstruct some of the officers, but they are surrounded and he can't see a way out of this. Agents from MI5 begin flashing badges and moving into place as well when Mabon grabs the pinned officers gun.

"Put the gun down! You can't get out of here. Release the officer and back away slowly."

"No way! We are going to leave with our package or we will die trying. We will take you with us if you make us." Tajo says snarling at all the officers.

A path begins to clear as a man steps forward. "Son, I am Aaron Hastings. I am with MI5. You are suspected of bringing a suspicious package through customs and we cannot let you leave here. We do not want to harm you, but you have to go into an interrogation room to be questioned and your package must be checked further." He says with a calm voice.

"You can't hold us! Tell your men to clear a path for us."

"We can't do that, son. We must follow protocols. We are not accusing you of anything. We just need to know more about your package, and who shipped it. Can you help us with that?"

"You know all that. It's written on the waybill. We are only picking it up. It's the batteries my boss ordered."

"Yes, but these batteries as you say, don't appear to be in proper working order."

"So! That's for my boss to figure out. If they are broke, he will contact the company he bought them from. It's none of your concern. He will be very mad if I come back without them. You will not get me fired because you think his batteries are broken.

"Yes, but it is our concern as you stated. We were informed that a suspicious shipment would be coming in which may contain weapons of terror. If this is true, we cannot let any suspicious shipment leave here. Therefore, you must surrender to be questioned or we will assume our information is correct and that you are a threat. Please don't make us use excessive force. Let the officer go and put your weapons down, now."

Tajo hearing that the authorities knew about his shipment begins to relax his grip on the officer slightly due to his puzzlement. At the same time Mabon fearfully fires off a shot near Tajo's ear at the MI5 agent deafening Tajo slightly. Mabon's shot misses Aaron Hastings but hits a BTP officer in the arm. People scream and duck for cover or drop to the floor if they have no place to hide hearing the sound of the gunshot in terror.

Three officers behind Tajo have clear access to Mabon and fire on him dropping him before he can fire again. Two other agents take aim at Tajo ready to fire but holding their position to prevent hitting the officer Tajo is still holding captive.

Aaron holds his hand up for everyone to hold their fire trying again to prevent more gunfire. "Son, please don't make these officers fire on you. You are surrounded so they will not miss. This doesn't have to go down this way. We only want to talk to you, but you have to let the officer go."

"No, no. I will not talk to you. You will let me go."

"Please son." Aaron says nodding his head slightly letting an officer behind Tajo know he has a go to fire his taser.

Tajo doesn't notice the nod and suddenly feels the lightning bolts shooting into his back from the taser gun being fired at him and loses his ability to stand collapsing to the floor quivering in a seizure like state. Officers move in quickly to handcuff their suspect and end the siege while the taser has him subdued.

Almir Nayja anxiously awaits Tajo and Mabon's return with his shipment. Watching the clock though, time ticks by and his men are not returning. Suddenly, news of the incident at the airport starts hitting the wire and replays on television and radio most of the evening. News of the incident goes international and cell phone videos posted to social media end up going viral along with airport security footage. Almir is livid! Not only has he lost his shipment, but he has also lost two of his best men.

The Pegasus Hotel in the heart of Kingston is one of Kingston's finest hotels. The rooms are rather expensive but Max wanted a balcony, so they rented a balcony room on the second floor.

Sam awakes fully refreshed and recovered from the rum he drank yesterday. "Good morning." He says to Max.

"Good morning. How do you feel?"

"Great! I feel full of hope."

"Hope? What are you talking about, did you have another dream?"

"No, I slept like a baby. Think about it, it's Tuesday and this is the first morning we didn't wake up in jail."

"Oh. I'm sorry, that's my fault."

"Don't worry about it. I didn't mean to place blame or make you feel bad; it's just waking up here in our hotel room feels like a real vacation. It helps that the sun is shining and it's a beautiful day."

"I see what you mean. What would you like to do today? I can take you sightseeing, or we go to the beach. We're in a tourist destination in the Caribbean; we may have a difficult choice trying to decide."

"I agree it may be a difficult choice. Right now though I'm hungry and want to grab a shower."

"I like the way you think Sam. Let's order room service and then you go shower first. When I get my shower, you can hang out on the balcony or look around to see if you see anything, you might want to do. We'll have a great view of the pool at least."

"Okay. I'd love some coffee though. Would you make us some while I shower? I don't want to have to wait until breakfast comes."

"Sure, no problem, that sounds like a good idea." Max says getting up.

"Great! I won't be long."

"Well, what do you think? It's a pretty island, isn't it?" Max says joining Sam on the balcony.

"Yeah it is. I couldn't really see it as a tourist spot when

158

we were driving around. It looks amazing from the visitor guide information I looked at."

"I know. We're in the city so you can't see all the wonderful beach views, but we grew up in Fort Lauderdale so beach hotels don't mean as much to us."

"You're right. I like this location. I was looking through the hotel guest info and it says Emancipation Park is across the street."

"Yeah it is."

"It says it's a good place to take a run. I feel like I haven't exercised in a month now."

"There's a gym downstairs also. After breakfast, we can check it out, or we can hang out at the pool or pool bar and enjoy the scenery. We can head out to other areas of the island if you'd like to see more. We could take a guide tour and fish some big fin. We can also get Byron to hang with us and do some tourist stuff since this is your first time here."

"Yeah, I would like to check out the gym and the park. I may take a run later to loosen up my muscles."

"Whatever you want. Oh it sounds like our breakfast is here."

"Good. I'm starving"

"Where would you like to eat sir?" The attendant says pointing to the balcony and around the room."

"What do you think Sam? Would you like to eat on the balcony?"

"No, let's eat in here. It's already starting to get hot out."

"Okay, here it is!" Max says to the attendant tipping him after he sets up their breakfast.

"Why don't we turn the tv on while we eat? I think they have a channel just for things to do on the island. It might give us some ideas." Max says clicking on the television.

The news is just finishing the day's weather report and

is switching back to the news desk when something catches Max's ear. "Hey Sam, listen to this." Stunned Max sits on the side of the bed and watches the news story. Sam's attention is also engulfed listening.

"It seems an international investigation is being launched as a shipment of chemical weapons originating from Jamaica was shipped to Heathrow airport and two suspects carrying false identification were apprehended yesterday attempting to pick up the shipment. Based on the reports, British authorities were tipped off that a shipment of possible chemical weapons were made to look like batteries and shipped as cargo for arrival at Heathrow on a British airways flight originating from right here in Jamaica. No one seems to know who shipped the package as the return address leads back to an empty field. The batteries however look like those manufactured at Silvan Enterprises one of our country's largest employers. A spokesperson for Silvan who refused to be identified or do an on camera interview, denies that Silvan manufactured the batteries in question. It is true, he said that Silvan does engineer and build military equipment for the US and other military's, but they do not build bombs or any sort of weapons. They limit their scope mainly to helicopters and other high tech large military equipment. It is up to the governments they build equipment for to build or acquire the bombs, bullets or whatever firepower the equipment will use. The spokesperson also stated that it is true that the Jamaican plant makes batteries of all sorts mainly those used in high tech equipment as well as a large range of battery types and states that a few weeks ago they noticed they were short one case of battery casings, but assumed the case had been misplaced in the warehouse. They can't see how it could have been stolen by whomever is behind this hideous event. When we asked why the missing case wasn't reported, the spokesperson stated that Silvan has no reason to believe their empty battery casings could or would be used for nefarious purposes. Due to their high level of security because of the work they do they have no reason to believe the missing battery cases are due to theft since they haven't had any breakdown in their security measures. They maintain that although the cases used to make these horrific weapons look like those they use, they did not come from their inventory. We asked about a recent event that occurred this weekend about an attempted break-in at the plant and we were told that the event in question was not a break-in, it was a prank by a couple of employees but their security measures held. They were detected before they entered the building or were able to do anything. We asked why the two were arrested and were told that they must have been detained on a nuisance charge because the company did not press charges against the individuals because the employee behind the prank is a known prankster. They say they have proof he has done pranks before on his co-workers. The employee was not aware of hidden cameras and other security measures in place. The man said quote, Since even our employees aren't fully aware of all of our security measures we are quite sure the missing casings are not the ones used to make or ship these weapons to England. Finally, the spokesperson stated that Silvan will co-operate fully with authorities in their investigation and are confident they will be vindicated in this matter. At this point, when we spoke to authorities to get a response we were told they could not comment on an ongoing investigation. Back to you Don."

"Wow!" Sam says.

"I know."

"Why do you look so stunned? Mark warned us this plan would become news. I'm glad it all worked out. I thought you'd be happy to know Mark was right and have proof he isn't a terrorist."

"Did you hear what they said? They know I'm a prankster and have done other pranks because they had hidden cameras and such that we didn't know about."

"Yeah, so?"

"What do you mean so? This means I was caught on the confetti prank Byron told you about. They must have known I did it and probably some other things too."

"If that's the case, why didn't they say anything that they knew? Why did you get away with it?"

"They must have decided it wasn't worth alerting the employees that they were being watched, I imagine."

"That makes sense. That also means you haven't been king of the pranks like you thought for quite a while then." Sam can't help but laugh at this.

"Oh my God! What if they are have hidden cameras at Silvan in Fort Lauderdale? Damn, I'm busted big time."

"Oh well, since you haven't gotten in trouble over it, then someone in security has had a few laughs."

"Yeah, I guess you're right."

Chapter Sixteen

Exploring the hotel facilities Max and Sam decide to check on the Ford Focus in the parking lot. With the bright sun and no storm clouds building this early in the day they decide to put the top back down to dry it out again. Hoping it will dry out before they have to return it to the rental company.

"You know, we still have time to have some fun."

"Yeah, we're going to take in some sights."

"No, I mean we have Wednesday and Thursday nights that we can party and I want to make the most of both nights." Max says.

"I guess so. Relaxing here at the hotel is cool, and seeing some sights would be nice, but a party would be fun."

"I'm thinking of calling that car rental gal Brenda. She could come to Byron's house tonight and maybe bring another girl with her for you. Are you ready to party, Sam?"

"Well, I did just break up with that crazy Jessica in Denver. But aren't you still with Peggy?"

"We're on a break, remember? I believe if she's not with me, I'm free to do whatever I want Sam. Live and let live, so far that works just fine."

"Wow! No commitment then?"

"Correct... Party?"

"Make the call." Sam says feeling he deserves some happy time. "We have two more days to relax, party, and drink rum with Byron and friends, and then it's back to reality." Sam pauses, "I told you Mark offered me a job and I don't have any ties to Colorado anymore since I broke things off with Jessica, so I'll probably accept it and then I can harass you since it looks like you are no longer the 'King of pranks' being you had the biggest prank of all played on you!"

Max bows his head graciously from his lounge chair saying, "I bow to Silvan Enterprises, the new 'King of Pranks'. I am in awe! As Byron likes to say, don't worry. Be happy!" Max laughs and they both have a good chuckle basking in the warm Jamaican sun. "Life is good!"

A light snow is falling and a strong wind blows around Sam's apartment building in Denver. It's one of the last spring snows for Denver. By noon, the movers are through loading Sam's belongings into a small van. The wind whips snow around as Sam loads the last of his essentials into his old Cherokee SUV. The moving van crackles through the snow-covered parking lot as it begins its long journey to Fort Lauderdale.

Sam takes a last look at his old apartment complex before getting in his SUV. He's a little apprehensive, but feels good about accepting the job at Silvan Enterprises. His new salary is nearly twice his old one. The benefits are better too, and his pay starts today. Mark is paying him to drive to Fort Lauderdale. Mark told him to take his first week at Silvan Enterprises to relocate and find a place to live, get settled in, and report the next Monday.

Working his way through Denver and onto I-10 eastbound, he decides to call his mom. She answers with her usual cheery voice. "Hello, Stormen residence."

"Hi mom. This is your Colorado son calling."

"Sam? Are you okay?"

"Yes mom, I'm moving back to Fort Lauderdale."

"Oh. You can't have your old room back. Dad made it into what he calls a 'Man Cave' and we gave away your bed."

"It's okay mom..."

"He bought a big screen TV and it takes up one side of the room. And..."

"Mom! I already rented an apartment."

"You were here and didn't stop to say hello?"

"No mom. I used the internet. It will be ready for me when I get there. Max is loaning me some furniture until my stuff arrives."

"That's wonderful, son. Will you be here soon?"

"I'll be there in a couple days."

"Wonderful! Your dad and I miss you."

"I'll be driving the old SUV back. I should be there by Thursday."

"I'll cook your favorite, potato pancakes and apple sauce."

"Okay mom, but I'm trying not to eat so many starches these days."

"You don't want me to fix it for you?"

"Please, its okay. Once in a while won't hurt me. I love your potato pancakes! See you Thursday night, I love you mom."

Due to the chain of events with Max, Sam realizes how much he misses his old hometown. *I'm actually looking forward to moving back to Fort Lauderdale and starting my new job at Silvan Enterprises. All the weight of thinking Max and I could be killed is gone and I'm going back to where I grew up. I think I'm enjoying this two thousand mile trip because I'm going home, home where I belong.*

Almir and Safar relocate to a small apartment in south London to regroup. Most of their guns, supplies and papers were lost due to a police raid when Tajo was captured and Mabon killed at the airport. Almir knew something went wrong as soon as the men failed to return. His men who were waiting to follow Tajo and Mabon when they left the airport saw the police transport arrive but couldn't get close enough to see what was going on. It wasn't until the ambulances started arriving that they suspected there was a problem. They called in to Almir to get instructions, but the events were already hitting the news. All they could do was to pack up quickly and run before the investigation lead to their location. They managed to get out minutes before agents arrived. Now sitting in their small living room, the phone rings.

"Almir, we have checked our comrades. No one has disclosed anything about your shipment. We have a contact at the University of Miami. We are sure he can break into the computer system at Silvan Enterprises and get information for us. It was not a coincidence authorities learned of our shipment and we need to find out what is going on. When we do, someone will answer for their treachery."

"I will wait to hear from you. It must be him; he is the one in charge there."

Four o'clock on Thursday, Sam enters the outskirts of town. "Hello Fort Lauderdale!" Sam shouts smiling seeing his hometown and dials Max.

"Hello."

"Hi Max. I'm in north Fort Lauderdale!"

"Great! I loaded some stuff into Peggy's truck. When do you want me to meet you?"

"I'll be at the Bridgestone apartments in a few minutes. I have to get the keys and sign some things. You're not very far away, so just head my way in ten or fifteen."

"Will do. I'll bring a six pack along to celebrate."

"Great! See you in a few."

"Ah, great timing. I just got the keys from the apartment manager. Let's get this stuff up to my new apartment." Sam says when Max arrives.

"Up? What floor?"

"Third."

"Damn, I guess I should have asked earlier. That's a lot of stairs."

"Don't worry; unlike my old apartment this place has an elevator."

"Excellent! I like this place already."

"Me too. I think I'm going to enjoy having an elevator."

"So where is all your stuff?"

"Almost everything is with the movers. I only brought the necessary essentials I need to get by until the moving company delivers the bulk of my stuff. Delivery is scheduled for a week from Saturday."

"So that's why you only borrowed a few items."

"Yeah, it'll tide me until my stuff comes. Let's load the elevator and take the stuff up."

"I like this over making multiple trips up three flights. Sam my man, I'm gonna like visiting your new place."

"Me too. I thought I might have some qualms about leaving Denver, but I didn't. From the moment, I gave my notice and started packing this move felt right. The trip back was very enjoyable and I feel at peace with myself again."

"What do you mean? I didn't know you were so unhappy there."

"Well, it wasn't that I was unhappy per se. I liked the area a lot and I had a few friends, but I never seemed to put down roots there or make it my home. It always felt a bit temporary. I'm sure my problems with Jessica only added to my uneasiness."

"I am so sorry Sam. I didn't know. Well you're here now. Have you been inside yet?"

"No. I just got the keys when you showed up."

"Well, what are you waiting for? Open the door to your new kingdom."

"Yeah, sure, I'm nervous. Happy, but nervous."

"I'm glad I could be here with you to welcome you home."

Looking around the empty apartment Sam says, "You know Max, this does feel like home."

Max opens a couple beers he brought and handing a beer to Sam says, "I christen thee Sam's Playpen!"

"Right! Let's hope I find someone to play with now!" Sam says taking a long sip of beer.

"I'll drink to that." Max says raising his bottle of beer. "Thanks." Sam says.

Sam sacks out early Sunday evening because he wants to be ready for his first day of work at Silvan Enterprises. He feels happier than he has felt in years.

Monday morning, Sam jumps in his SUV heading to Silvan. Turning his SUV onto Silvan Drive, he marvels at the scenery splashed along the only entrance to Silvan Enterprises. Swaying palm trees; perfectly mowed bright green grass, and narrow canals sit on both sides of the road. Near the end of the drive, two large sand cranes are casually drinking from the canal along the right side of the road.

The two-story company building sits dead ahead on the road, driving slowly to obey the speed limit, a large metal barrier suddenly comes up out of the road in front of him. He slams on the brakes hard to avoid crashing into it. Just as suddenly, the barrier recedes into the road again. His car thumps a little going over the receded barrier wall.

"What was that about?" He says before remembering Max telling him the government forced Silvan to install the walls because of the secret nature of some of their projects. The heavy steel barriers can rise up in seconds to stop a possible intruder's vehicle from getting to the main building. The remotely controlled walls rise to lock down the plant whenever necessary.

Sam knows Max somehow managed to get access to the security area to do this as a way of welcoming him to Silvan Enterprises. Finding an open slot at the far end of the massive parking lot, he swings into the slot. Walking up to the front main doors, he stands outside for a moment, taking a deep breath before walking inside.

A very attractive brunette woman at the reception desk looks up from her work as he enters smiling at him.

"Good morning, sir. How may I help you?"

"Hello. I'm Sam Stormen. This is my first day of work here." He says smiling back at the receptionist.

"Yes, Mister Stormen. I have a note here to expect to see you this morning. Let me ring personnel to get you started and get you a badge." Dialing a number, she requests someone to come check Sam in. Jane comes a moment later to escort him to the new employee check-in area.

"How are you today?" Jane asks while walking down the hallway.

"Oh, I'm fine. I'm a little excited to be joining the company."

"Have you worked in a company like this before?" She asks, smiling at him.

"Sort of, I mean I've done this kind of work before, but my previous company didn't have this level of security." He responds.

"Yes, our security protocols are very high. We do a lot of sensitive work here plus we have several government contracts we handle." She says.

"I'm just really happy to be here."

"Then I hope you enjoy it Mr. Stormen."

"Thanks and its Sam."

"We're here." Opening the door to the security office, she offers Sam a warm smile before following him inside.

"Hi Clark," Jane says when Clark enters the office.

"Mister Stormen is a new employee. We're just finishing his new hire paperwork; he needs to get a badge."

"No problem. Just stand over here." Clark says directing Sam to stand in front of a blue screen. "We'll have you outta here in just a few moments. Give me a couple minutes while the computer creates your badge and we'll get someone to take you to your area."

"I'm supposed to start work in the research lab." Sam says receiving his badge.

"I can walk you there," Jane says. "It's not far from here and it's on my way. If you don't know where you're going, you can end up going around in circles. I recommend you learn to navigate using our multi-colored hallways. They will guide you. Your employee packet will explain the color coding."

"Hello Albert, this is Sam Stormen, your new coworker."

Sam gives Albert a quick look noticing he is about six feet tall just like him, but maybe in his fifties. Albert is wearing a starched white shirt, denim trousers with a belt buckle that has a small image of a dartboard on it and calf-high black boots. "Hello." Sam says offering a hand to shake.

"I'm glad they finally got some help for me." Albert says shaking Sam's hand.

"I'm here to help however I can."

Jane interrupts to say, "I'll leave you with Albert now. It was nice meeting you Sam."

"We're testing a new ionization process here." Albert says pointing to a set of electronic instruments and asks, "Are you familiar with these instruments?"

"Yes, I can handle all of these."

"You may want to get a pair of boots for in here. Sometimes they come in handy if you spill something. You can get your feet wet, so to speak, on this test rig for now."

Showing Sam the details of the tests to perform, Albert can tell Sam knows how to operate the equipment and leaves him alone to work. The tests are easy for Sam. They are similar to what he did at his job in Colorado, so the morning passes by swiftly.

Just before noon, Max stops by to say hello with a broad smile on his face.

"Hey, I heard you met the barrier walls this morning."

"I should have expected that." Sam says.

"How's the job going?"

"A piece of cake. These tests are like what I did at Tech Store Corporation."

Albert approaches them as Sam says, "Albert, this is my friend Max."

"I know Max. Everyone knows Max! The number one salesman and number one pain! Just kidding Max. Let's get some lunch. Sometimes the cafeteria has good food, and I'm hungry!"

"Okay, but I have to find someone after lunch. It shouldn't take very long." Sam says.

"Someone I know?" Albert asks raising an eyebrow at Sam.

"Yeah, you know her." Max interrupts.

"Her name is Ann. She works in accounting." Sam says.

"Oh, you want to go see sexy gray eyes, don't you?" Albert says.

"Yes, I just want to say hi and see how she's doing."

"You know her! You just started here. How do you know her already?" Albert asks.

"We met a few weeks ago briefly. I, um, I was kind of rude to her and want to apologize and say hi."

"Admit it Sam. You like her." Max ribs.

"Maybe I do. It doesn't mean she likes me. I just want to clear the air and apologize. It bothers me how I treated her although I didn't have a choice at the time."

"What did you do Sam? It sounds like I missed part of the story here." Albert says.

"Um, no offense Albert, but I really can't get into it." Sam responds looking at Max who's trying to keep his mouth shut for a change.

"Oh so you just started here and already you have secrets huh." Albert dismisses.

"It's not like that. We met accidently while she was doing a project for Mark." Quickly changing the subject, Sam adds, "I like how bright and cheery the halls are here. They're nothing like the drab olive walls at The Tech Store. I assume the multicolored walls and shiny vinyl floor tiles have meaning to help you find various departments."

"Yes, the cafeteria has yellow corners. Each department has different colored corners." Albert says.

Sam breaths a silent sigh of relief that his trick worked, he was afraid it might not. "I wondered why there are so many colors. I guess it will make sense to me when I've been here for a while." Sam gets his food tray and sits down next to Max and Albert as Jake joins them.

"Do you play darts, Sam?" Albert asks.

"I can throw them."

"There's a small bar called CC's right near the entrance that has a regulation dart board. Maybe you guys can stop by after work to see if you can beat me and Jake here at darts."

"Peggy just went out of town until Saturday." Max adds.

"If you go, I'll go." Sam says.

"Jake, can we beat these rascals?" Albert asks.

"Yeah, why not. I can beat any of you clowns at darts!"

"Watch who you're calling a clown!" Max says.

"I'm so sorry." Jake says feigning a smile. "I'm just trying to get you mad so you will throw badly."

Sam suddenly notices a blonde woman across the cafeteria briefly looking at him between her conversations. She doesn't look his way long enough for him to see her face and she leaves with friends before he can get a close look at her.

Leaving the cafeteria after lunch, the guys all head in different directions. "Listen Albert, I'll only be a few minutes." Sam says.

"That blonde chick?" Albert says. "You can try, but I think you're wasting your time, she won't date you. We all believe she's gay. She's never dated anyone who works here."

"See you in a few."

Sam wanders around the huge building until he sees green corners ahead and reaches the accounting department. He spots Ann sitting at her desk in a small office with a window. *Is she blushing?* Sam thinks feeling strangely elated that she must recognize him.

Nearly a month ago he only saw her for a few minutes, yet he can't forget her. He is compelled to see her again. Gently rapping on her door, he steps into her office.

"Hello Ann, I'm Sam. Remember me?" She looks just as beautiful as he remembers.

Her long blonde hair is draped over her left shoulder. Looking up from her computer monitor, her eyes meet his. An awkward pause occurs before Ann turns her eyes back to the monitor. "Yes, Sam. I remember you." She finally says.

"Um, I hope you will forgive me for kicking you out of my car! It was a case of mistaken beliefs. I thought you were one of the bad guys."

"It's all right; the boss told me what happened. I'm glad it's over. It was quite distressing for me having to lie."

"Oh, I'm sorry."

"When I got out of your car, I was a little scared. I called Mark and he came to pick me up."

"I really am sorry. At the time, I was trying to save my friend's life. I didn't want anyone to find out where he was, including you. I thought someone wanted to kill him and maybe me too! I knew someone was tailing me!"

"Yes, that was Mark."

"Well. I thought he was a bad guy so I did some evasive maneuvers. Believe me I was pretty scared myself."

"We both had more excitement than we wanted that day. I think I'm glad you kicked me out! Just pretending to be Max's friend with you was all the stress I could handle. I hate to lie about anything and I barely knew who Max was. I felt really uncomfortable lying about being a good friend of his."

"I'm glad it's over too! Listen, I know this is a bold move, but if you have nothing going on Friday night..." Pausing, she doesn't cringe or turn away so he continues, "I'd like to take you to dinner to make up for my misunderstanding."

Chapter Seventeen

Ann looks down and fiddles with some papers on her desk, trying to hide the sheepish grin on her face. It's an incredibly long time before she finally looks up smiling. "Umm... That sounds like fun, but you have to promise me you won't throw me out of your car again!"

"Okay... but you'll have to give me another big hug."

"What! Oh yeah, I was trying to be a spy when I hugged you! I was supposed to be a worried friend of Max's. Guess I'll keep my day job!"

"Oh, you did a swell job! I was convinced until you said we only had an hour to find Max. You couldn't have known that unless you heard my phone call with Max."

"Like I said, I'm not cut out for the spy business! Anyway, here's my number and address."

"Great, Friday it is then. Well, I gotta get back to work." It's really nice meeting you again." Sam says backing out of her office.

A co-worker of Ann's comes ambling into Ann's office after Sam leaves. "Wow! Some dish Ann. Did I hear you're going on a date with him?"

"Well, yes Victoria. He's nothing like the other guys."

"I heard Max thinks no one can get a date with you."

"Hey, I'm not a prude! Why would Max think that? I'm just more selective, besides Max isn't my type."

"Just a conversation I heard. Well, if you don't hit it off with this guy, let me have a try at him."

"I think we hit it off already." Ann says smiling.

Hurrying down the hallway to get back to work, a crazy thought pops into Sam's mind remembering what Chet said to him on the plane. "Someday, if you're lucky, you will meet miss wonderful." *Maybe, I just did.*

Armo Najya summons his oldest son Almir to him in Afghanistan.

"You are a fool!" He shouts. "I have a report the Orange Cloud is a fake! The Americans used it to track and destroy us! They succeeded to kill two of your good men. If you were not my son..."

"Two men?"

"Yes, two Almir, Tajo took his own life rather than be questioned about us."

"I hadn't heard. I left London soon after hearing the news. Tajo was a good man. Father, give me a chance to avenge myself!"

"This man Mark Goodman, he has others involved."

"I must go to the US, I must destroy these men. Please let me do this father!"

"Almir, our troops are angry. I fear our opposition's strength may be growing. In addition to the Americans, England and others are beginning to work together against us. They are losing their fear and striking hard at us. I will send you to strike new fear and remind them, and hope you will inspire all of us. I suggest you take Safar with you. Your two minds can surely outwit these infidels."

"Yes father, thank you. You will not be disappointed I promise!" Almir says leaving the room.

"Where are we going?" Safar asks Almir.

"Jamaica. We are going to Jamaica. We will look into this American company and our shipment. We will make them pay for deceiving us."

Max and Sam join the others at CC's Bar and Grill as planned to play darts. The four guys chat and nibble on peanuts while shooting darts and drinking beer.

"Hey guys," Sam says looking at his watch. "I think I'll

head out. It's nearly eight o'clock and it's been a long day for me what with the new job and all."

"Party pooper!" Jake shouts after finishing his third beer. "Let's have one more!"

"Hey Jake, I'll hang with you." Max says. "Peggy's out of town again."

"Where did Peggy go this time?" Sam asks.

"She went with some girlfriends to Disneyworld. They are staying at the Hilton Hotel for a few days. She says she'll be back on Saturday or Sunday. Since I don't have any desire to see Disneyworld, I'll be alone for a few days. Drive safe my friend. See you in the morning."

"Good night, guys!" Sam says waving at the trio walking out of the bar.

At home, Sam relaxes and turns on his TV. There is a brief story about more unrest in the Middle East on the news.

"So what's new?" He says to himself. The last report he'd seen was from a masked spokesperson deep in Afghanistan. The man was supposedly from the terrorist group that ordered the Deadly Orange Cloud weapons that the London authorities confiscated. The scarf the man wore across his face was bloody on the right side. Sam remembers feeling the hatred in the man's eyes.

"I promise we will have revenge for our loss! Praise Allah!" The man shouts.

"Who wouldn't be upset? They paid big bucks for those weapons and got nothing! Mark's plan worked in spite of Max and me!"

Thinking about his adventure with Max, brought his thoughts back to his upcoming date with Ann on Friday. *I think we have a lot in common. There is something special about Ann. My only regret is not asking her to go out before Friday. I wonder if giving her a few days to think about it, that she might cancel out. For the first time in my life, I feel like maybe she is too good to be with me.*

"Well Almir, we're here. How do you propose we get started?"

"I want you to contact your cousin at the University of Miami. His computer skills will aid us nicely."

"I thought you might feel that way. I already informed him we were coming and asked for his help. He says he will be happy to help the cause."

"Very good. See if he can hack into the computers at Silvan Enterprises. Also have him check news wires and social media and other channels for anything strange going on the week before and after our shipment."

Max and Sam join Albert and Jake the next two days after work at CC's. Sam enjoys the camaraderie he's developing with his co-workers and playing darts.

Wednesday evening Jake loses two games in a row, as Max throws a bulls-eye at the start of the next game.

"You stepped over the foul line! That doesn't count!" Jake shouts taking a gulp from his beer.

"You're crazy!" Max says. "You're just a sore loser!"

Jake leaps off his stool and wrestles Max into a headlock choking his wind off.

"Hey, stop that!" Sam shouts, but Jake keeps his hold on Max.

It looks like Jake is trying to strangle Max. Sam grabs Jake's shoulder to separate the two wrestlers but just as Jake releases his hold on Max, he takes a roundhouse swing at Sam.

Sam's Judo training kicks in and he raises his arm instinctively and blocks the punch by contacting Jake's wrist with his forearm. Sam hears a snapping sound and

Jake screams in agony.

Max regains his breath as Jake sinks down to the floor holding his damaged wrist. The wrist appears to be broken. The bartender seeing the commotion dials 911. Albert stays with Jake to console him while Max and Sam move off to a corner to wait although they want to leave. They know they need to wait for the police and paramedics to come.

"Great, Jake's probably going to file assault charges on me for breaking his wrist. Great way to start my new job."

"Don't worry Sam. He attacked me first and you only tried to break things up when he tried to assault you too. Everyone here saw me in the chokehold and with the marks on my neck to prove it there's no way you can get in trouble here."

"I hope you're right Max."

"Come on Sam, let's get out of here."

"I'm ready! At least no charges were filed against me. You were right. I have to say, I'm relieved."

"Yeah, it was easier for everybody to just call it a draw so no charges were filed on anybody. Although I was surprised he told the cop he's going to kill us for breaking his wrist." Max says.

"They must not have believed him. They probably assumed this all started because he was drunk."

"Probably. I haven't been in a fight in years. If I remember right, my last scuffle was in grammar school with a kid named Johnny. I don't even remember why we were scrapping. Really, it was more of a wrestling match than a fight though. It couldn't have been for anything major though because we eventually just gave up and went back to being friends again."

"That sounds like you Max. You've always been a

happy-go-lucky kind of guy. You rarely ever get upset or mad at anyone."

"Yeah, but I should have seen this coming. I've been noticing how upset Jake was getting if we were scoring better than him, enough so I found myself intentionally missing a few shots just so we'd lose."

"Why did you do that? It was only a game."

"Exactly, it was just a game and I just wanted to have fun. If we won great, if we didn't, well it was no big deal. I knew you felt the same way so it wasn't worth ruining the evening."

"I saw it too, but I don't really know the guy. Knowing you, I just assumed he was acting that way because he's been drinking a lot since it's not like you to hang with unhappy people."

"Normally he isn't like this. Come to think of it, I don't remember seeing him drink so heavy either, even at the holiday Christmas parties."

"Almir, I just spoke to my cousin Mo. He says this Silvan Enterprises has a very secure firewall on their computer system so he wasn't able to get in. He says he can get around it though. He's writing a malware file that you can send in an email. As soon as the email is opened the program will install itself creating an opening he can get into."

"Won't their virus checkers find it?"

"He says no. I asked that question. He said because it's not a virus, most virus programs won't detect it. The malware program won't look suspicious or harmful so it isn't caught. He says most people accumulate so much malware everyday just by surfing the web, emails and other sources and never know it until finally their computers begin to run so slowly. He also says this type of file writes itself into the operating system making it tough to locate yet it will grant him the access he will need."

"When will this be ready?"

"He says he will have it done for you tomorrow. In the meantime, he says he did find something for you."

"What's that?"

"He says he was checking social media sites like you requested and a guard in the police department was bragging about how he spent the weekend babysitting these two guys in jail after they were arrested breaking into Silvan Enterprises. He said they played poker and had fun telling stories all weekend and that's why he hadn't been online for a few days. He didn't give the names of the guys, but Mo then hacked into the jail's computer system. He said most government places like that have weak security so it was easy getting in there."

"What are the names? Did he find them?"

"Yes he did. There isn't an arrest record, but there is a note in a detainee file stating that Max Merchado and Sam Stormen were being held for breaking into Silvan Enterprises on the Saturday before the shipment and were released the following Monday. It also stated that both men were company employees and the company chose not to press charges but requested they be held on a nuisance charge."

"Why would they do that and why would the police department go along with that?"

"This is a small island and Silvan probably gives many kickbacks to the police here."

"You're probably right. I drove by the plant to check it out to find an isolated area to grab Mark. I also checked out several hotels in the area to see if Mark Goodman was registered. I found the one he stays at but they say he is back in the states. I was hoping to find him here so we could take him and make him talk."

"Why can't we do that in the states?"

"We can, I just thought it would be easier here because this island has very poor security. The police here are a joke compared to those in the states, but no matter, we will get him."

"How would we get him to Miami if he was here?" Safar inquires.

"I arranged for a boat. It will take us to Miami so we will not be monitored by Homeland security in the US. My plan is to bypass security and customs. We will be just a few guys returning from a fishing trip."

"Will that work? What about their coast guard?"

""There will be no reason for the coast guard to notice us. They are looking for suspicious activity for those running drugs and refugees trying to enter illegally. I think they call them boat people."

"Yes, but we are entering illegally. What if we are caught?"

"Relax Safar. They don't check papers here. The Americans have nice shiny boats and like to go fishing. As long as the boat is licensed and we have the appropriate gear onboard in case of a spot check we are just a few guys enjoying the waters."

"What kind of gear is the boat supposed to have?

"Oh, just the typical stuff like life jackets and safety gear, nothing for you to worry about."

"How do you know so much about the Americans? Have you been there?"

"Yes, I was there many years ago. Like others, my father wanted me to go to school there. I learned much, and the Americans are lazy and think they own the world. Like you, I have contacts who can help us. Let's head to Miami and meet up with Mohammed. We can send the email from his computer with the malware."

After the incident with Jake, Max and Sam decide to stay away from CC's and go home Thursday after work.

Wanting something to do, Sam decides to read a book until he remembers the invitation from Chet Hatter, the lead guitarist of the Danglebatts. The clock on the microwave shows six o'clock as he tentatively dials Chet's cell phone.

"Chet here."

"Hello Chet. This is Sam. We met on the flight from Denver a few weeks ago."

"I remember. How are you doing?"

"Great. I hired on at Silvan Enterprises here in Fort Lauderdale."

"So you're in Fort Lauderdale again?"

"Yes, I threw out the anchor. I'm back to stay."

"Great! Listen Sam, the guys from the band are camped out here for a few weeks until the concert. You know we have a concert here in a couple of weeks. Why don't you come over to my house, we can jam a bit?"

"Really! That sounds super. What about the other guys? Will they mind having me there, are you sure?"

"Yes, I'm sure. If you haven't eaten, we're having a seafood night. All kinds of eats from Smith's Catering."

"I didn't mean to impose on your hospitality, man. Do you want me to bring anything?"

"Just bring your appetite and your guitar. Actually, we have extra guitars. Just come on over!"

"What's the address?"

"We're in the Blue Lake Estates. I'm at 246 Lux Lane. The guard will call me from the gatehouse and he can direct you to my place. Just pull onto the circular driveway. I'll meet you there."

"Okay, Chet. I should be there in thirty minutes."

"Great! I look forward to seeing you again."

Sam remembers searching the internet out of curiosity for the 'Danglebatts' after getting back from Jamaica and discovered they've sold millions of albums, including 17 number one songs on the hard rock charts. They also made millions on tour all over the world. Sam found it surprising that a band he'd never heard of could be so famous.

It starts raining a few minutes later as Sam gets into his SUV, but he is happy to have this chance to meet the band because he wants to learn more about them after what he saw on the internet.

Arriving at the guardhouse and pulling under the overhang the guard is expecting him and the directions to Chet's house are simple. Driving along Sam can't help looking at all the massive houses on the way. Chet's house is an impressive three stories, which is unusual for Florida. A wide circular driveway runs around the front of the house with two-car garages on each side of the house. Driving onto the driveway, the garage door on the far side starts opening.

Chet comes out motioning him to pull into the garage, having Sam park right next to a blue and gold Boxster convertible.

"Hello my friend. I thought you might prefer parking inside, out of the rain." Chet says wearing a black bathing suit, a blue robe, and sandals.

"Thank you. This is really an impressive house Chet."

"Well, it keeps the rain off us. Anyway, we just got through taking a dip in the pool. It's an indoor pool you know. That keeps the rain off too. Come in and meet Katie my wife and the other guys. I'm going to change into some clothes in a minute. The caterer just delivered the food and we're ready to eat."

Following Chet through a large exercise room Sam enters a huge living room. Near a large fireplace on one side of the room, four chairs have guitars beside to them and an electronic drum set sits next to them.

"The guitars are all wireless, hooked into the PA system over there." Chet says pointing to a bank of speakers and a lit panel.

Off to the right side is a dining room with a large mahogany table and ten high back chairs. The other band members are already seated and eating. Alongside the main table, along one wall, a lengthy counter is full of food the caterer brought. A young blonde haired woman, obviously pregnant in the dining room, begins walking toward Sam.

Smiling at her, Chet says, "Sam, meet my wife Katie. She is the love of my life. Go with her and get a plate. I'll be back in a minute." Giving her a kiss, Chet heads off to change. Taking Sam's hand, Katie leads him into the dining room and introduces him to the rest of the band.

Sam loves seafood and digs in to the food with the band members. After dinner, Chet sits Sam down next to a Gretsch G6122 guitar and after tuning up; they all begin playing hits like 'Tragedy of Love', and 'Tangled Love'. Sam is learning the chords to their biggest hit song, 'Dangling My Love for You' and is really liking the 'Danglebatts' music becomes a fan.

Looking at his watch, Sam says, "Hey, guys, its ten o'clock and my fingers are raw. I haven't played for weeks. I guess my fingertips need toughening again."

"The three of us are going bar-hopping in a bit. Do you want to join us?" Dan Batts, the lead singer asks.

"Thank you for the offer but I think I'm ready to call it a night. I have to go to work in the morning. Thank all of you for a great evening," Sam says. "You guys are so far ahead of me. I learned some new riffs though. The food was excellent, and was only surpassed by your hospitality."

"Glad you enjoyed yourself," Dan says. "It's fun just to jam sometimes."

"Well, good night everyone." Sam says walking back to the garage with Chet.

"Hey, I think you should come to our concert. I want to give you some complimentary tickets. Find a babe to bring along and see if you like our on stage music." Chet says.

"I don't have a girlfriend right now. I just moved here but I have my friend Max. I can bring him along if I can't find a date."

"Does Max have a girl?"

"Yes, her name is Peggy."

"Okay, then I'll give you four tickets. Surely, you can find someone to take with Max and Peggy. You have a couple weeks so that should be enough time for a handsome bachelor like yourself."

"Well it sounds like fun."

"The seats are second row, near the center. All I ask is that you cheer like Hell! The rest of the crowd will be cheering so just join in. Hopefully you will all become fans and have a great time."

"I'm already a fan Chet. You guys are better than I imagined."

"Thank you, I'm glad you enjoyed yourself tonight." Chet says handing him the tickets, and patting his back. "Sam, this lifestyle is really great and I'm glad I can afford it, but I would give it all up if I had to, to keep Katie. When you find your soul mate, it will mean everything to you. It's worth the wait."

"You seem totally content with Katie."

"I am. I am a happily married man."

Chapter Eighteen

On Friday, Max and Sam meet for lunch. "Hey Sam, What's up?"

"I went to a jam session last night."

"You did, who do you know that's in a band?"

"Chet Hatter, remember the guy I met on the plane a few weeks back."

"Oh, hey do you want to come over for dinner tonight? We could throw some steaks on the grill."

"Nah, I can't. Tonight is my date with Ann from accounting."

"Oh yeah, gray eyes."

"Her name is Ann, Max. I'd appreciate it if you show her some respect. I really like her and I want this date to go well. If it does, she may go on another one."

"Boy, you're really into her. I'm sorry man; I will refer to her by her name from now on, okay?"

"Thanks Max."

"So what are your plans for your date?"

"I made reservations at the Café Del Mar for dinner."

"Oh man, you really are trying to impress her. I hope you saved your pennies to go there."

"Come on Max, it's not that expensive. Haven't you taken Peggy there recently?"

"No, and I'd appreciate you not putting fancy ideas in her head." Max says jokingly.

"Aw no wonder she leaves you all the time. I may have to take her out for a nice dinner myself sometime to show her how she should be treated."

"Who are you kidding? Peggy loves me. No fancy dinners are gonna turn her head."

"If you say so Max, if you say so."

"Why don't you come over tomorrow? Maybe we could

hang out or something?"

"We'll see. I'll have to let you know. Well let me go finish some tests. I'm hoping to head out a little early today."

"Hey, I heard Jake hasn't been to work yet since he got out of line the other night. He is AWOL and hasn't called in or anything."

"He's probably taking some sick leave to nurture his wrist. Well wish me luck with Ann tonight."

"Yeah, I guess I'll go home and watch a movie. Enjoy!"

"Mohammed, have you managed to get access to the computer system at Silvan since we sent the email?"

"Yes Almir, I have. Once I was able to get through their firewall and into their root directory system, the rest was easy. I have downloaded their complete personnel file. It also has all their clearance access codes. I expect to be able to create a duplicate system with the information I have access to."

"Why do we need a duplicate of their system if you have their personnel files?" Safar asks.

"Ugh, you don't get it. The duplicate system will act as a mirror allowing me to gain further access."

"Access to what? Not everybody is a computer geek like you."

"I will gain access to passwords and other security measures. We can get banking info to transfer funds or access other security files. I have found they have limited access into the government's computers also because of the work they do. With a little time, I can get into the governments computer mainframe by using Silvan's computer as an access point."

"Wow!" Safar says.

"Yes and the government's computer system isn't separate for different departments meaning once we get in, it's just a matter of writing programs to break the security protocols, then we'll have access to all of the US."

"Won't that take a lot of time, though?" Almir asks.

"No, not really. These Americans think they are so smart that no one would try to break into their computers and their so-called protection is weak. The weakest area is the Treasury department. I think that will be my first entry point."

"Very good Mohammed, you make us proud. I do have a question; can your access be traced back to us?"

"Nah, I can route the servers to so many countries around the globe they will never find us or... I can partially route it so they can find a destination, say like the Chinese or whoever you want to pin it on."

"Excellent! Safar, get a couple of guys together, now that we know where this Mark Goodman lives we will start with him."

Late in the afternoon on Friday Mark is still hard at work when his cell phone rings. "Hello."

"Mark, I need you to listen to me very carefully."

"Um, okay."

"I have a car waiting for you outside. You need to drop what you're doing, take nothing with you and leave now."

"Why? What do you mean take nothing?"

"Just what I said. Leave your jacket, briefcase and anything else you normally take with you. We suspect you have been compromised."

"Compromised? I don't understand."

"Listen Mark! I'll explain everything once you get outside. Oh and leave your cell phone. Don't say anything to anybody that you're leaving."

"Okay." Mark jumps up a little frazzled and heads to the parking area. Walking towards the door, he runs into

Sam.

"Hey boss."

"Oh Sam, how's it going? I'm sorry I haven't had the chance to welcome you aboard. Are things going okay for you?"

"Yeah, they're great."

"Good, I'm glad. If you need anything, just let my secretary or me know. Are you on your way out?"

"Yeah, I finished up and wanted to leave a little early today. I have a date tonight."

"Excellent! You must be settling in. Listen, I'm in a hurry and don't have time to chat right now."

"Okay, see you later." Sam watches Mark rush outside and jump in the passenger side of a waiting dark sedan that drives off quickly as soon as the door closes.

"Are you going to tell me what's going on? What's this about being compromised?"

"You know you and your family have been under surveillance for security purposes ever since this project started."

"Yeah, so?"

"Well, about an hour ago two men tried to abduct your wife when she got home from the grocery store this afternoon."

"What! Is she all right?"

"Yes, she is. She is a little shook up, but she is fine. They were scared off by the neighbor's dog before we could grab them."

"How do you know they planned to abduct her then?"

"Because we found evidence at the scene they dropped while trying to get away. We found a slip of paper with your address, some zip ties and a black hood. That's not the kind of tools a legitimate person would be carrying."

"You're kidding, right?"

"No Mark, I'm not. We knew that you or your family might become a target once that shipment was discovered to be a fake. That's why I've had you and your wife under surveillance ever since you agreed to do this."

"How did they know where I lived?"

"We are still trying to figure that out. That's why I had you leave everything behind at your office. It's possible a bug may have been slipped to you."

"A bug? How? Where?"

"I don't know. It could have been dropped in your jacket pocket, or placed in your cell phone or briefcase or attached to your car. I will have your things checked to see what we can find. In the meantime, you and your wife will be placed in protective custody until this is over."

"How long will that be?"

"As long as it takes; look Mark, we talked about this in the beginning. Until these people are captured or killed, this will not be over."

Riding up to his third floor apartment, Sam knows it's still too early to pick up Ann and turns on the TV. FOX News shows another battle scene in the Middle East.

Nothing new. He thinks, deciding to take a quick shower. After his shower, he changes into his dark gray suit. It's his favorite "make me look great" suit. Grabbing a multi-shaded tan and black tie to wear he sat down to watch the evening news again while tying his tie. The weatherman predicts a clear sky for the evening.

Briefly walking to the dresser mirror, he checks himself before leaving. Determining he looks good, he says to himself "You're a handsome devil!"

Leaving the apartment, and walking to his car in the

moist evening air he thinks, *Thank God for air conditioning*. Having been away from Florida, he'd forgotten how unusually warm evenings are for early spring. The night temperatures aren't like the Colorado air that he's become accustomed.

Loading Ann's address into his GPS, he follows its directions toward her apartment. The evening traffic is still heavy but he left early enough to take his time. He feels a twinge of excitement and nervousness swinging the SUV into a parking place right next to Ann's front door. Getting out of his SUV, he stands and straightens his tie.

"Show time!" he says before walking to her door.

Knocking on Ann's door right at 7 p.m., he's surprised to see her door open almost immediately. She smiles at him with her gray eyes, standing in her doorway wearing a black evening dress, with a thick pearl necklace, and pearl colored fingernails. She looks beautiful to Sam. For a second she takes Sam's breath away causing him to wonder why she isn't already married. Realizing she has chosen to date him leaves him stunned.

"Wow!" He finally manages to say. "You look beautiful. Um, I mean hello."

"Thank you Sam." She replies, her face flushing a little. "You look pretty handsome yourself."

"I guess we're ready to go." He says offering his hand to walk her out. "Shall we?"

"Yes!"

Accepting his arm, he can feel what he can only describe as an electric shock going through him from her touch; a feeling unfamiliar to him.

"Chivalry is not dead." She says as Sam opens the car door for her.

"My pleasure!"

Driving to the Café Del Mar, he feels unusually elated. He has been on many dates with beautiful women before. However, he's never felt quite as happy as he's feeling about this date with Ann. There is something different about her; something he can't yet grasp. He feels an instant bond he's never felt before. Maybe it's because of the entire Orange Cloud thing that is causing him to feel this way.

As he stops the SUV in front of the restaurant, Sam remembers how elegant it is inside and how great the service and food are. He hopes to impress Ann with his apology dinner. He sees Blair, the valet as he comes to open Ann's door.

Handing his keys and a tip to Blair, he walks Ann into the restaurant.

Ah, this is the perfect place, Jake thinks inside his car as he stops across the street from the Café Del Mar as he watches Sam and Ann go in the restaurant. Earlier, Jake went to Sam's apartment complex wanting to slash Sam's tires but when he arrived, he saw Sam getting in his SUV all dressed up. Curious, Jake followed Sam from his apartment to Ann's apartment. At the time, Jake did not realize whose apartment Sam had gone to because although he wanted to know where Ann lived, he could never learn that information. It didn't take long before Sam and Ann came out. Jake realizes that somehow Sam has managed to get a date with the woman he's been trying to date for a very long time.

This new revelation heightens Jakes' anger. It's been a difficult time for Jake before Sam's arrival. Since his arrival, Jakes' life has taken a turn for the worst. He doesn't take loss well, and is accustomed to his friends letting him win. Ever since that night at the bar when Sam broke his wrist after disgracing him at playing darts Jake hasn't coped well. He never should have stopped taking his meds, except that he'd come to convince himself he didn't need them any longer. He was fine. Other people he believes are his problem so why should he have to take meds so he can function amongst them. Sam assaulting him and breaking his wrist with his fancy Judo moves broke what little Jake had left of his grasp on reality. After stewing for days, he'd decided it was time to retaliate. Sam and Max would pay.

Now watching from across the street as Blair parks Sam's SUV and goes back to the front of the restaurant, Jake sees his opportunity. Easing out of his car and casually walking across the street into the parking lot of the Café Del Mar, looking around and seeing no one he reaches down and slashes Sam's right front tire with his Stiletto. He jerks back a little surprised hearing the loud hissing as air escapes the tire and breaks into a stifled hysterical laugh. *I'll teach you to break my wrist!* As he laughs, he walks to the rear of the car and stabs the rear tire. He muffles his laughter until he gets back to his car. Inside his car, he roars with a crazy man's laugh.

The maître d' greets Sam and Ann near the entrance.

"I have an eight o'clock reservation."

"Very well sir, please have a seat. You are a little early."

"Yes, I know we're a little early." Sam says handing the man some money.

"No problem. Right this way sir. We do have a table in a rather secluded area. Will that do?"

"Perfect." Sam says following the man to a table.

"Thank you." Ann says to the maître d' as he seats her.

"So here we are." She says to Sam. "I'm glad you asked me out. I heard you were working in Denver, Colorado before this. That's a long way from Fort Lauderdale! How did you hire on at Silvan Enterprises? Did Mark lure you away from your job in Denver?"

"Yes, and I'm glad you agreed to going out tonight. Mark made me an offer I couldn't refuse. I found out a lot about Mark because of that Orange Cloud thing. He's a good person. I guess he liked me, too. This job pays better, and has better benefits. Frankly though, I was getting tired of the mountains. This is really my old stomping grounds. It's where I grew up. Max and I grew up here but in different areas of town. We have been friends for years. I believe it will be a better life for me here, and of course, I met you! Enough about me, tell me about you."

"I worked basically as a barmaid at a Holiday Inn until I graduated as a CPA. You cannot imagine how many creeps I met working there! So many of the men think because they buy you a drink or give you a big tip they can do whatever they like! Anyway, I applied for work at Silvan Enterprises and just got lucky that there was an opening. It's really the best job I've ever had. And Mark is a great boss just like you said."

A waiter approaching them asks, "Would sir and madam care for something to drink?"

"I understand your house Rose is excellent." Sam says.

"Yes, it has a wonderful light taste. We import the wine from Italy of course. Would sir and madam care to try a glass?"

Ann nods her head at Sam's questioning look. "Yes, we would. We'll order a little later."

"As you wish sir." The waiter says handing menus to Ann and Sam bowing slightly before walking away.

"You said you and Max grew up together, so was he always like he is now?"

"Pretty much. Although we were both raised in Fort Lauderdale, we went to different high schools. Our parents knew each other, but we didn't become friends though until we met at the University of Florida and were roomies in the dormitory. That's when I learned he is a major prankster! We made a pact back then never to play any pranks on each other. I'm glad we have that pact."

"So you went through college with him as a roommate?"

"Not really, we both left after the first year. I wanted to get into electronics and it takes too long at the University. The engineering program didn't get into any serious electronics until the third year of college. At least that's what it looked like to me. I went to a trade school called Electronic Technical School here in Fort Lauderdale. I met Max again at the trade school that next year. At that time, I guess he wanted to be an electronic tech, too. We were already best friends but became even closer friends then. We had some good times together, some fun times. He did some crazy pranks while we were at school." Sam paused for a moment. "When he called me a few weeks ago he sounded desperate. I thought he was in grave danger. I don't handle danger very well, but he's my best friend and he called on me to help him."

"Oh, you came here, to help Max?"

"Exactly. You know Max, he tends to get excited easily and he is extremely patriotic. He thought Mark was trying to snuff him out! As you know it was really an elaborate plan to help stop terrorism."

"Let's hope there are no repercussions over it." She says as he sees a brief scared look on her face but an instant later, she returns to her cheery smile.

"Well, I think they believe we have nothing to do with that shipment being confiscated in London. Mark's plan apparently worked well."

Chapter Nineteen

"I have a question… You know I have never been married, but I can't believe no one has latched onto you. Have you ever been married?"

"No, and I was thinking of asking you the same question, but I didn't want to seem forward. I used to date regularly but the guys I met were usually bar flies. I guess they were all after the same thing! I dated one guy for nearly a year. I thought we would get married but he turned out to be a cheater. It hurt me very much when we broke up. After that I somewhat gave up on dating. Then I hired on with Silvan Enterprises. Now, some of the guys there flirt with me. Jake in shipping seems a little weird and flirts with me a lot. I don't encourage any of them. I haven't really been interested in dating guys from work because it can cause problems at work running into them if things don't work out. Since I didn't think any of the guys who have tried to get me to go on a date were potential real relationships, I just decline their advances. I guess the right guy just hadn't come along for me. After a while, I got used to not dating. You're the first man I've gone out with in a long time. Now, I'm talking too much! What about you?"

"My dating life hasn't been stellar by any account. My last girlfriend Jessica was studying to be an anthropologist at the University in Denver. She ran off with another anthropologist student. Go figure! She told me I didn't have enough in common with her, so she said goodbye!"

Continuing to talk, while sipping wine and eating they learn more about each other and their interests.

"I think Mark's Orange Cloud was a genius' plan." Sam says when the conversation lapses.

Frowning a little Ann says, "I know we aren't supposed

to talk it even now that it's over, but I still pray nothing happens to us or Silvan Enterprises because of it. Oh, by the way, would you like to come to church with me on Sunday?"

"Church?"

"Yes. I think you'll love it. We have a great pastor. He calls himself Big Ben. His real name is Pastor Ben Gless. He gives wonderful sermons. I think you will enjoy coming, and he's a Gator graduate."

"Um... Okay. What time should I pick you up or is it out my way?"

"You can come get me. It's near my place." She says.

"Okay, maybe you could wear a bathing suit under your clothes and we can go to the beach after church."

"Maybe, come over early Sunday morning. We can have coffee before we go. The beach sounds like fun."

Chatting and laughing he finds her smile to be enchanting, and her voice is like music to Sam's ears. Enjoying the evening and their time together proves to be a pleasant and romantic time for both of them. Touching hands occasionally, they feel a bond building between them. Sam's never experienced feelings like this before. Feeling a sense of peace within himself he's never had, and not just because of consuming a lot of wine happy.

Leaving the restaurant, Sam hands his ticket to the valet. Holding on to each other arm in arm, they wait for the car to arrive from the parking lot continuing to enjoy their remaining time together.

A minute later Blair returns without the car and has a worried look on his face. "I can't bring your car out sir. Both your right side tires are flat!"

"What!" Sam exclaims.

"Yeah, I noticed the car was tilting over a little. I checked and sure enough, both tires are flat on the right side. I'm really sorry, sir. We've never had any vandalism here. What would you like me to do?"

"Just call a cab for us." Sam says trying to hand Blair a tip.

"Right away sir," Blair raises his hand to refuse the tip Sam offered. "I'll be right back. We'll get you a cab." Running inside he informs the restaurant manager and phones for a cab, Blair is shaken by the incident.

Sam shakes his head looking up at the sky saying, "Why me, Lord?"

Ann tightens her arm around him, "I'm sorry, too."

"I'll send someone to fix the tires tomorrow. Don't worry about it, Ann."

Returning, Blair says, "I spoke to the manager, he's very concerned. He says the cab is on us and we can have your car towed to a place of your choosing, on us of course."

"Thank you, but don't worry about it. I'll have a repairman come get it in the morning; you'll be closed then."

"Yes sir, are you sure you don't want the car towed this evening."

"Yes, it will be fine here. I'll let them know where to find it so they can come early and fix it." Tightening his arm around Ann's waist, he is annoyed yet happy at the same time.

I know the valet parking area is open to the public so anyone could have let the air out of my tires. Nothing like this has ever happened to me. It's bad enough to have flat tires, but it's even worse to have them when I'm on a great date! Just some bad luck, he thought. *Peaks and valleys.*

A taxi arrives quickly and Sam opens the rear door for Ann to get in before getting in himself.

The cab ride to Ann's building seems to end all too soon. Sam doesn't want the night to end. The evening was a big success in his mind even though his tires were flattened.

Getting out of the cab to let Ann out, Sam staggers a little before extending his hand to help Ann. He starts to feel the effects of too much wine.

Stepping out of the cab, Ann is a little unsteady on her feet too. She realizes they are both tipsy. Smiling at Sam she says, "Would you like to come in for a nightcap or a cup of coffee? I can drive you home later."

"I'd like that!" *Only a fool would turn down that offer!* He thinks and leans inside the cab for a second to tell the driver not to wait.

Ann realizes walking toward her apartment; that she drank way too much wine. Embracing Sam and enjoying holding on to steady herself they make their way to her door laughing and giggling.

Stepping inside, as soon as Sam shuts the door behind him, she surprises him. She put her hands on his waist trying to steady herself, and looks up at Sam with her sexy eyes. "I'm a little off balance." She says slurring her words as they taper off.

Wrapping his arms around her to help steady her he feels she needs help to stay upright. "Hey, let's have a seat on the couch."

"Okay. I don't feel..." Sam immediately feels the weight of her body in his arms as she leans into him and passes out.

Holding on to her and leaning against the door to steady himself and keep from tipping over, he stands still for a moment. Having her pass out helps sober him up, a bit. Gently reaching down and cradling her in his arms, he carries her into her bedroom. Laying her on the bed, he sits down next to her gently speaking to her calling her name. Slowly her eyes show she is starting to come to.

"Ann! Hey there, are you okay? You passed out. I carried you in here." He says as she starts looking around trying to determine where she is.

"I'm fine. I think. The room just started swimming. Would you be a dear and get me a glass of water? There is cold bottled water in the refrigerator, if you don't mind.

"Sure, no problem. I'll be right back. Do me a favor and scoot onto the bed more. I don't want you to fall off while I'm gone."

"Okay." She mumbles scooting in and rolling over onto her side. "Is this good?"

"Yes. Thank you. I'll be right back with your water." He says smiling.

Rushing to the kitchen, he grabs a glass from the cabinet and a bottle of water from the kitchen, and hurries back to check on her. This is not how he wanted the evening to end, but now he just wants Ann to be okay. "Here you go," He says coming back in her bedroom.

Propping up on a myriad of pillows, Ann starts to feel better. She glances at Sam and sees he is teetering slightly.

"You don't look so steady yourself you big hunk," She says.

"I've got to admit, I do feel a bit tipsy. I was nervous about our date and drank too much wine while we were talking."

"Me too! I hate to say it, but I'm glad. I feel a little ashamed getting drunk enough to pass out. I finally go on my first date in a long time and I get drunk. I hope this hasn't ruined your opinion of me?"

"Of course not, I can ask the same to you."

"I'm afraid I'm not up to driving you home as I promised."

"I can call a cab to take me home."

"Well, you could spend the night on my couch. I can drive you home in the morning."

"That sounds fine. I think I need to lie down too. I'll take you up on that offer."

"Here's a pillow," She says grabbing one from her bed and handing it to Sam. "You can grab a blanket from the hall closet. Thank you, goodnight."

"Good night, Ann." Sam says looking at Ann for a moment before staggering into the living room. Finding the hall closet, he retrieves a blanket and a moment later settles on the couch and crashes.

Saturday morning Sam wakes up feeling a gentle kiss on his cheek. Opening his bleary eyes, he focuses on a beautiful woman staring down at him. Ann's hair has cascaded around her face, and she is still wearing her black formal dress.
"Good morning handsome. It's almost eight o'clock."

"Holy cow!" Sam says sitting up on the couch and rubbing his eyes.

"I drank too much wine. I'm not used to drinking that much."

"Me either. I hadn't intended our date to end this way. We talked a lot, and that pesky waiter kept filling our wine glasses. I wanted to impress you and make up for ditching you. I hope you can forgive me."

"Done! I had a great time. I loved talking and the wine, but I wish we hadn't drunk quite so much. I hope you can forgive me for passing out on you."

"I can if you agree to another date sometime?"

"What about church and going to the beach tomorrow? Doesn't that count?"

"Yes, but no! I want another date like last night, if you'll accept."

"Okay, I'll think about it, but not so much wine. Let me fix some coffee. I've got some cinnamon rolls we can have for breakfast too. Are you hungry?"

"Hmm, yes I'm hungry." Before she can move to get up he grabs her head, draws her face to him, and gives her a long kiss on her lips. He immediately thinks about apologizing for the kiss, but then she returns his kiss and doesn't pull away.

Caressing and kissing, they sink onto the couch. Sam feels her passion as his own stirs up. The whole world seems right for a moment, until she suddenly brakes away.

"Whew!" She exclaims breathing hard as she stands up. Waving a hand in front of her flushed face she dashes away to the kitchen. "I'm going to make some coffee now. Maybe you can turn on the TV to see what the weather will be like today."

In a daze, Sam acts like a robot obeying orders. He fumbles with the remote and turns on the TV. Switching to a news channel finally a weatherman comes on. The forecast is clear and sunny for the day. Smelling the coffee brewing, he walks into the kitchen and wraps his arms around Ann.

"Um..."

As he holds her, Sam sees a stuffed Gremlin sitting on her kitchen windowsill. "What's that?"

"My lucky Gremlin. I won it at the county fair a year ago. I just like it sitting there, greeting me in the morning. It makes me remember how lucky I am."

"I feel lucky, too." He says squeezing her a little before turning her loose and helping her carry the coffee and rolls out to the dining table. Still clad in their formal attire, they enjoy breakfast smiling and chatting, this time without wine.

"I guess I need to change so I can drive you home."

"I suppose, I didn't think we would be having breakfast together. I wouldn't mind hanging with you today, though."

"Surely you have things you have to do, like find out about your car."

"Yeah, and there's something else important I have to do today... I just can't think of what it is right now."

"I'll drive you home. Maybe you'll think of it then."

Arriving home, he waves goodbye to Ann. He heads for the elevator and notices a large moving van parked next to his apartment building. *My stuff is here! That's what I forgot. I knew there was something.*

A heavy man is heading for the driver side of the truck cab and looks to be preparing to leave. Sam hustles over to the man. "I'm Mister Stormen. Are you here to deliver my stuff?"

"Mister Stormen, Yeah, I was getting ready to leave. The paperwork says you wanted a morning delivery."

"Yes, yes, I apologize. I ran into car trouble or I'd have been here earlier. Please... can we get this done now?"

"Yeah, it's 303 right?"

"Right, I'll see you up there. The elevator is right over here." Sam points toward his left.

Calling his old friend at John's Auto Repair Shop Sam explains what happened to his car. "Can you just go there and inflate the tires and drive it back to your shop?"

"No problem Sam, I'll send a couple guys over to the res-taurant. They can pump up the tires and drive the SUV to the shop. I'll check it over when it gets here and give you a call."

"Hello." Max answers.

"Max, you won't believe what's happened!" Sam says somewhat annoyed.

"What! No hello? What happened?"

"Someone flattened my tires at the restaurant last night? We had to take a taxi home!"

"You're kidding?"

"Yes, both right side tires."

"I didn't do it."

"Yeah, I know, it just upset me since my date was important to me. I've never had a problem like this before... and at the Café Del Mar, no less."

"It does seem a bit mean to do two tires. Does anyone have an issue with you?"

"Not that I know of, it just seems like a lot of strange things are happening lately. I guess someone wanted to show me it wasn't just a normal flat tire thing. I had to call John's Auto Repair shop. John is sending a couple workers over. They'll pump up the tires, and get it to his place. He will call me when it's ready. Can you pick me up to go there later?"

"Sure. Why don't I bring you over here and we'll play some cards or something?"

"I can't, the movers are here. I want to stay and unpack things."

"Well, let me know when you're ready to go."

"Okay thanks, wait! Here's John now, let me take his call and I'll get back to you.

"I hate to tell you this Sam. I sent my guys over to reinflate your tires, but they have been sliced on the sides. You know when a radial tire gets a cut like that on the side it's not safe to patch. You're gonna need new tires! I'm gonna have my men tow it here. Then we'll pull the wheels, and replace the tires. While we're at it, we'll give her a once over to see if anything else was tampered with, just in case. I can get the tires this morning and replace them if you want me to go ahead."

"Wow! Um...Yeah, go ahead and replace them. Call me when it's finished." *Peaks and valleys.* Sam thinks. *Damn, I had a fantastic date last night and now an expensive repair job.*

Well let me focus on getting my stuff arranged while the movers bring it so I can have this finished by the time my car is ready.

Chapter Twenty

Max hangs up the phone with Sam and hears the front door open. Peggy comes in carrying her purse and an oversized handbag. He sees her wave back at her friends.

"Bye now, and thanks for the ride! Be careful driving home!"

Peggy sees Max standing near the kitchen. She drops her bags and hurries over to him. She gives Max a long kiss and hug before he can put away his phone.

"I missed you." She says still hugging him.

"Oh boy it's great to have you home! These last few days have been strange."

"Why do you say that?"

"Well, Jake tried to strangle me at CC's, and..."

"What! That rat! I remember you told me he's flakey. Why did he try that?"

"It's a long story. I'll tell you later. Anyhow, Sam pulled him off me and broke his wrist."

"Sam's wrist is broken!"

"No, Jake's, but listen there's more. Last night someone flattened two of Sam's tires while he was on a date."

"Sam went on a date already?"

"Oh yes and with the woman none of the guys at work could date. Anyway, I'm glad you're home. Sam's furniture came today. I'll need to bring home the stuff he borrowed."

"So you'll need to drive my pink truck again."

"Yup."

"Well, let me unpack. I brought you a rubber Donald Duck. You can add it to your rubber duck collection."

"Gee thanks. It looks too nice."

"Should I whip something up for lunch?"

"Yes. Another reason I'm glad you're home, but first maybe..."

Peggy presses her lips to his as they kiss several times. Embracing a while, Max suddenly lifts her off the floor and walks into his bedroom.

"I guess you really are glad to see me." Peggy manages to say.

Outside Max's house, Jake casually walks into the carport. He looks around and sees no one. *You too!* He giggles. Taking out his Stiletto, he bends down and slashes the right front tire on Max's Corvette. Hearing the air hiss out, he covers his mouth hushing his laughs and after stabbing the rear tire as well, quickly walks back to his car laughing. Jake seems to have more and more trouble controlling his laughter and feels overjoyed with his latest accomplishment in broad daylight. Back inside his car, he roars with laughter. *This is so much fun! I must think of something else to do...*

"Hey Max, the movers just left a little bit ago. I'm all settled in now, I guess. Oh, speaking of which, guess what?"

"Um...You want me to come get the futon and stuff?"

"Well yeah, but I meant about my car. John called me, it seems my tires were slashed instead of the air being let out."

"Wow! You're kidding! That's a crappy thing to do to someone. Who would do that?"

"I don't know. I haven't been in town long enough to piss anyone off. Other than that one night when things got a little out of hand when we played darts after work, nothing strange has happened. Do you think it's because of that, or could someone at work be jealous about my date with Ann?"

"Well, you did just blow into town and wrangle a date from the ice lady. Nah, I'm just kidding. I can't think of anything. A game of darts isn't serious enough to warrant behavior like that and besides, it didn't happen at home and no one other than me knew where you'd be last night."

"That's what I thought. I just don't get it. Sure anyone has easy access to vehicles where they park' em, but it's hard to believe it's just a random act of violence when no other vehicles were hit."

"I know what you mean. You're sure no one else was hit?"

"I doubt it. The valet and manager seemed thoroughly surprised. Ann and I were talking and she keeps saying she hopes that we won't have any repercussions over that Orange Cloud thing."

"How could we? They got the guy when he picked up the package at the airport. Well just think, Jake's right wrist is broken and he slashes your right tires. That may be the connection."

"That's a strange coincidence... Yeah, but something's nagging at me. I don't know why, I just have a feeling I can't shake."

"Oh come on Sam, It's done and over. Don't go stressing yourself out over something that is no longer an issue. Mark's government contact is convinced and they would know if they didn't get the right guy."

"Yeah, I guess you're right. Regardless, it's an expensive act of vandalism."

"That it is. When will your SUV be ready?"

"I expect John to call me anytime now. Is Peggy back home yet?"

"Yes, happily she came back just a little while ago."

"Maybe you can bring her truck and we can load your stuff up. By then my SUV should be ready."

"Sounds good, but let's take the stuff to my house first to unload before I drop you at the repair shop."

"Okay, see you in a few." Sam says.

Max hangs up the phone. He smiles at Peggy.

"Thank you for coming home early!"

"This is nice," She says kissing him on the cheek.

"Guess I'd better get dressed, and go see Mister Stormen." Max says slipping into a pair of shorts and loafers preparing to go to Sam's apartment. "See you later beautiful."

"I'll have something cooked up when you return."

"Thanks, love."

Max grabs the spare keys for the truck and walks out to the carport.

As he walks between the truck and his Corvette, he sees the two right tires on the Vet are flat.

"What the..." He mumbles and bends over to examine the tires. They each have a long slash on the outer side.

"Oh no! This is too much!" Max dials John's Repair Shop.

"Hey John, you have another customer. Someone slashed two of my tires." Max gave him the size of the tires. A moment later, he pounds on the steering wheel of the truck before he cranks it up and heads for Sam's apartment.

After Max helps Sam load his stuff in the truck, he drives on not saying much. He can't help thinking about all the nasty things he wants to do to Jake and daydreams about taking all the slashed tires and tying them to Jake and tossing him into the ocean. His daydream is interrupted by Sam.

"Hey Max, do you really think Jake slashed your tires too? What are we going to do now?"

"I don't know. Who else could it be? Jake is the only person who would want to hurt both of us. He said he'd get even that night, but I thought it was just drunk talk. I never thought he'd actually try anything. I wish I knew where Jake lives; I'd go there and torture him! The guy is a nut case. You would think he knows the wrist thing was an accident. This is too much retaliation." Max drives on with an annoyed look on his face.

Riding on in silence Max turns onto Clifton Street and Sam sees Max's red Corvette looks tilted in its parking spot on the right side of his triple carport as Max parks the truck.

Sam doesn't understand why Max chooses to live in an older house. It's a mystery to Sam. *Max is a cool guy and is one of the smartest people I've ever met and he's a super-salesman. It still seems strange why mister modern age would choose to live in an old frame house. Nevertheless, true geniuses tend to be eccentric*, he thinks.

When Max pulls into his carport, Peggy comes dashing for the truck.

"Hi there stranger." She shouts as Sam slips out of the truck. "I heard from this one you came in town while I was at Disney World with my friends."

"Hey Peggy, how are you?" Sam asks giving her a big hug.

"Boy, am I glad you are living back here again. With you gone, Max has been driving me crazy with his pranks."

"I guess you heard, this time the prank is on him, along with me of course."

"Yeah, I heard. I feel so bad for you, getting thrown in jail for trying to help a friend."

"Yeah he owes me big time now."

"Hey, would you two stop talking about me. I'm standing right here. It's not polite." Max has an annoyed look on his face.

"Max, you have no right to tell me about being polite.

It's not polite to be constantly pulling your pranks on me, the woman you're supposed to love."

"I do love you. You know that."

"Do I?" She says placing her hands on her hips.

"Peggy," Sam interrupts jumping in to break things up before they got out of hand, "When did you get back? Max told me you were away with friends."

"I came back a little early. My friends dropped me off this morning. Since you're here, let's have a barbeque, drink some beers and hang out. That way I can catch up with you. How is Jessica? How is she handling your move?"

"Um, we broke up."

"Oh no! That's too bad." She says giving Sam another hug, sticking out her tongue in jest at Max. "When did this happen? Well come, tell me all about it after you unload."

"I'm sorry Peggy; I've got to go to the repair shop. They are replacing my sliced tires."

"Oh yeah, Max told me."

"Yeah, they're replacing the tires."

"Holy cow! Who would do that?"

"I don't know. I was on a date at the Café Del Mar when it happened."

"I can't believe that. Oh, wow! That's such a great restaurant. Things like that don't usually happen there."

"I know. The manager felt so bad he paid for a taxi for us and offered to have my car towed."

"Well come on in later. Do you have plans after you get your car back? Maybe we can have that barbeque after all. It sounds like we have a lot to catch up on since you're only in town a short time and already dating. So, who is this woman that you'd take to the fancy Café Del Mar anyway? Maybe we should invite her too. I may need to check her out and..."

"Let me see about later. Maybe I can bring Ann another

time. I'm not quite ready to share her."

"Oh, so this is serious, then. Well now, I definitely want to meet her! She must be a..."

"Peggy, the man told us another time. Don't crowd him. He'll bring her by when he's ready. Right Sam?"

"Right." Sam replies.

"Well let's finish getting this stuff unloaded before she starts planning your wedding."

"Max! I'm going to make you pay for that."

"I'm sure you will." Max says under his breath. "It's nice to have you back, Peg. By the way, if you look around your truck you'll see my Vet has two flat tires too."

"What happened?"

"They're slashed just like Sam's tires were."

"Wow! You think it's this Jake guy we talked about?"

"Yes. Right now, I'd like to shoot Jake. The guys from the repair shop should be here any minute to replace the tires. Well, let's get this stuff unloaded." Max says as he walks to the back of the truck.

Arriving at John's Repair Shop, Sam's SUV is sitting in the parking lot waiting for him.

"Do you want me to wait until you get your car back?"

"No, go on. Thanks for bringing me. I'll see you around two o'clock?"

"Okay, see you then."

"Hello John."

"Hey, Sam. I'm sorry about your tires. I have the bill ready and the SUV is ready to go."

"Wow! Those tires aren't cheap!"

"I put Michelin tires on. They're extra heavy duty tires, and the same as the old ones."

"I guess that's why they make credit cards."

"Sorry about the cost, I wish you could arrest someone

for this! I wonder if they realize how much damage they did! You should at least report it to your insurance."

"I already did this morning. My agent hasn't called me back yet. I'd like to catch whomever and stuff this bill down their throat! Well, thanks John."

Max arrives back at his house, as his old Vet tires are being loaded in the back of a van. He pulls into the carport and stops as Peggy comes to greet him.

"Hi, Max. I thought Sam would come back with you."

"Hi. I think he's going home to unpack some more. He's coming over about two or so to go fishing."

"Rats. I mixed up some tuna salad. I know he likes that. We can save some in case he hasn't eaten."

"Sounds good. I like your tuna salad too. Let's go eat and think about how we can get even with Jake."

"He seems to be on your mind today."

"And he will be until we resolve this problem with him." Max says, as the technician is getting ready to leave. He shouts, "Thanks, Guy. See you in a while."

Guy waves at Max and drives away as Max and Peggy go inside to have lunch.

"Sam thinks it could be that Arab guy causing trouble. I still think its Jake." Max says.

"Well come, sit down and eat. Maybe you can think of how to stop Jake after you have some food in you."

"You might as well know Sam made me promise to stop doing pranks on you."

"Really? You think you can do that?"

"Yes. I never want you to leave again."

"Aw Max. That's sweet!" She kisses him and sits down to enjoy the tuna salad.

"Hello handsome!" Ann says sounding unusually cheery

when she answers the phone.

"Hi beautiful, I have my SUV back, but I had to buy a pair of new tires."

"My God! That's awful!"

"Are you sure you don't have a jealous ex-boyfriend?"

"No, I told you I haven't had any relationships for over a year since I caught my 'ex', Paul with another woman. He did get upset when I broke up with him, but he has never done anything bad that I know of. He's married now. However, that guy Jake in shipping keeps asking me out and I keep turning him down. He seems a little creepy and I've been trying to discourage him from asking. Other than him, there isn't anyone else I can think of."

Wondering for a few seconds, *Jake has to be the culprit.*

"Nothing like this has ever happened to me. I guess I'll have to chalk it up to bad luck and hope my insurance will reimburse me."

"I know. It does sound like you had some bad luck last night."

"You're kidding, right? You're the luckiest thing that's happened to me in a long time!" *Maybe ever.*

"That's sweet! I had a nice time, Sam. Will I see you at church tomorrow?"

"Yep! I'll come over a little after ten. Is that good?"

"Yes, that'll be fine handsome."

"Um, would you like to go fishing with Max and me to-day?"

"I'd love to, but I think I'll let you boys go by yourselves. I have some things I need to do."

"All right, I'll see you in the morning."

Leaving John's, shop, Sam decides to head to Marcy's Place, an old mom and pop restaurant just a few blocks from John's Repair shop. A quick glance in the rear view mirror suddenly makes the hairs on Sam's arms stand on end. *Damn, that black Escalade looks like it's made every turn I have since I left John's. That's definitely not Jake. There's no reason for anyone to follow me. I must be paranoid because of my tires last night. Probably someone's just headed in the same direction as me.*

Oh good, they kept going when I turned. My imagination must really be working overtime. Sam fails to notice the older model beige Ford Escort following Sam by hiding in the shadow the black Escalade.

"Hola, Sam!" Marcy shouts seeing Sam walk inside.

"Hi Marcy. Look at you; you haven't changed a bit. You look the same as you did three years ago when I last saw you. Just as gorgeous as ever!"

"You charmer, you. You also lie. I'm old and fat."

"It doesn't show Marcy. You're beautiful to me."

"That's why I love you Sam. You're good for a girls' ego. When did you get back in town?"

"Just over a week ago. I came back for a new job."

"Wonderful! We sure miss you around here. So what can I get you today?"

"Do you still have that delicious clam chowder?"

"Yes, sit! I'll bring it."

Before sitting down, Sam checks and sees that his and Max's pictures are still hanging in the same spot making Sam happy, and he sits contentedly at his favorite table to wait.

"Thanks Marcy. The chowder was excellent as always. I'm glad to be back, I miss eating here."

"You're welcome Sam. Next time you come by, bring Max with you."

"I will Marcy, I will." He says kissing her goodbye on the cheek.

Chapter Twenty-One

Driving to Publix to get a few groceries, Sam catches himself checking his mirrors frequently even though he sees nothing strange. After unloading the groceries, he plops down on his nice fluffy couch, and closes his eyes to take a catnap. *I'll just rest for a few minutes before I leave to go fishing with Max and Peggy.*

Just as he falls asleep, he suddenly sees an image of Jake with a group of angry people.

"Why did you do this to me?" Jake is shouting holding his broken wrist and screaming in agony. A small crowd gathers around Jake to console him. Everyone begins staring at Sam with menacing eyes and humming while shuffling closer to Sam.

"It was an accident!" Sam shouts.

"No it wasn't!" Jake says. "You deliberately hit me. You knew it would break my wrist!"

"It was an accident!" Sam shouts again. "It was only a reaction to defend myself."

"I think you and Max riled me up so you could do this to me. You set me up so you could test your Judo out on me! I have to get even now. You and Max are responsible for this. It's only right for me to do something to you now!"

"It was an accident! An accident!" Sam shouts.

The crowd begins encroaching on Sam as Jake looks at him and starts laughing cynically. Just as suddenly, the image of Jake and the crowd fades away.

Sam shouts loud enough to wake himself up. "I'm sorry Jake." He says to his empty apartment. Looking at his watch, he's running late and rushes out of his apartment to Max's house.

"Hey Sam, you get hung up in traffic or something?" Max

asks a little annoyed.

"No, I dozed off, sorry. When I got home, I just crashed on the couch for a while. I had a strange dream..."

"Well, I've already loaded all the gear into the truck." Max says interrupting Sam. "You ought to get that strange dreaming stuff looked in to, Sam."

"I know. It's getting annoying." Sam says.

"Let's get going!" Max says climbing into the driver's seat and cranking up the engine. Peggy slides in next to Max and Sam gets in closing the door.

In a few minutes, they arrive at the yacht and are ready to release the moorings on Max's boat. Firing up the twin 250 horsepower Mercury engines, they idle along the waterway until reaching open water.

"Hold on!" Max shouts as he pushes the throttles wide open. "I want to get to an area about five miles from here where the blue fish usually swarm this time of year."

"It's nearly dark; I guess it's time to head back in. I want to dock while I still have some light." Max says cranking up the engines.

"Yeah sure, we can scale and fillet the fish once we get back to the boat dock."

"You better!" Peggy interjects. "I don't want all those fish guts and scales at the house. You can put the filets in this cooler I brought."

"Aye, aye, mi Capitan!" Max says sarcastically to Peggy.

"You just get us in Mister, and don't even think about playing any of your pranks tonight! When we get back to the house you need to get the grill fired up so I can throw some vegetables and potatoes on while you unload the truck."

"But I was..."

"No but's Max! I want to have a nice dinner and spend

some time with Sam, and I don't want to be on the lookout for your pranks." Max nods his obedience to Peggy.

"The meal was excellent Peggy." Sam says.

"Yeah it was great babe. Can you grab me another Michelob while you're up?"

"Okay, do you want another one Sam?"

"Sure. It's great being back in Lauderdale. Thank you for cooking Peggy, and both of you for being great friends!"

"We love you, too Sam."

"Thanks, you guys are great!"

"Ah shucks, man!" Max says.

Sam says, "What can I say, Max? I am enjoying the journey! I stopped by Marcy's Place for lunch today. Marcy is still right there next to Electronic Tech School and still has that great clam chowder. Our pictures are still hanging on the wall. Do you believe that! We had some great times hanging out there."

"We should plan a dinner there. I haven't been to see her in years!"

"Have I ever been there?" Peggy asks.

"No silly, but you'll love her. She is a sweet old woman. She loves all of us who ate there when we went to school. It's just her way." Max says.

"Hey, it's been a long day. I think I'll go back to my place and sack out early. I promised to go to church tomorrow with Ann."

"Oh really? This relationship must be serious. I'm going to have to meet this girl Sam. You can't get serious with her until I check her out."

Chuckle, "Okay Peggy. I'll be sure to plan an evening or something, I promise. Well good night all."

On the ten o'clock news, a TV reporter in Afghanistan is

talking to a group of rebel forces. The men are clothed in brown smocks with dark tan scarves wrapped around their faces masking their identities. There is no new information to be found regarding the Orange Cloud weapon, however these men insist they will get even with whomever caused them to lose their shipment.

Just another nut case. Sam thinks turning off the TV. *The Brits will have to deal with them.* Stripping down to his underwear and crawling into bed, Sam falls asleep quickly after his afternoon on the water and the beers he drank while boating and with dinner.

Sound creeps into Sam's brain as someone is pounding at his front door. *Who would be calling on me at this late hour? Why didn't they just ring the doorbell?* Getting up still dazed and staggering out to the living room, the front door bursts open with a loud crash before he can get to it. Two Arab-looking men in brown smocks with dark tan scarves across their faces rush in. Trying to turn and run Sam's feet seem locked in place!

One man waves his gun at Sam and yells, "You come with us!"

"Who are you? What do you want?"

"No talking! Put your hands behind your back! Tie his hands!"

The other man swiftly cinches Sam's hands behind his back with a long black tie-wrap and blindfolding him before forcing him out of the apartment causing him to brush against the splintered doorframe.

"Ow! Where are you taking me?"

"No questions!"

"Can I get dressed?"

"No! No questions!"

Barefoot and clad only in his underwear, Sam is pushed down the hallway and into the elevator to a waiting car.

Feeling the car start moving it stops a few minutes later and Sam can smell ocean air when the door opens. Tripping and staggering they hustle him onto a boat. Onboard, one of the men pushes him onto a bench seat. Just before the noise from the engines starts, he hears familiar voices nearby. Trying to decipher the voices, the surge of the powerful engines causes the boat to lurch forward at high speed knocking him backwards.

His blindfold is suddenly ripped off and he sees Max and Mark sitting on the side bench across from him in pain. Blood is oozing from their arms and faces. Mark's pajamas are soaked in blood and Max's clothes appear blood-soaked as well. Looking at each other, they see someone has cut their arms and faces with a knife.

"What's going on?" Sam shouts.

Max says, "They're going to kill us! They think we killed their shipment of those weapons so they're going to kill us. As soon as we get closer to the shark infested area near Key West, they're going to throw us overboard."

Laughing behind the scarf on his face one of the Arab-looking men starts approaching Sam with a razor knife. Trying to wriggle himself free Sam thrashes about, but it is no use. Sam starts screaming as the knife begins slashing his arms.

"Stop!" Sam shouts sitting bolt upright in his bed still trashing from the ties that bound him. Looking around the room reality floats back to him. Somehow, in his thrashing about he managed to tangle himself in his bedding. "Good grief!" He exclaims to himself.

Max is right! I need to get help! There is no way those men could get into the US and hijack us like that. I can't keep having nightmares like this or I'll give myself a heart attack! My heart is still racing and the bed is soaked from sweat, I need to get up, take a shower and change my sheets.

Shrugging off a nagging worry about the tire incident, the Jake incident, and the stupid dream last night, Sam thinks. *It's time to pull myself together. Ann is like a shot of adrenaline for me. I feel great and I'm full of energy around her. Peaks and valleys, and today's going to be a peak! I'm looking forward to going to church with Ann and spending the afternoon with her at the beach. I love Fort Lauderdale beaches. There are no sandy ocean beaches in Colorado.*

"Hello bold one! Would you like a cup of coffee before we go?"

"Yes, that sounds good. You look great! Aren't you dressed to the nines."

"Why thank you. This is my favorite navy blue dress. I wanted to look nice for you so I thought I'd wear my matching navy blue shoes."

"Okay and I see you have a hat and gloves as well."

"Busted, you caught me. Since you said we were going to the beach after I thought why not wear a dark blue wide brim hat. It will come in handy later."

"Okay, so how do long white gloves come into play. Aren't they for evening or something?"

"You got me there. Once I added this and that, I just felt the outfit wasn't complete without them. Do you think they're over the top?"

"Not at all. I'll have the best-dressed lady in the congregation on my arm, so I can't complain. Besides, I kind of remember old ladies like to wear hats and gloves to church."

"Oh, so you think you're a comedian also."

"We aim to please." Sam says laughing.

Walking to the table, she pours coffee into a glass cup for him.

"Here you are, handsome. How's your car with your new tires."

Sam is nervous trying to think of a gentle way to tell Ann about Max's tires. Finally he decides there is no easy way to do it. "I hate to do this, but I have something I need to tell you."

"Oh my God, what is it?"

"Yesterday when Max was on his way to my house, he noticed that someone had also slashed his tires."

"At his house?"

"Yeah."

"Who would dare go to someone's house to slash tires? Are you sure they weren't just flat?"

"Yeah, they were slashed just like mine. The amazing part is it didn't happen at night like with mine. Whomever did it slashed them in broad daylight."

"Poor Max, how is he?"

"He's okay. He was upset because the only person we can think of who'd want to hurt us both has to be Jake. The situation is just too odd to be coincidence."

"Did you report it to the police?"

"No. I reported mine to my insurance because I didn't know at the time that it might be Jake. I'm sure Max also contacted his insurance company, but we don't really have any proof that it was Jake. If it wasn't and we go make a report saying it was, that could cause even more problems so we decided to let it go since no one was hurt."

"I know Jake is a little strange, but why would he want to hurt you and Max?"

"Well, we seemed to have upset Jake a few days ago. We all went to CC's to hang out, drink some beers and play darts. You may not know it, but Jake gets nasty when he drinks."

"I could guess that." Ann said sipping some coffee.

"I had to break up a fight he started."

"You broke up a fight?"

"Yeah, he got mad when Max and I won the dart game and he grabbed Max in a head lock and was choking him. I had to try to break them up and Jake tried to lunge at me when my back was turned. I caught the movement from the corner of my eye and my reflexes kicked in. I put my arm up to block his shot and when he struck me, his arm broke. The cops had to be called, but no charges were made since Jake was the only one hurt. Max could have pressed charges, but didn't feel it was necessary. We both thought it should be dropped and forgotten. Jake made some threats about getting even, but he was drunk so no one really believed him. It sounded like idle rantings that he wouldn't remember when he sobered up. I wanted to apologize, but he hasn't been at work since it happened."

"What did you mean by your reflexes?"

"I was working towards a brown belt in Judo back in Colorado."

"Really? I learn a new side of you each day. Breaking his wrist could be a reason he'd be upset with you."

"It was just a freak accident. I reacted instinctively. He swung hard; I blocked with my arm and hit his wrist. Believe me Ann I haven't been in a fight since grammar school!"

"Well just in case, let's do some praying at church. It can't hurt!" Folding her arms across her chest, she stared at Sam.

"What are you thinking about?"

"Oh, nothing. So you really think Jake is responsible for the tires? It's possible I guess." Smiling at him for a second, he could tell something was bothering her even though she wasn't saying what it was. "Well let's go cowboy before we're late." Carrying a small orange tote bag along with her small blue purse, he closes the door behind her.

"What's in the bag?"

"Just some walking sandals and other stuff. You did want to go to the beach after church, right? Do you have your bathing suit with you?"

"Yes; and yes I do."

After church, Sam and Ann leave to spend the rest of the day at the beach. Driving to a small café along the beach road called 'Topy's', he parks as close as he can to the café.

Getting out of the SUV, they strip down to their bathing suits. Sam can't help but stare at Ann's trim body.

"Why are you looking at me like that?"

"Oh, just admiring your sexy two piece bathing suit, and its contents!"

"You men are all alike!" She muses striking a modeling pose for him. "I guess I'd be upset if you didn't stare a little. You look pretty good, too."

Sam starts to lock the SUV when his phone rings.

"Hello, Max. What's up?"

"You guys at the beach yet?"

"Yes, we're going to Topy's for lunch."

"Mind if we meet you there?" Max asks.

"You and Peggy, sure."

"We're almost at the beach now. See you there." Max says and hangs up.

Peggy taps Max's shoulder. "See, I told you. Sam is okay with us meeting him and this Ann gal. I want to see her."

"I know. It's like an obsession with you. You sure you're not after Sam now?"

"No way, Max. He's like a brother. I want to protect him

from evil."

"You think Ann is evil?"

"I don't know. She might be."

"Trust me, she's a sweet gal."

"We'll see."

Max shakes his head smiling and finds a parking spot near Topy's.

Walking to Topy's café Max sees it looks as faded as ever just like its faded red and yellow sign outside. He finds Sam and Ann sitting out on the back patio jutting over the beach as a gentle breeze sweeps by.

"Hello Sam." Peggy says hugging Sam as he stands up. "Holy cow! You must be Ann."

"Yes." Ann says.

"I'm Peggy and you know Max." She continues her big long hug on Sam.

"Don't be jealous," Max says to Ann. "She always does this."

"We're more like sister and brother." Sam offers as Peggy releases her hold on him.

"Okay, let's eat." Max says a little annoyed.

Chapter Twenty-Two

"We're going to head back to the SUV and get our towels." Sam says. "Maybe wade in the ocean. The water is slightly choppy but it might not be too rough to swim."

"Okay sounds good." Max says. "Peggy and I'll be wading along the shore."

"Yes. I wouldn't want you to get swept away from me." Peggy says holding on to Max.

"See you in a few."

Max walks down to the shoreline with Peggy and sticks his feet in the ocean. He coaxes Peggy to follow him until he is waist deep.

"Oh boy, the water is cooler than I expected." Peggy says. "The sun is warm though. It feels good. What are you doing?" Before she can move away, Max throws himself into the surf splashing her in the process. He swims a short distance and comes back to the shore.

"It's a little too cool for me." Max says walking back on the sandy shore. Peggy hands him one of their beach towels, and he wraps it around his shoulders.

"Hey Max." Sam says as he and Ann join them.

"Hey, just got back from a swim."

A woman shouts, "Hey, how about playing some volleyball with us?"

Looking toward the voice, an athletic woman holding a volleyball stands next to a loosely set up net.

"Hi Victoria." Ann says. "How are you doing?"

"We need four more players."

Max and Sam look inquisitively at Peggy and Ann. They get a tentative okay. "You got it!" Max shouts as he finishes drying off.

"Let's not split up." Ann pleads to Sam. "I don't want to play against you."

"Me neither." Sam says. "We want to stay on the same side." He shouts at the rest of the players.

"You guys aren't newly-weds are you?" Someone teases.

"No, maybe someday. We just like to play together!" Grinning at Ann, Sam sees her flush a little, as she stares up at the sky.

Max, Peggy, Ann, and Sam make the blue team and win all the games. After the umpteenth losing game, someone on the red team wants to trade couples to even out the players, but everyone is tired. One of the guys sprawls out on the sand. A moment later, his girlfriend flops down beside him. It's time to stop.

"This was fun." Victoria says. She hugs Max and Sam. "You guys should have let us win at least one game, though."

"Well..." Ann starts to speak.

Walking up to Ann, Victoria leans against her whispering. "Did Sam win the bet?"

"What bet?"

"He bet Max he'd score with you." Victoria whispers.

"What! I don't believe that."

"He's not as nice as you think. Would I lie to you?" Victoria says breaking away from Ann pointing a discrete finger at Sam.

At a loss for words Ann stares at Victoria until Sam nudges her. *Victoria must be wrong.* She thinks to herself.

Sam and Ann finish saying good-bye to everyone and walk to the SUV.

"That was fun." Sam says. "I feel bad about winning every game, though."

"No you don't!" Ann chuckles. "You savored it each time we won by cheering."

"Yeah, you're right." He says as he sings a line from a Mac Davis' song. "Oh Lord, it's hard to be humble, when you're perfect in every way..."

"Okay, that's way too much bragging!" Ann laughs putting her hand over his mouth.

Laughing Sam starts the car. Ann seems sleepy to him as she kisses him on the cheek and leans against him.

When Sam parks the SUV at her apartment complex, she gathers up her clothes and bag. Before starting to get out, she suddenly turns and kisses Sam on the lips. Her kiss is like an electric shock to Sam. For a second they just stare at each other before she backs out of his car.

"Goodbye Sam." She says stepping out.

"Wait! Do you have to go?"

Leaning inside his window she says, "I had a good time Sam but I... I'm really bushed. I need to get some sleep. It's back to work tomorrow you know."

"I'm offering a totally relaxing back rub! Interested?"

"I'm really tired from all our frolicking on the beach. I'm sorry. I think I'll just go sack out early. Goodbye." She says turning, walking toward her apartment door.

"I'm pretty tired myself. See you in the morning. I'll miss you tonight!"

"Miss you, too." She says waving a hand back toward Sam without turning around.

He blows a kiss toward her and watches her walk to her door and go inside. As he starts up the car to leave, it puzzles him how she just walked away.

Arriving home, Sam feels the day catch up to him. *Boy it really was a long day. Now I understand why Ann wanted to rest. I forgot how the sun and fun of living in Florida can take it out of a guy. I should get some water to hydrate and take a cool shower, then go to bed early myself.*

Sam wakes up bouncing around on a small sailing ship.

Somehow, he knows the boat is sinking. Jake is alongside the boat standing on the edge of a small freighter and tosses down a rope ladder. Sam climbs up nearly a hundred feet to get aboard Jake's ship where Jake is standing at the edge of the bow.

"I've come to take you back home Jake. You've done some bad things." Sam says.

"You'll never take me alive! I'm staying here, deep in the Atlantic Ocean. If you come for me I'll feed you to the sharks!" Jake shouts.

"You can't beat me! I know Judo!" Sam starts running towards Jake who is holding a red cloth draped in front of him like a toreador.

Diving for the cape to grab him, Jake swings the cape to the side. Sam follows the cape like a bull trying to gore a toreador leaping into the air. Jake isn't behind the cape causing Sam to fly off the bow of the freighter a hundred feet high in the open air heading for the Atlantic Ocean! Nearing the water, a Great White Shark with its enormous mouth open is waiting for him! The last thing he hears is Jake roaring with laughter.

Jake's bellowing laugh wakes Sam up. His heart's pounding as he comes fully awake. *Max is right. I should see a shrink. Are my dreams really expressing some omen or are they just bad dreams?*

Safar receives his orders from Almir and drives to Sam's apartment complex early Monday morning. From the minivan, Safar cautiously looks around the parking lot. Seeing no one, he gets out and carries a small coil of wire and a small can of accelerant into the elevator. He pushes three. When the doors open on the third floor, he quickly finds apartment number 303. Securing the wire around the doorknob and to the railing alongside of it, he renders the door impossible to open. He opens the lid of the can and starts to pour accelerant on the door when he hears the elevator stopping at Sam's floor. He quickly shuts the accelerant lid, and hurries to the stairwell exit and disappears through the door.

As he steps out of the stairwell on the ground floor, people are walking about preparing for the workday. Safar hunches his shoulder hiding his face as best he can and swiftly walks to the stolen minivan with the accelerant tucked inside his shirt. Driving away, he goes back to the abandoned warehouse where Almir is waiting.

"I have failed you Almir," Safar says. "Just a few seconds longer and I would have accomplished the mission. There was too much activity. I should have gone there earlier."

"Bah, these people are trying my nerves! You should have waited and gone back."

"Almir, people were starting to come out. I did not want to be seen or caught there. I can try again earlier tomorrow."

"No Safar, I have better plans."

Monday morning arrives and Sam does his exercises, before getting ready for work. Eating breakfast, he has mixed emotions because his dreams are starting to worry him for a moment or two, until he thinks about the great time he spent with Ann.

Ready to retrieve the newspaper from outside his front door Sam unlocks his front door and turns the knob. When he pulls the door, it won't open. Turning the knob again and pulling on the door, it still won't budge. *What the..., why won't the door open? The doorknob seems to be okay, so why won't the door open.* Pulling on the door several more times, Sam stands there confused and frustrated when his phone rings. The caller ID shows its Ann.

"Hi, are you ready for a new day at Silvan Enterprises?" She says sounding cheery.

"Hello my love! Will you come rescue me! My front door won't open!"

"What do you mean your door won't open?"

"Just that, I unlocked it and turned the knob, but the door won't budge. I'm trapped inside."

"What? You can't get out of your apartment!"

"Exactly! Would you be a dear and come by. I'd call the super, but you can get here quicker."

"I'll come over right away, but what do you think I'll be able to do?"

"I don't know. Maybe if you push on the door while I pull we can get it to open. If not, I guess we could call the fire department or something."

"I'm on my way now. I'm already in my car. What do you think would cause the door to stick like that? Have you been having trouble with it opening and closing?"

"No, it's been opening and closing with ease, that's what I don't understand. I thought for a minute that the door might have swollen and that was causing it to stick, but that doesn't happen that quickly, so I dismissed it, especially since it's been moving with ease until now."

"Wow, what a way to start your Monday morning."

"Tell me about it. I even woke up last night because I had a nightmare."

"A nightmare?"

"Yeah, I have a tendency to have nightmares when I'm stressed. Ever since Max called me to come help him, I started having nightmares again. I hadn't had any in years, ever since I lived in Colorado."

"So basically ever since you moved away from Max."

"Um, I guess. I never thought about it like that. So Max

is the cause of my nightmares."

"Not necessarily, but you said he's always into something or another with his pranks and such. Maybe you're a more sensitive person and although you find some of his pranks funny, you don't like how they affect the people they're played on."

"That's true. I never thought about it that way. Although when the dreams started this time at first it was because of the stress of Max thinking people were trying to kill us. Afterwards, that situation with Jake has been bothering me. Last night's dream was about him. I dreamed he was still after revenge against me and Max."

"That must mean you really believe Jake was behind the incident with the tires."

"Yeah, I do. If it had just been my tires, I'd think it was random vandalism. With Max's tires also being slashed, and right there at his house, I can't help but believe Jake is making good on his threat to get even. It must not have been idle rantings of a drunk after all. He may just be deranged."

"That's possible, but if you feel that way. Maybe you should consider filing a police report. If you're right, this might not be over. What if things escalate? How far do you think he will go. It sounds like you're worried more than you realize if you're having nightmares."

"So how did you get so smart? In just a few minutes, you've figured out my psychological problems. Who needs a shrink when I've got you?"

"Remember that when I send you my bill"

"Oh, I will, so far you're earning every bit of it."

"I'm here now. I'll be right up. Which apartment is it?"

"303. It's right there as soon as you get off the elevator."

"Okay, I'll be there in a sec, the elevator is almost at three."

"Okay baby, I can wait a few more seconds for you to rescue me."

"Oh my God!"

"What? What's wrong?"

"Your door! It isn't stuck; someone has wrapped wire around the doorknob and attached it to the railing. Wait, what's that smell? Oh no! I think that's gasoline!"

"What? You're saying someone intentionally trapped me in my apartment and was going to set a fire!"

"Yeah, it looks that way. I think we should call the police. Maybe they can get some prints off the door or railing. Since you're not in danger at the moment, I think we should call them before I touch anything. I could destroy evidence trying to get you out."

"I don't believe this. Jake needs to stop this!"

"Let me put you on hold and call the police."

"Okay."

"911, what's the nature of your emergency?"

"I'm at my boyfriend's apartment because he couldn't get out of his apartment and his door has been wired closed and some sort of accelerant was poured on it. He's trapped inside. I don't want to destroy evidence or prints trying to let him out."

"Okay ma'am. Give us the address and we'll send an officer."

"Okay, thank you."

"Hey there, they're sending an officer."

"Thank you. It never dawned on me when I asked you to come by that this was intentional."

"Yeah well at least you're safe. What if Jake had set the fire he intended? You would have been trapped?"

"He must have been interrupted. Thank god for that."

"Are you sure Jake did this?"

"Who else could it be? Jake is the only person who has an issue with me. How did Jake even get my home address though? Maybe I mentioned it sometime when we were at CC's."

"That makes sense if he's the one who slashed your tires."

"In what way?"

"If he knew where you lived, he could have followed us to the restaurant."

"That makes sense. He hasn't been at work since the incident, which means he's had time to follow both Max and me when we left work to find out where we live. If that's true, and he followed us to the restaurant, he also knows where you live."

"Oh my God! I never thought about that."

"If he's upset that you're dating me, I wonder if that made things worse."

"I hope not. I always felt like he was a little off. He just didn't seem normal when he was trying to get me to go out with him. The average person would stop asking after once or twice, but he kept asking me, like I'd never rejected him. That isn't normal and he was starting to make me feel like he was stalking me."

"Well let's hope this will end it. Since there will be a police report now hopefully, they will at least talk to him and that will scare him into ending this. Whatever this is."

"Let's hope. A police car just pulled in, they'll be here in a second."

"Okay. I guess I'll see you soon then."

"Yes you will. Let me go and talk to the officer. Could you call work and let them know we'll be late."

"Sure thing."

"Hey Sam, why were you late for work this morning? I

swung by your lab this morning. Peggy wanted me to tell you she approves of Ann."

"Oh man, you won't believe it when I tell you. Let's hit the cafeteria and get a table by ourselves. I have some news. I was going to find you so I'm glad you came by."

"Why, what's going on?"

"I had to file a police report on Jake this morning. There was another incident. A serious one. Let's eat and I'll tell you about it. I expect the cops will speak to you also."

Chapter Twenty-Three

"Well it's half past five." Max says slapping Sam's shoulder giving him a start. "Are you nervous about something?"

"Oh! No, I'm just buried in this test. Are we still playing cards tonight?"

"Yes, Peggy is cooking some vittles. Bring some wine if you have some."

"Did you hear from the cops today?"

"Not yet, I heard an officer came by Silvan today and spoke to someone in personnel. I thought they would come see me while they were here, but they didn't. Maybe they'll come by later at home."

"Why do you think they came by here?"

"Probably to get his address. You couldn't give it to them."

"Yeah, I guess. I just assumed they get it from the DMV when they pull up his license."

"Maybe they did and the address on record wasn't correct. Who knows with that guy, at least the cops are onto him. He's not our problem anymore. I'm sorry about what he did to you, but it's good to know we don't have to keep looking over our shoulder anymore."

"Yeah, especially if he's that far gone. Anyway, I'll pick up Ann about 6:30 and head over to your place. She's making some kind of appetizers to go with the wine."

"Well, see ya later. Let's hope we have a quiet evening. I haven't told Peggy about what happened and I don't want to scare her. Can you let Ann know so it doesn't come up tonight?"

"Sure thing." Sam nods in agreement and starts wrapping up his test.

Ringing Ann's doorbell at six thirty, Sam can tell something is bothering her because of her weak smile upon opening the door. "Hello love. You look beautiful as always."

"Hi, I..." She says turning her face down from him, staring at the appetizer tray in her hands.

"What's wrong Ann?"

"It's nothing."

"Come on, tell me what it is."

"Well, I guess it's just everything that's happened."

"Ann, we will make it through this okay." He says reaching out to hold her and assure her. "You know between Max and me, we will get this cleared up."

"It's more than that. I can't believe what happened between us this weekend. I don't want you to think I'm so carefree with everyone I date!"

"That's what's been bothering you? That you drank too much and passed out!"

"Yes! I feel guilty! You could have had your way with me. I lost control and then that guy on the beach asking us if we were newlyweds..." Ann's eyes begin tearing up.

"Ann, let's sit for a few minutes." He says taking the tray from her hands and motioning her back inside. Hesitating for a moment before agreeing, she sits on the couch next to him.

"Ann, something is very different between you and me. I don't mean that I slept in your home on our first date, not that I normally sleep in a woman's home on a first date. I hope you don't think I took advantage of you."

"No, I know you didn't, but I wanted you to and that scares me."

"Let's blame it on wine or maybe it's because I feel like I have known you forever. I think we have something special. There is something magical about us, just us! Almost every time I touch you, I feel this electric charge of excitement go through me. I think maybe we were meant for each other, to quote an old saying."

"I feel that way, too. I'm just not sure about all this."

"Why?"

"Let me ask you a blunt question."

"Anything." Sam says.

"Did you bet Max you could get me in the sack?"

"What! That's crazy! No! Why would I do that?"

"Victoria said she heard you make a bet with Max."

"Victoria? She couldn't have heard that because it never happened. Did you notice her making eyes at me all afternoon at the beach? I think she wants me to..."

"Oh my God! She wants me to stop seeing you so she can step in! Okay, now I have another problem."

"Spit it out my love."

"Before I met you, I was doing fine. I was used to not having a man in my life. I could have gone on that way forever!" Sobbing she says, "But its different now. If something happens to you, I don't know if I can handle it! With all these problems with the cars and all, it's scary. Maybe Jake really is crazy. Do you understand what I am saying?"

"Yes, I do. Trust me; everything will be okay, especially now that we filed that police report this morning. He'd be crazy to continue pulling these stunts." Reaching out to her face with his hands, he kisses her lips. "Don't worry Ann. Everything will be okay."

"Do you really think so?"

"Yes, I do because now we know that he's after us. He doesn't have the element of surprise anymore and the police are following up on things. By the way, I told Max at lunch about what happened. Later he asked me to tell you he hasn't told Peggy because he doesn't want to scare her unnecessarily. Being the cops are looking into things he feels there's no reason to worry her."

"Okay, I won't say anything. I just wish it were over already."

"Me too. Well we should go. Max and Peggy are waiting for us."

Thinking about things while driving along, several thoughts were in Sam's mind. *I want to be with Ann forever. I never thought I'd feel this good not being a carefree bachelor anymore? I am so comfortable for the first time ever, but what if I lose her because of Jake? If anything happens to Ann, I couldn't handle that!*

"When's dinner?" Sam asks after chatting for a while.

"Why? We've already eaten the spring rolls and are on our second glass of wine." Ann says.

"I can't help it if you're a good cook. The spring rolls were amazing." Sam says.

Peggy says, "Don't worry Sam; we're almost ready to sit down to eat as soon as Max brings the food out. Why don't you guys go sit at the table? He's bringing in a big bowl of Pepper Steak and rice."

"Wow that sounds wonderful." Ann says.

"Yeah, Peggy's quite a good cook." Max says winking at Peggy. "Why else do you think I keep her around? Most of the other women I tried may have been as pretty, but they couldn't make tea. Never mind make my stomach happy." Max gives Peggy a sassy look.

Ann looks at Peggy to see her reaction. Pausing, Peggy suddenly just sticks her tongue out at Max.

"She's also such a great orator as you can see." Max says smiling proudly.

"I've got a question to ask." Sam says retrieving four tickets from his pocket and waving them in the air. "I have four complimentary tickets to the Danglebatts concert in a couple weeks. Would you all like to go?”

"I love the Danglebatts!” Peggy says. "How on earth did you get free tickets?”

"If you told me a month ago I'd be going to a Danglebatts Concert, I'd say you were crazy! However, I met Chet Hatter on the plane trip down here a few weeks ago.”

"You know Chet Hatter? You know the lead guitarist for the Danglebatts?” Peggy exclaims.

"Yes I do. Anyway, we hit it off. I went to his house last Thursday night to jam with him and the other band members, and before I left he gave me four tickets, second row center, no less.”

"You were at his house? You jammed with the Danglebatts! That's so cool! Second row center tickets Max, we've gotta go!” Peggy says bouncing up and down like a little girl.

Raising his hands Max says, "Okay, we'll go Peggy. Calm down.” Turning to Ann he says, "What about you, Ann?”

"I guess I can go.” Ann says shrugging her shoulders. "I'm not a hard rock fan, though. Aren't they a hard rock band?”

"Sam knows this girl,” Max teases. "She renamed herself Chet-ah to show how much she loves Chet. I know she would do anything to go to the concert with Sam.”

"Oh yeah, I totally forgot about meeting her.” Sam says.

Grinning, Max adds, "She's maybe twenty years old with a great body, too! She seemed to think Sam was 'the bomb' being he personally knows Chet.”

"Never mind Miss Chet-ah!” Frowning Ann looks at Sam. "I'm going!”

"Excellent! Then we'll go.” Smiling at Ann Sam says, "I think you'll enjoy it. It'll be fun just to be that close to the band.”

"It'll be loud. I hope you have ear plugs for us." Ann says.

"We'll get some." Sam tilts his head at her. "Chet says some of the female fans get really excited and throw under garments at them."

Ann and Peggy shake their heads in unison.

Max shouts, "Don't be throwing your bra Peggy unless it's at me!" They all laugh a little.

"Well, dig in everybody before it gets cold." Peggy says.

After dinner, Max and Sam retire to the living room. Ann begins helping Peggy with the cleanup. Sam waits until the girls are in the kitchen to speak.

"Have you heard anything yet about Jake?"

"Nope… nothing." Max says.

"Do you think he'll try again now that I filed a police report?"

"I don't know. I guess that depends on whether the cops were able to catch up to him yet. Since they came by personnel to locate an address for him, tells me they still hadn't found him. Even with his address, there's no guarantee they've been able to talk to him yet. Do you think he'd attack the girls?"

"That's not a good thing to think about. Why would he do that?"

"He might just for spite, just to harass us."

"The girls need to be extra cautious then until we catch Jake. You should probably tell Peggy what happened this morning. You don't want her to find out if the cops come by to question you. Do you think Jake really is the one who cut our tires?" Sam asks.

"Who else would be so bold? You're right, I don't want to scare her, but I think it's foolish to leave her in the dark considering. I think I'll tell her later tonight after you guys leave."

"She can't watch her back if she doesn't know there's a problem. I think it's a good idea."

"What's a good idea?" Peggy asks coming back into the room.

"Just something I wanted to talk to you about later after our company leaves." Max responds.

Ann says, "Let's call it a night. It is a work night after all. Peggy, dinner was wonderful, thank you."

"You are very welcome. Thank you for keeping this one out of trouble. I can sleep easy knowing wild women like Chet-ah aren't after him."

"My pleasure." Ann says.

"Well I guess it's time to call it a night. Are you ready babe?"

"Sure. Thank you guys for a wonderful dinner." Ann says.

"Ya'll come back and see us, ya hear!" Max says.

"We will." Sam says walking outside. Turning around to say goodbye he sees a flame on the side of Max's house. "Hey! What's that?" Sam shouts pointing toward the fire.

Just then, fire flashes near the bottom of Max's house near the dining room spreading quickly.

"Oh no!" Ann cries seeing the flames too. "Your house is on fire Max!"

In the short time Sam and Ann are looking at the flame, it doubles in size as Sam dials 911. Adrenalin kicks in and Max comes to life grabbing a hose, cranking the faucet on and quickly running toward the flames. He begins dousing the fire, but it doesn't seem to do much good.

Suddenly the fire flares completely across the left side of the house reaching its way for both the front and back doors. Max thinks; *If we'd stayed inside a few more minutes, the fire would have been out of control and we would have been trapped inside.*

A fire truck arrives and within minutes, the flames are out, but the whole side of the house is damaged.

"Nothing like a little fire to sober you up." Max says walking back to the front to meet the fire chief.

"Sir we found a charred timer right where Mister Stormen says he saw the fire start and an accelerant was used to spread the flames so quickly. This is arson, someone tried to burn your house down. The police may add charges for attempted murder as well."

"Wow!" Max says. "We have a suspect. We think it's a guy named Jake Crocker. We think he's already slashed our tires and tried to kill my friend Sam here in a similar manner."

"You'll need to talk to the police officers on that. We will provide them with our assessment with what happened here."

"Okay."

"The officer will speak to you in a minute; he's finishing up taking pictures of the device and the damage."

"Thank you for getting here so quickly."

"No problem sir."

"What did he say Max?" Sam asks as the fire chief walks away.

"He said it was arson and that the fire spread so quickly because a timing device and an accelerant were used."

"Wow, you're kidding right?"

"The whole side of my house is burned up, so yeah, I'm kidding."

"Oh man, I'm sorry Max."

"You know, this morning someone trapped you in your apartment and put an accelerant on your door, and tonight someone used accelerant and a timer and set fire to my house. This is getting serious." Max says. "We could have all died here tonight.”

“Mister Merchado as you know, the fire chief and I believe this was an arson. I’m concerned that in addition to an accelerant being used that the party who set this fire also used a timing device.”

“You have to do something, Jake is crazy. First he comes to my house and slashes my tires after slashing Sam’s tires, and now after attempting to trap Sam in his apartment this morning and setting a fire, he comes and sets my house on fire!”

“What makes you think this Jake person is responsible?”

“How can he not be? There was an incident recently at CC’s pub where he attacked me and attempted to choke me until Sam broke him loose and then he tried to attack Sam. There’s a police report for it. He swore he’d get us and that this wasn’t over. Next he follows Sam and slashes his tires Friday night and then Saturday he came to my house and slashed my tires right here in my driveway.”

“And did either of you see this man slash your tires?”

“No sir, but he isn’t well balanced.”

“Did you file a police report for either tire incident?”

“No, we didn’t. When Sam’s tires were slashed we thought it might just be vandalism, but when my tires were slashed just hours later, Jake is the only person who has an issue with either of us.”

“Okay, now you said he tried to trap Mister Stormen in his apartment with the intent to set a fire, was a police report filed on that incident?

“Yes sir it was.” Sam says.

“Can you tell me more about what happened? How were you trapped in the apartment?”

“Wire was wrapped around my doorknob and tied snugly to the railing. My door was wedged tight and I wasn't able to get out. I called my girlfriend and she came over to help me get the door open and found the door had been tampered with and called the police."

"Okay, I'll check into these other reports. You should have reported the tires as well because we may have been able to find finger prints if he leaned against the vehicles to bend over. Without proof he damaged your vehicles we won't be able to add that to the case to show a progression in events."

"I understand. I should have reported it."

"Well, we will be investigating all the events reported since there does seem to be a pattern here with the fire and Mister Stormen being trapped as he was. And you are both sure there isn't anyone else who has an issue with you two."

"Yes sir." Sam says. "I just moved here a couple weeks ago from Colorado for a new job. I haven't been here long enough to have an issue with anyone."

"And how do you know this Jake Crocker, Mister Stormen?"

"He works at Silvan Enterprises with Max and me."

"So you met him when you started working then?"

"Yes, that's right."

"And how do you know Mister Merchado here?

"We've been friends since childhood."

"Okay then. Mister Merchado, do you have a place to stay tonight or are you planning to stay here?

"I'd prefer to stay here. I'm afraid he might try to come back and finish the job."

"Well I'm going to phone in and see if I can get protection with police surveillance for each of you at least for tonight since both of you have had these events. It may only be for tonight as there needs to be a clear and present danger, which may not apply as time goes on. We will review the previous reports and put out an APB on this individual if he has not been interviewed yet. If he has, we need to speak with that officer to get an assessment. Can you give me the particulars on him?"

"Yes, I can. I know him well. So does Ann. She also works at Silvan and he has been stalking her."

After giving the police officers all the information on Jake, it was after midnight and the fire truck was finally driving away after making sure there were no hot spots that could re-ignite. To ensure this, some of the siding had to be pulled away creating even more damage to Max's property. At least they hadn't needed to use axes to break holes into the interior. He didn't get so lucky with water damage, especially in the dining room.

Standing outside with Ann and Sam, Max seems stunned by what happened.

Finally Ann speaks. "That fire could have burned us all to death!"

"We're lucky we came out when we did!" Sam says.

Looking at Peggy Sam knows she is worried sick. She didn't find out about Sam's incident until this happened since Max never had the opportunity to tell her.

Sam offers, "We're all a little shook up. Why don't you guys come to my place tonight? I have a spare bedroom and I doubt Jake will come back tonight. If he is watching from somewhere, he's probably pissed that the fire was put out so quickly."

"No!" Max says firmly. "I want to stay here just in case he comes back. Besides, the officer said he was able to get approval for security for both of us for tonight. He said they will revisit further surveillance tomorrow and let us know."

"Okay, at least there is a record of the incidents so later we can tie Jake to them. Then we can press charges against him for this and the other stuff too."

Wrapping her arms around Sam, Ann says, "I'm shook up, and really tired, can we go?"

"Yeah sure, good night Max and be careful!" Sam orders.

"We will. See you in the morning."

Chapter Twenty-Four

"I think my place is safer than Max and Peggy's. If I wasn't so worried I'd love to have you stay over." Ann says to Sam driving home.

"I'd love to have you stay at my place." Sam offers.

"Is that another bold move?" Ann replies moving her hand to his chest and patting him.

"In all seriousness, are you going to be okay at your place?"

"Yes, besides, my apartment complex has security and cameras and is safer than your place."

"Yeah, but Jake may know where you live if he followed me the other night when I came to pick you up.

"Are you sure you aren't just wanting me to stay at your place?" Ann asks giggling.

"If that will get you to stay with me, then yes. Please stay at my place. I don't want to be alone."

"Now that's a bold move!" Ann says. "Could you just stop in for a few minutes before you head home?" She asks leaning against his shoulder a little harder.

"How could I turn down the invitation? I really wanted to do that anyway so I can make sure you'll be okay." He knows all the mysterious events are worrying Ann. He's also concerned about all the recent events. *We're like two scared rabbits looking for a place to hide from the adversities of life.*

"Ann."

"Hmm."

"Wake up Ann, we're here. We're at your apartment."

"What time is it?"

"It's almost one. Let's get you inside."

"Okay. You're gonna stay for a while right?"

"Yes, I'll stay."

"Here are my keys, will you unlock the door?"

"Yeah, sure no problem." Opening the door, Sam senses something isn't right, but he can't place what it is. He smells a faint unfamiliar odor inside her living room causing his body muscles to go on alert.

"I'll just fix us a glass of wine." Ann says smiling, now wide-awake and alert heading for the kitchen.

"Sounds good." Sam says looking around for what's bothering him. Not able to find anything he can see, he thinks maybe it's his imagination and sits down on the sofa.

Ann suddenly screams causing Sam to jump up and run for the kitchen. Ann's face is ashen as if something's sucked all the blood out of her. She's holding her lucky stuffed Gremlin toy that she keeps in the windowsill for good luck. Staggering slightly she manages with his help to reach the living room. Sitting on the couch with Sam sitting down next to her she's still clutching the Gremlin toy.

"I'm scared. Someone has been in my kitchen! My lucky Gremlin always sits on my windowsill. I never move him. Someone slashed the right side of his face then threw him in the trash! Some of his stuffing is falling out." Tears well up in Ann's eyes and she shakes before speaking again.

"Why would someone do this? How did someone get in here?" Pausing for a moment, she looks into Sam's eyes. "Would you mind, I mean, uh... if I stayed at your place? I don't think I can stay here tonight."

"Yeah, sure, anything you want. Good grief! Jake is messing with you now! How did he get into your apartment? Let me check out the kitchen and the other doors and windows to see if I can find out how he got in. Why don't you go grab some things and pack an overnight bag while I look around? We'll leave as soon as you're ready. It's

late, so we'll call the authorities tomorrow to report this."
Sam feels the knot in his stomach tightening. It distracts
him from being happy about her staying with him.

Wrapping her arms around Sam she says, "I love you
Sam Stormen!"

"I love you, too!" He blurts without thinking. Staring at
each other for a moment with a shocked look on their faces,
they both smile. Kissing him quickly she dashes away to
pack a bag.

Needing a minute to recover from the shock of what just
happened; Sam remembers he needs to check out the place
to see how Jake got in.

"Come here." Ann shouts from the bedroom. "The bedroom window is open."

Sam rushes into the bedroom. He examines the window
and sees the lock is broken. "Well, now we know how he got
in."

"Stay in here, please. I'll just be a minute packing."

"Yes, I'll see if I can secure the window." Sam finds some
screws to secure the window in its track.

A quick look around determines that everything else is
in order, all the other windows are locked and show no evidence of having been opened.

"You know, tomorrow we should get with security as
well as the police. It's possible a camera somewhere in the
area caught Jake approaching your apartment. If we're
lucky, the angle might have been right to catch him busting
the window lock." Sam says, but thinks, *I just can't believe
that Jake has the guts and is agile enough to bust a lock or
to sneak around and set fire to a house full of people without being caught. He doesn't move like a person who can do
this. He proved that when he tried to hit me. His move-
ments are awkward and gangly and he is anything but sub-
tle. I easily saw his punch coming. Being I was griping his*

back, he should have been able to get at least one blow in before I pummeled him. This whole thing doesn't smell right, but we don't have another suspect so I'll have to wait and figure it out tomorrow.

Deciding to have a seat while waiting for Ann to finish gathering a few things, a new thought begins running through his mind. *I really just met Ann a few days ago so what am I thinking? I just told her I love her. Why do I feel like we're soul mates, we just started dating. Did I say I love her because I really do or is it a simple reflex? Somehow, it doesn't feel like a reflex, but how can I fall in love so quickly?* Leaning back on the bed, he puts his hands behind his head, takes a deep breath and exhales as Ann finishes packing her small suitcase.

"I'm ready. Did you really mean what you said?" She asks with a sheepish grin on her face. It was the same grin she showed him when he first saw her at her desk at Silvan Enterprises. Even though her eyes are teary, he still feels his heart skip a beat when she looks at him.

"You mean the 'I love you'?" He asks timidly.

"Yes! Of course I mean the 'I love you'!" She still has that cute grin on her face.

"I think I've been smitten with you since the first time I saw you."

"Oh my God!" She blurts. "I mean it, too! I was just so glad you came to see me on your first day at work. I wanted to jump up and down! That's why I was grinning so much when I saw you that day."

"I remember," Sam says. "At first I thought you were laughing at me. You know, all the silly things Max and I did, but you were so... beautiful... and nice..."

"And you looked handsome all dressed up. I saw you in the cafeteria earlier, but you were so engrossed in conversation with Max and the guys, I didn't want to interrupt.

Then later you came to my desk to say hi, and I think I was staring at you so much."

"Not at all! I was the one staring at you!" Pausing, he asks, "So what do we do now?"

Ann's smile changes back to a scared expression as she recalls her damaged Gremlin and the other things that have happened. "Let's get out of here!" She whispers. "My own apartment is giving me the creeps!"

Locking the door, they hurriedly get into Sam's SUV. Driving off he can't help being thankful he still has all four working tires. Funny how a simple thing like four inflated tires can give a man comfort. At one something in the morning, they finally arrive at his place. Mentally on guard, he walks ahead of Ann just in case.

Stepping out of the elevator, everything looks normal. He's glad he noticed the marked police car sitting in the parking lot facing his door when he pulled in making him feel a little better. Opening his door and stepping inside first, he looks around; then motions for Ann to come inside.

"Would you like a glass of wine?" Sam asks.

"Yes, please. I know it's late, but I think it will help settle my nerves."

Sam can tell the wine she drank earlier has worn off and she is anxious.

"What's going to happen to us? These attacks seem like a vendetta, not just pranks. I'm afraid to do anything. I think we should consider this could be someone other than Jake. I never considered Jake to be... how do I say this? Jake doesn't seem smart enough and coordinated enough to do some of these things."

Retrieving a half-empty bottle of wine from the refrigerator and grabbing two glasses, he knows it will be a long night.

"You know, I was thinking the same thing back at your

apartment. When he picked that fight with Max and me, he was so uncoordinated I can't imagine him being deft enough to break in or to set the fire at Max's with everyone right there. Plus, how would he know about using a timing device. That sounds more like a professional, but why would a professional be after all of us."

"I know what you mean. As much as I'd like to convince myself Jake is behind this, more and more I'm finding that hard to do."

"Well, there isn't anything we can do about any of this tonight. I think we should talk with Mark in the morning. After that, we'll have to see what the police say after they check things out. There has to be a way we can thwart this, but right now, I think we had better try to get some rest. Look, I know you're still worried; but there's nothing more we can do tonight. Until we get this situation resolved, we need to go into survival mode. That means rest and sleep when you can. Not being rested will make things even worse. We can't be alert and thinking clearly, if we're exhausted."

"But how can I sleep? I'm scared out of my mind."

"I know, but you're not alone. I'm here, and I won't let anyone hurt you if I can help it. Let me double check the deadbolt and get you settled in my room. I'll stay with you until you fall asleep if you want, and then I'll sleep in the spare bedroom."

"No, please don't leave me. I don't want to wake up and you're not there. I don't think I can even go to sleep if I know you'll leave me."

"Okay, if you're sure. I'll sleep on top of the covers then. I don't want you to feel like I'm trying to take advantage of the situation."

Without saying anything, she grabs his arm and leads him toward the master bedroom. Turning back to him, she put her arms around him gives him a long kiss. Sam tries to keep thinking about everything that's happened in the past few days, however all the memories fade away with the deep desire he feels for Ann. He can tell she feels the same way. He's never experienced feeling so good about anyone before.

Standing in the bedroom doorway for a moment looking into Sam's eyes, she starts unbuttoning her blouse. Then they both nearly tear off the rest of their clothes. They embrace as they fall onto the bed. This time Ann does not back away. All the fears and anxiety built up inside her seem to rush out in passionate desire. For a short time, all the world is right as they make love. After their energetic romp, they fall asleep in each other's arms. Sam sleeps like a dead man - all his worries are gone for a while.

Sam wakes up Tuesday morning with the alarm clock buzzing in his ear. It's six o'clock in the morning. He hears his shower running and then it shuts off a moment later. He sees Ann come out of the bathroom with only a large towel wrapped around her. She looks at him with a big smile.

"Good morning my love," She says in her cheery voice. Coming to him, she presses her hand on his shoulder, and kisses his cheek.

"Good morning beautiful. I have lots of stuff in the fridge if you want to eat something. I want to take a quick shower."

"Okay. I hope Max and Peggy are all right. Will you call them when you get out?"

"Good idea. I'll call right now." Turning on the speakerphone, he dials Max. The phone rings four times before Max answers.

"Hellooo..." Max slurs.

"Are you okay?" Sam asks. "You sound like you have a

bad hangover."

"Yeah, I stayed up all night watching my house. I was hoping that SOB would come back and try to burn my house so I could feed him some lead! I'll have to call in sick today, Sam. Maybe you can tell Mark what's happened. Don't you think he should know about this?"

"Totally! It's probably good that you didn't get to shoot him though. Maybe Peggy should stay with you today. I'm keeping Ann close by me for now, too."

"Did you pick her up at her place already?" Max asks.

"Um," Sam realizes Max doesn't know what happened after they left him. "Oh… Um… no, not exactly. There was another incident."

"What! What happened?" Max says coming fully awake.

"When I dropped Ann off we found that someone had broken into her place. Since my place had police surveillance and it was already so late, we just locked up her place and she came back to my place to stay. This morning, we need to get with security at her place and see if they have anything on video and then contact the police. I'm starting to think this might not be Jake."

"Who else could it be?"

"I don't know, but I just don't see Jake as being able to do all these things. These things just don't seem like they're things he'd do. I can't explain it other than to say these things other than the tires seem like they're more grown up than the sort of childish things he'd do."

"I see what you mean, but no one else has a beef with all of us. Who would want to harm Ann?" Anyway can you tell Mark about the house and the tires."

"Okay, I'll tell the boss what happened. I think we're also going to take the day off, but I'll call Mark later after we deal with the cops. I'll see you later." Sam says ringing off.

"Can you believe Max stayed up all night?"

"Yeah, I can. If someone had set fire to my house, I doubt I'd have gotten a wink of sleep either."

Sam finishes showering and shaves. Donning a white shirt and tan slacks he comes out of the bedroom while Ann is brushing her hair into its long silky flow, and is fully dressed. She has breakfast on the table ready to eat and he smells the pleasant aroma of coffee brewing from the kitchen. Ann even has the newspaper placed next to his plate.

"I can get used to this. A man can endure a lot when he has a good woman to share things." He says and kisses Ann before sitting down for breakfast. His thoughts ramble on as he starts eating. He is unusually contented for a moment and looks across the table at the woman he loves. She is smiling as she eats and looks beautiful.

"Did you call work yet to let them know we won't be in today?"

"Yes, I did it while you were showering. I agree with what you told Max. We need to deal with the security people at my place and then notify the police. We probably should have called them last night, but after the fire, I was exhausted and just wasn't up to it. Maybe we can talk to the officer stationed outside before we leave. The officer from the fire last night probably isn't on duty."

"Good idea. Well, are you ready?"

"Yep, let's get this over with."

Just as Sam is getting up, he notices something in the paper. A name pops out at him as if it was on fire! "Almir Najya!" Sam says remembering it was the name on the email for the shipment of chemical weapons! Sam's eyes grow wide as he reads the brief article.

"Ann, look at this!" Sam exclaims. "He's here!" Sam

steps around the table to show Ann the article.

"Apparently, Homeland Security believes that the terrorist Almir Najya is in America hiding in a cell group somewhere in South Florida! They make no comment about why they believe he is in Florida, nor any explanation for how he was able to enter the United States." He reads that they are determined to find him and prosecute him for alleged war crimes against the US in Afghanistan. Sam is sure that Almir Najya isn't just in Florida, but more specifically, that he's in Fort Lauderdale! "I bet he's the guy. He's the guy! It has to be!" Sam shouts.

"Oh my God!" Ann says in a shaky voice looking at the brief article. She gets up from the table and throws her arms around Sam as he feels her shaking.

"I'm so scared!" She finally whispers. The relaxing morning has ended. Sam just hopes someone will capture Almir Najya before the assaults become deadly.

Sam recalls how Mark discretely fooled Almir Najya and knows he is one of the Afghanistan leaders. Perhaps the man thinks he and Max caused the loss of his shipment, but how could he even know about him and Max. This must be Almir Najya's revenge for the order of weapons! This is news he must share with Max. Sam decides its best not to call Max but instead to go to his house to talk to him. Standing there holding Ann he tries to think about what to say.

Chapter Twenty-Five

"I want to go to Max's house first. He needs to know about this development. I don't want to talk on the phone about this." He looks down at Ann and she holds him even tighter.

"Are you all right?"

"No!" She cries. "Don't leave me. Don't ever leave me! I need to pray for a while. I will just be a minute. Then we can go to see Max and Peggy."

"Okay. I'm right here, my love. Do what you have to do."

Ann prays silently for several minutes. She finally looks up at Sam and brushes her hair back over her shoulder. He sees her steel gray eyes are damp with tears. She gets up and leans against him burying her head in his chest.

"It will be all right." He says trying to calm her and hoping his own words will calm him, too. "We will make it through this, my love. He can't continue this way without someone catching him. We will be okay. Trust me!"

"He's going to kill us!"

"Maybe he will try but he can't get away with murdering us! He's already caused us, especially you, a lot of angst and worry. Let's hope that's enough to satisfy him."

"No, I know he's not done," She cries. "He's a terrorist, he has no conscience about harming people."

"Let's go." Sam says grabbing the newspaper and heading for the elevator. He fails to notice a man standing at the far end of the hallway who dashes into the stairwell.

Sam presses the lobby button. The elevator doors close and the elevator begins its usual whirring sound as it starts to descend. Suddenly everything goes black and silent. The elevator comes to an abrupt stop as the whirring stops.

Ann screams and sinks to the floor.

"It's okay, Ann. It's probably just a power failure. It should be back on in a minute or so."

Five minutes pass and then ten. The only light Sam sees is the occasional blinking from their cell phones. Ann scared, sits praying on the floor of the elevator. He reaches down and puts a hand on her shoulder. He can feel her shaking. Holding onto her shoulder, he wonders when the power will come on again.

Jake casually walks out of the elevator control room after shutting down the elevator. Happy with himself he skips down the hallway and out of the building laughing along the way. He can no longer control his laughter. More and more he feels like laughing hysterically and making up rhymes. He tries to contain his laughter as he heads back to his car.

Along the way, he breaks into song saying, "I'm a wild man! Yes a wild man! I'm a cool alligator messing with Sam's elevator!" He laughs hysterically. "Oh, yeah! Next time my attacks - will kill Sam and Max!" Laughing uncontrollably he continues heading for his car.

Officer Kelley sitting in the Bridgestone Apartment parking lot has just finished speaking to the overnight officer he just relieved. Pulling up the description for the APB on Jake Crocker, he takes a look around the parking lot and notices a man fitting Jake's description coming from the building and acting strangely. The man is laughing and staggering talking to himself like some sort of mental patient. From the report he just read, this man appears to be the suspect everyone has been looking for. Getting out of his car quickly, he approaches Jake unseen being Jake is in his own little world laughing.

"Sir, hold up! Can I see your identification?"

"Huh! What? Turning to see the officer standing near

him with one hand on his holster, Jake freezes.

"What's your name? Are you Jake Crocker?"

"Uh..." Jake looks around wildly but refuses to respond to the officer.

"Put your hands up and interlace your fingers behind your head." The officer says pulling his taser.

Seeing no way he can run away fast enough to not get tasered or shot, Jake obeys and the officer places him in cuffs.

"Do you have any weapons or contraband on you?"

"Yeah, I have a pocket knife in my pants pocket."

"Anything else?"

"No."

"Why didn't you tell me who you are? Are you Jake Crocker?"

"Um."

"Um, what? Are you telling me you don't know your name?"

"Yeah, I mean no."

"Do you have any ID on you?"

"No."

"How did you get here, did you drive?"

"Yeah."

"And you don't have ID on you. So where is your driver's license if you drove here?"

"It's in my car."

"Okay, so again I'm asking you, what is your name?"

"Jake. Jake Crocker."

"Now was that so hard to answer? Why wouldn't you identify yourself when I asked you originally?"

"I was scared."

"You were scared? What had you been doing that you needed to be scared?"

"Um, I was just walking."

"You were just walking, but you don't live here. So where were you walking from? What's back there where I saw you come from before I stopped you?"

"I don't know, I was just walking."

"Dispatch, this is Adam 7." Officer Kelly says into his shoulder mic. "I have a suspect in custody at the Bridgestone Apartment Complex matching an open APB for Jake Crocker. I observed the suspect coming from the building acting suspiciously and apprehended him. I'm requesting backup to my location."

"You're arresting me? I didn't do anything."

"Yes, I'm arresting you because there is an APB on you and you can't account for yourself and what you're doing here." Officer Kelly says walking Jake to his patrol car.

"Watch your head. I'm going to leave you here until backup arrives and go investigate where you came from when I saw you. Sit still and don't cause any problems."

Closing the door of the patrol car with Jake secured inside, Officer Kelly walks to the area where Jake appeared from and notices a lock on a utility door has been pried loose. Opening the door carefully, he sees it's the maintenance closet for the elevator. Further inspection shows the main for the elevator has been shut off. Nothing looks amiss so he throws the main to the on position and the elevator starts up. Closing the closet door and walking to the elevator, a man and a woman step out visibly shaken.

"Officer," Sam says. "We need to talk to you. I think we're in danger."

"Your name?"

"Sam, Sam Stormen and this is Ann Picard."

"You're the party in the complaint against Jake Croker. I apprehended him a short while ago. It looks like he broke into the elevator maintenance closet and shut it down with you in it."

"Oh my God!" Ann blurts.

"Yes ma'am. He's in custody now and backup is en route. Here's the backup now. Would you two come with me?"

"Okay." Sam says as he and Ann follow the officer to the car of Officer Kelly's backup.

A quick explanation of the events from Officer Kelly to his backup put things in action. Sam and Ann are asked to standby as an officer retrieves his fingerprint kit from his trunk and heads to print the maintenance closet. Officer Kelly contacts the building superintendent and has him come down to ensure no damage other than the lock has been done to the closet. A report of the events is written up. Statements are taken from Ann and Sam stating that they were indeed trapped in the elevator making Jake's mischief an intentional act being he waited until Ann and Sam had entered the elevator.

"Since the two of you were trapped in the elevator when he shut it down, we are charging him with assault and kidnapping. The super says there isn't any other damage to the elevator other than the closet lock so we are charging him with vandalism as well."

"What about when he trapped me in my apartment?"

"We don't have any witnesses placing him at the scene, but it's obvious he knows where you live and was caught on premises this morning for purposes of mal intent so the DA may extend charges on him on that as well since he seems a likely suspect."

"When I took Ann home last night, we discovered her apartment had been broken into. Jake's been following me so he also knows where she lives. He's also been stalking her at work. Can you have someone come by her place to finger print and check things out. That's where we were

headed when we were stuck in the elevator. We were coming to talk to you and then see if we can get video from the
surveillance cameras at her place."

"So your place has cameras? Give me the name of the
complex and I can call and get them to pull a copy on the
way over. Do you have the number for the super?"

"Yes, it's the same as the leasing number. Let me write
it down for you. Should we head over there?"

"Yes, but I need you both to sign the complaint for this
event first. It will be ready in just a minute. My partner is
finishing up his portion. Let me check with him and update
him on the events at your place ma'am."

"Okay." Ann says to the officer.

"I guess we have to wait before going to Max's place.
Maybe we were wrong after all. Maybe this was Jake all
along." Sam says to Ann.

"I know. Let's hope this was all Jake because the other
is unthinkable. If it was Jake, then at least this is over and
we can get back to normal."

"Amen to that." Sam says.

"Well, we've dusted the bedroom window for prints and the
area around the kitchen where you said your doll was sitting. We also dusted the kitchen and bedroom door frames
for prints. I'm sorry, but the finger print dust makes a bit
of mess I'm afraid. We found some prints but we'll need to
get prints for the two of you in order to rule them out. We
didn't do more surfaces to prevent making a mess for you
so we may not find any prints that are useful."

"I understand." Ann says pouting looking at all the
black print dust all over her previously white surfaces.

"We are going to need to analyze the prints taken and
the video. The video does show someone lurking around,
but the face of the person isn't clear. The lab will have to

enhance it to get a better image. For now, the man in the video seems to fit the same basic height and weight of Mr. Crocker, but we can't say for sure it was him. It could just have been a random break in. I know that's no comfort in light of the other events."

"I understand. Thank you Officer."

"Yes ma'am, you're welcome, goodbye."

"Wow, what a day?" Sam says when the officer leaves.

"So this may have been Jake after all." Ann says.

"I don't know if that makes me feel better or worse."

"I know. It was one thing for Jake to bother me at work, but to think that he could have broken into my apartment and touched my stuff makes my skin crawl."

"It's okay Ann, they got him. He won't be back here. Not now that he's been caught. Hopefully he won't be able to make bail."

"I hate to say it, but amen!" Ann says.

"Well I guess I should call Mark now." Dialing Silvan the receptionist answers.

"Silvan Enterprises, how may I direct your call?"

"Hey Marilyn, this is Sam Stormen. I'm calling to talk to Mark."

"Let me transfer you Sam."

"Mr. Goodman's office."

"Hey Sue, this is Sam Stormen. I'm calling to talk to Mark."

"I'm sorry Sam, but Mark isn't in. He left early last Friday without saying anything to me and hasn't been in since. He hasn't contacted me so I don't know when he'll be in."

"Oh, well I guess I'll call him on his cell phone then."

"I'm afraid that won't work. He left it here with his jacket and briefcase. He never does that. I've called his home to check on him, but there's no answer."

"That is strange. Well if you hear from him, would you have him call me, it's important."

"Sure thing Sam."

"Bye."

"What was that about?' Ann asks.

"Sue says Mark left early last Friday without telling her and didn't take his stuff with him and hasn't been in or called since."

"Wow, that's not like Mark. He always has his cell with him."

"Well let's go see Max and fill him in on everything. Maybe we can all go get lunch or something."

"So Max, what do you think? Do you think this was really all Jake now that they caught him red-handed or do you think it could be this Almir Najya?"

"I don't know. I'd like to say it was Almir Najya, but he would have no way of even knowing about our involvement or non-involvement in his shipment, whereas Jake had cause and opportunity and was caught in the act."

"I know that's what's bothering me too."

"Well there's not much we can do about it. We can't really go to the police and claim a terrorist might be after us because then we'd have to explain about Mark's sting and we were sworn to secrecy even though it's over. Mark was working with the government on that and we don't know who his contact is to report things and we can't talk to Mark so we're stuck for now."

"I know and that bothers me. At least Jake is in jail and if all is good, he won't get bail which means things should calm down now."

"I saw the article in the newspaper this morning." Mark

says to his contact.

"Yes, we didn't want to release the information, but my boss felt we might get some tips if the public was made aware. Extra eyes and all that stuff. There have been calls coming into the tip line, but so far they're all cranks. The article didn't list a description of Almir Najya so unless someone who knows him personally comes forward I don't see much credible information coming through."

"But what about Max and Sam? They'll have seen the article. You don't want them to get ideas and think they're in danger. You know how Max is."

"Good point. I'm sure everyone has noticed you aren't at work and haven't called in. Maybe you should call your secretary and tell her you had to leave for a personal family emergency. Just say your wife's sister took ill and you've been with family and that's why you've been out of touch."

"I need to tell her something. She'll worry since it's not like me to be out of touch. I can say I was so upset when my wife called that I forgot to take my cell when I ran out."

"Very good. Just be careful and don't give anyone any location details where they can look for you. How's your wife holding up?"

"She's concerned, but at least we're safe here. I'll call you back after I call the office."

"Hello Sue, this is Mark. I'm sorry I ran out and didn't talk to you last week."

"Yes sir, I was very worried that something had happened when I couldn't reach you."

"Yes, I'm sorry. I didn't think. My wife called and there was a family emergency. It caught me off guard and I just ran out."

"When I discovered your jacket and cell were still here that bothered me, but then I noticed your car was still here too.”

“Yes, I was too shook up to drive safely so I called a cab. I’m sorry I worried you.”

“Don’t worry about it boss. I’m glad you’re okay. I hope everything is okay with your family.”

“It’s still touch and go, so we’re praying. That’s all we can do.

“Is there a number I can reach you at?”

“No. We’ve been in the ICU most of the time and moving around to different family members. It’s best I just call you when it’s convenient. I just didn’t want you to worry. I don’t know how long I’ll be out.”

“Okay. Oh, Sam Stormen called you this morning. He asked that you call him because it’s important he said. There’s nothing else that can’t wait. Do you need his num-ber?”

“Yes, please. I’ll call him. Thank you Sue.”

Chapter Twenty-Six

"Sam. My secretary said you called and it was important."

"Yes, I did. Thanks for getting back to me. Are you okay? Sue said you left suddenly and hadn't contacted her."

"Yes, I apologize. We've had a family emergency we've been dealing with. I was distraught and didn't think when I ran out."

"I hope everything will be okay."

"Me too. So what's up? What's up that's important?"

"I hate to have to tell you all this when you're dealing with family issues but I thought you should know.

"Know what? You're scaring me. What's going on?"

Sam relays all the events of the past week and then admits when he saw the paper this morning that he thought maybe this wasn't Jake after all until the cops caught him at his place this morning.

"Oh my God! Are you all alright?"

"Yes. We're a bit shaken up, especially Max. His house suffered a lot of damage. If another few minutes had lapsed we all could have been killed."

"You've caught me off guard here. I'm still trying to process all this. I had no idea. I'm sorry. I've been involved in my own issues."

"That's okay boss. Being we all work for you, and with the recent events, I thought you should know before the cops contact you or you read something in the paper. You know how news people can be. Since we all work at Silvan they might bring the company into things just to hype the story."

"I appreciate you considering that. I have to go, but I'll check back with you in a day or so. Feel free to call Sue as I'll be checking in with her."

"Adam, I called Sue and gave her the story we discussed, but she said Sam called and said it was important so I called him. I gave him the same family emergency story, but he had a horrendous one to tell me. I think you need your people to look into it. Let me tell you what I learned."

"Mark, you're right. We looked into the events you mentioned. I agree that some of them were perpetrated by Jake, but we believe at least a couple of them may have been Almir Najya."

"That's what I was afraid of." Mark says.

"Yeah I believe the attempted arson at Sam's and the fire at Max's were definitely Almir Najya or his crew. I don't know how he could have learned about them or why he is targeting them. My people believe that your computer network at Silvan has been hacked and that may be part of how they have obtained information."

"You're kidding, right?"

"No, I'm not."

"I considered bringing them into protective custody also, but it seems anyone in the company could be at risk at this point so that's not going to work."

"So what are we going to do?"

"We're working on it. I'll have to get back to you. We think we need to form a plan that will pull Almir out into the open where we can nab him once and for all. It means putting you and Max and Sam in the line of fire, with protection of course."

"Whatever, this has to end! I can't stay in hiding forever and I don't want my wife to be in danger any longer."

"Okay well, let us put a plan together and get back to you."

"Hey Mark. Since we know you're computer system and

email have definitely been hacked, we think we should use that. We propose that you send Max and Sam an email to their company accounts stating that you want to have a meeting with them about the 'Jamaica thing'. We think using those words will get Almir's attention. We're going to make arrangements for you to have a secret meeting out of the office. That will also get his attention, but before we do anything we've decided to print an article in the paper stating that the government now thinks Almir has left Florida and possibly the US so he'll let his guard down thinking he no longer has to be careful."

"That sounds like a good plan. I need my people safe. It was one thing when this revolved only around me. I was willing to help my country to catch a few known terrorists if we could or even just Almir, but this whole thing is now out of control. I've learned that Dave, one of my security guards was mugged after work and his wallet and Silvan ID was taken. More and more of my people are coming under fire."

"I understand. Mark you've gone above and beyond to help your country and since we got you into this, we are working to get you out of it."

"Good, the sooner the better."

"I'll be in touch soon with a plan."

Wednesday morning an article appears in the local paper stating that the terrorist Almir Najya has been sighted in Europe. Authorities believe he was secreted into South Florida near the Miami area for a meeting where he'd been sighted, but has since left to meet up with cell members in London where authorities believe has been his base of activities for nearly a year now. Attempts to learn more about his activities here in Florida have been unsuccessful.

Another article also appears in Wednesday's paper.

> Several weeks ago, Silvan Enterprise's Jamaica plant was at the center of a suspicious shipment of possible chemical weapons being shipped to London, England to a terrorist cell located there. Although Silvan Enterprises does not make weapons of any sort, it was suggested that they had been the source of the suspicious shipment intercepted at Heathrow Airport. The return address for the shipment led to an empty field in Jamaica, but the shipment looked like a shipment of batteries that Silvan Enterprises does produce in their Jamaica plant. It had been suggested that a shipment of battery casings might have been stolen from Silvan causing them to be implicated. A multi-national investigatory committee has completed their investigation and although they do not have a suspect in the incident, Silvan Enterprises has been cleared of any involvement whether directly or indirectly in the suspicious shipment. A spokesperson for Silvan stated he was glad to see the company has been vindicated in this situation and that the company would never have any involvement in such a deleterious act.

"Good morning Mark. Did you see the articles in this morning's paper?"

"Yes, I did. Thank you. It was good to see the article clearing Silvan Enterprises of involvement in the shipment."

"Yes we hoped that if Almir sees that article and then sees the email you're going to send that it will entice him into action."

"So you've come up with a plan then?"

"Yes we have, we are just fine tuning it and getting things in place."

"When do you want me to send out the email?"

"We'll draft it up and send it to you. All you'll need to do is copy it into your company email and send it. You will have it in a couple hours. You can plan on going into work tomorrow. We're going to keep your wife in the hotel for another day."

"Okay, good."

Mark sends an email addressed to Sam and Max. The subject line says 'Staff Meeting'. The body says:

Hey Guys,

I'm sure you've seen the article in today's paper vindicating our company in the 'Jamaica thing'. This is very good news. It makes me very happy that this article was placed here in Florida for all to see instead of just in Jamaica where the incident happened.

Now that we have been cleared, it's time that we meet to discuss this situation further and plan where we intend to go from here. I'm sure you both also saw the article stating that Almir Najya is back in London. I know you may have had some concerns, but all has worked out as I anticipated.

I have planned a private meeting for the three of us to have a late lunch at the Hampton Inn near the office, so that we may talk freely. I have leased a limo to carry us to and from the hotel and have leased a private conference room where lunch will be catered by the hotel. This privacy away from unwanted ears will ensure we have no leaks in planning our next step.

Thank you for your trustworthiness and assistance in this matter.

Mark

"Hi Max. I need you to do me a favor."

"Sure boss."

"I need you to call me back at the number I'm going to give you, but you can't use any phone connected to you. If you can run out somewhere quick and use a public phone, the better."

"This sounds ominous."

"Please Max, it's important."

"Okay. Give me the number and I'll call you right back in a couple minutes."

"Hello."

Hey boss, what's up with the cloak and dagger?"

"I need you to get with Sam after we talk, but do it in person and not over the phone, understand?"

"Yeah sure."

"Did you see the paper this morning?"

"Yeah. That's great what it said. Almir Najya has left the country."

"Well that's what this call is about. The article was a fake. My contact Adam had it placed because we have a plan to pull him out in the open where he can be apprehended once and for all. My wife and I have been sitting in protective custody since last Friday and we suspect many of the things you and Sam have been through are also related."

"You're kidding, but they caught Jake red-handed. Sam told me you were dealing with a family issue."

"Yes, my own. Jake's deranged vendetta has definitely muddied the water, but your fire and several other events were likely due to the Jamaica situation. I'm told that Silvan's computer network has been hacked. It appears my email was the source of the infiltration and how they learned of yours and Sam's involvement."

"Why didn't you say something?"

"I didn't learn about the email and computer hacking until late yesterday. When Sam related your events over the past few days I realized that I wasn't the only one in danger, and now it's extending outward to other employees as well who had no involvement. At this point, everyone in the company could be a target so we've come up with a plan to end this."

"Wow! So we're still in danger even though Jake has been captured."

"Sort of. I'm having Fred Holland order around the clock surveillance for you and Sam until tomorrow evening. I understand it had already been ordered so he is merely extending it. It's already been done."

"Thanks boss. I don't know if I could sit up another night trying to watch my house."

"Yes, that's why I'm calling. I've sent you and Sam a dummy email to your work account. It was designed to draw Almir Najya and his people out in the open. When

you read it, I need you both to play along. Several under
cover government personnel will be around some of whom
will be at work and other places. An army of tactical staff
will be around to capture and seize these individuals. This
means you can't comment on any new faces you notice
hanging around. We don't want to blow this."

"I understand boss. Are you sure this plan will work?"

"I believe that when you see the email and it's wording
that you will agree it was designed to incite anger and get
these people to strike. The article this morning was designed to make them feel like the pressure is off if the government believes they have left."

"Okay. I'll check it when I get home. I'll call Sam and
have him come over and fill him in. I have a question
though."

"What is it?"

"You said Fred is putting surveillance on just Sam and
me, but what about Ann?"

"She can stay with you guys or go to a hotel. For now,
we're trying to keep the scope of this directed at you, Sam
and myself for anyone watching. No one knows about any
involvement by her and we're keeping it that way. Anything that's happened to her is probably because of her relationship with Sam."

"Oh, okay."

"When you discuss this with Sam, I'd appreciate it if you
don't disclose any more to Ann than is necessary. We need
her to act normally since we don't know who may be watching."

"Understood. I think Sam will prefer that anyway. She
has taken this pretty hard and may not be comfortable
knowing he and I are still in the line of fire. What should
we say is the reason for the security being extended?"

"Good point. Just say that the police are attempting to

make sure that Jake didn't have an accomplice in his vendetta against you. No one will question the actions of a
madman. You can tell her that I fully intend to dismiss him
from the company so she won't have to deal with him at
work anymore. That should make her feel better."

"Yeah, it will. Thanks."

"I hope you and Sam are okay that I need to use you to
help end this, but there really isn't another way. Being
three of us have already been targets, it was decided that
if we are together making it easy for them to attempt to get
us all at one time, they may make their strike. The email
is pretty inciting if I say so. Adam wrote it intentionally for
that purpose."

"Well, I think we'll all be glad to have this behind us. I
never imagined things could turn so crazy." Max says.

"Alright, well I'll see you tomorrow at work. Be careful."

"Will do."

"Hey boss, you're back."

"Yeah, good morning Sue. Do I have any messages?"

"Yes, they're on your desk. Nothing urgent. Tony wants
to talk to you about something with the computers. He
didn't say what."

"Tell him I'm swamped today, but I'll meet with him tomorrow."

"Yes sir. Anything else?"

"Yes. I scheduled a late lunch today. Max and Sam will
be joining me to go over a new project. A limo should be
here around two to take us to lunch. Oh, and I hired some
extra security people being I heard that Dave was mugged
and his credentials were taken."

"Okay. I'll send out a memo. Are they here long term or
temporary?"

"Temporary."

"Hey Sam, are you ready to head out for lunch?"

"Yeah. I haven't really been able to focus today. Albert noticed so I had to tell him it was due to the fire at your house and the antics of his friend Jake."

"He apologized. He said he didn't know Jake was so un-balanced. He knew he was a little off, but never imagined he was crazy. When I told him we were having lunch with Mark this afternoon he assumed it was to make up for Jake, so I let him believe that. He wondered why we were having lunch late though, so I just said it was probably be-cause Mark was swamped on his first day back."

"Sounds like you handled him well."

"It seemed like he was okay with things."

"Hey Sue, is the boss ready to go?"

"I think so, the limo is here and I believe he is finishing up an important call. He should be right out."

"Hey guys. Let's roll, I'm starved. What a day. I guess that's what I get for missing a couple days."

"Yeah, same here. I miss one day and I couldn't believe the calls and emails." Max comments.

Chapter Twenty-Seven

"Well boss, lunch was great but it doesn't look like Almir took your bait." Max says.

"Max, we were the bait." Sam says.

"Okay boys. There may be several reasons why nothing's happened. Maybe some of the security here was noticed or there may not have been enough time allowed for this lunch since the email was sent. We know the email's been hacked, but we don't know how closely it's being monitored. I was hoping to end this today, but it may take another day or two. I'll make sure you both have protection until this is over."

"That makes sense. I guess it was foolish to hope we could get this over this quickly." Sam says.

"True, but when Adam set this plan, I hoped since there had been so many events these last few days for all of us that we were striking while the iron was hot and we had their attention." Mark says.

"I guess all we can do is head back to work for now. I'm sure Adam will come up with another plan." Max says.

"Yeah, after the past few days, I can't see him stopping now unless it really was Jake after all."

"I doubt that. Adam said his people looked into your events and there's no way it could all be Jake. He had a behavioral analyst look at everything and he agrees."

"Well thanks for getting the limo." Sam says getting in. "I've never ridden in one before."

"Really?" Max says getting in behind Sam.

"Well, enjoy it Sam. I know Max uses one every now and then when he's trying to woo a new client." Mark says closing the door behind him.

The window separating the driver partially lowers just enough so that the drivers' eyes are visible acknowledging their entry in the car. "Where to?"

"Back to Silvan, Tom." Mark says.

"Sam asks, "Isn't the driver supposed to get out and as-sist you into the car?"

"Maybe for regular limo service, but I use this company a lot and Tom has a hip problem so he knows I don't hold him to those expectations. He's an excellent driver and dis-crete."

They begin moving and just as Mark finishes talking, the window comes down more showing that Tom isn't driv-ing the limo.

"Who... are you? Where's Tom?"

"Ah, that is the question isn't it?"

"Tom has been removed you could say. My name is Sa-far. The three of you have caused me much difficulty these past days."

"Why? What do you mean? What's this about?" Mark yells.

"Let me have my friend here explain." Safar says as Al-mir sits up smiling.

"Oh my God!" Max yells.

"Yes, you understand Max. Too bad your house wasn't totally destroyed. You and Sam here could have been dis-posed of so that I only needed to find Mark and deal with him. It was nice of you to make this easy for me so I could get you all at one time."

"What are you going to do to us?" Sam manages weakly.

"Ah, yes, that is the question isn't it. Well for starters, I foretell that you will die today. However before I carry out my deadly plans I want you all to suffer first. I intend to take out all of Silvan Enterprises before I end the three of you. This company has caused me much money and loss and now you will lose."

"What do you mean you're going to take out Silvan?"

Mark asks.

"What I mean is I intend to blow Silvan Enterprises to smithereens as you Americans say. You see, we planted explosives all over the building. You see, your security man was careless and we were able to rob him easily enough and get his clearance ID along with vital security codes he was nice enough to carry in his wallet. Overnight, we were able to plant devices to make it go boom. You understand boom right? I'd hate for you to be confused here. My plan is so sweet that you need to understand that I am tired of playing with you."

"No! You can't do that?" Mark yells.

"Ann." Sam says quietly.

"Ah, yes Sam, your girlfriend also works at Silvan. I'm sorry to say you won't be seeing her again, alive."

Tears are streaking down Sam's face. Max's eyes are wild with rage and fear as Mark is sinking into submission.

"Don't fret guys. We will arrive at Silvan shortly so this will all be over soon." Almir says smiling.

Max covertly retrieves his cell phone from his pocket without excessive movement so as not to be noticed and sends a text to Carl his friend in security that says 'limo 911'.

"Okay boys, now that you know my plan, you'll pardon me if I ask you to lace your fingers behind your head. I wouldn't want you to think you could try anything not that you could from way back there, but better safe than sorry as you Americans say."

Max is glaring now at Almir and would love to lunge for him except that Almir is holding a gun on them.

"Safar, once we get off the main roads speed up. The access road to Silvan is long and I'm in a hurry."

Yes Almir. We're almost there."

"How do you intend to set off your bombs?" Max asks.

"Yes, I left that part out didn't I? Well I have a detonator here. I only need to push the button once we are in range. We must get close so you'll have a front row seat, don't worry. Then Safar and I will jump out and you will drive into your precious burning company. Of course you will each have a bullet in your heads first of course."

"Don't be so sure." Max yells his vile ranging higher.

"Aw, see Safar. Even when they are licked, these Americans don't know when to give up. They always think they can win even if they can't."

"Almir, it looks like we are being followed. Not closely, but there is a car following us."

"Yes!" Max yells. "We are being followed. You are not as smart as you think you are."

"Max shut up!" Sam whispers. "You're antagonizing him. You're going to make him shoot us sooner."

"Listen to your friend Max. He is scared as he should be."

"Yeah well, you're going to kill us anyway so I'm going to say my peace."

"You are brave I see. Too bad that won't help you. So who is it that is following us as you say?"

"Government agents. They know you are still here and used us as bait to catch you."

"Too bad. Didn't you know that it never works out for the bait."

"Maybe we'll just shoot you after the explosion and use the chaos to get away. We only need a short head start to get far enough away to dump the limo."

"Where is Tom?" Max asks.

"Don't worry, he's nearby. In fact, he isn't far behind you. The trunk is quite roomy."

"Is he dead?" Mark asks weakly.

"Ah, I'm afraid so, but don't fret. He never saw it coming."

"Here's the access road Almir."

"Good, hurry. Let's get in range, push this button and get away in the confusion of the explosion."

"I am sorry I will only have a few seconds of pleasure watching each of you die. My plan for you was so much better, but this will do also! As long as you suffer and die, I am happy."

Mark is at a loss for words. He can't believe things have gone so badly. All he can do is pray silently that somehow this will end without his company blowing up killing hundreds of employees. This was not what he anticipated when Adam approached him months ago to help them. Naively he never thought anyone but himself would ever face any danger. Now, realizing he has doomed an entire company is too much for him to cope with.

The limo races along the access road approaching the front of Silvan Enterprises' main building. The driver is speeding along above sixty miles per hour!

Sam feels his heart pumping yet his mind is fuzzy. None of his dreams have been this horrifying. *Another minute and it will be all over! This is it, our final ride!*

Almir Najya smiles broadly at Max. "Well Max, just another few seconds. How convinced are you that you will win now?"

"Ah, pretty good actually." Max has been watching carefully ever since they entered the access road to Silvan. Sitting in the middle and with the visor down they can all see out the front windshield. Off to the side of the road sitting low to the ground are small lights that are used to light the private access road at night. As expected, he saw a quick flash of the lights closest to the building notifying him that his message has been received.

As Sam looks onward to his amazement, the large steel barrier walls rise up suddenly out of the roadway. The Limo can't stop in time traveling at such a high rate of speed. They are so close to the steel wall when it comes up they only have seconds to stop. Almir never sees it happen, as his back is to the windshield as he holds his gun on the trio and confidently converses with them. Safar sees the wall come up too late to do anything and screams out. He tries to call out to Almir, but Almir doesn't have time to turn around before the limo pummels into the wall at full speed.

Mark, Max and Sam all see the wall when it rises suddenly, but fully expect to die in the crash. Max's last thought before the crash is that at least they are unable to get within range for Almir to set off the explosives. The wall is too far away so even though he may die, his text has saved everyone else. The men were all able to fasten their seat belts before learning of their kidnapping, but at such a high rate of speed, they will likely not survive.

Sam hears a single gunshot as they crash and all goes dark. The final ride is over!

Take away the pain!" Sam is screaming inside his mind. Then he feels like he's floating on a cool breeze as everything fades away. The sky goes black and his mind goes blank.

Later when he becomes aware, the first thing he feels is being scared, frightened. He has no idea where he is. He imagines a wistful peaceful melody is playing from a church organ from somewhere. He suddenly feels overjoyed instead of scared. Old friends are standing around him and smiling. Some of the friends are children from his grammar school days. They are humming to the melody the organ is playing. He remembers the old church hymn from his childhood. The experience is peaceful. He is lost in the enjoyment of the music and the humming. He is at peace with the world.

As he lay there in peace and happiness, a faint beeping emerges from the distance. The sound grows louder and begins to nag at him. It is out of sync with the melody. The steady beeping continues to grow louder and louder. He begins hearing faint voices in the distance as the music and humming fade away completely. He tries to force the beeping noise from his head. He wants the melody to come back. The beeping just grows louder until he awakes and opens his eyes. He realizes he is lying in a bed.

Everything he sees as he looks up is white. He thinks, *Am I in Heaven?* Until the sounds of hospital monitors beeping and nurses chatting nearby brings him back to reality. There is a pain in his right shoulder.

He looks to his left, and sees Ann smiling and staring at him as she sits by his bed. As he focuses on her, he sees her eyes are red from crying. Her blond hair falls over her shoulders and her steel gray eyes are starting to water up. She still looks wonderful to him!

"Hello, Sam," She says. "Welcome back, my love!"

"What a sight for sore eyes!" He says but his throat is dry and his voice is raspy.

"You came back to me."

"Where am I?" He asks.

"You're in Holy Cross hospital. You all made it. You have some scars but you made it! I thought you'd want to know that right away."

"Everyone made it? Max and Mark, too?"

"Yes, but the bad guys were both killed. They died instantly. The driver and Almir were killed when the Limo smashed into the barrier. Mark broke his right wrist and

received a good bump on the head. He had a slight concus-
sion. Max has some bruises from the seatbelt, and mild
whiplash, go figure.

How am I?" He questions suddenly worried about himself. "Why am I in bed hooked to machines."

"You're going to be fine." She assures him.

"So why do I have all these tubes if I'm okay?"

Ann nods and smiles again. "Yes, love. Everything
should be all right. You have been in a coma for several
days, but the doctor told me all the tests are fine. He said
as soon as you wake that means things are returning to
normal."

"A coma? What happened?"

"When the limo crashed into the barrier, Almir was in
the process of turning towards the front to see what the
problem was, but still had his finger on the trigger of the
gun and it went off in the crash. The bullet struck you in
the shoulder and between the impact of the limo hitting the
wall and the bullet hitting you; you were thrown against
the side doorjamb hitting your head hard. The force of the
impact was severe and the authorities say the only reason
you all survived was because of the extra length of the limo
over that of a normal sized car. It also helped that you were
all in the back seat the farthest away from front because
the limo looked like an accordion after the impact. As it
was, they needed to cut you guys out of it.

By the time the paramedics got to you; you'd lost a lot
of blood from the gunshot wound. Then because of how
hard your head hit, you had some swelling in your brain.
The doctors felt it best to induce a coma to allow time for
the swelling to subside. That's why you're hooked up to machines. They only removed the breathing tube last night
after your last MRI showed the swelling was nearly gone
and they started the process to reverse the coma. At that

point, it was touch and go because they needed to be sure you could breathe on your own and you did. Next, we needed to wait until you awoke on your own because that would mean the swelling was gone and your brain was healing. You'll need to go for some tests, but the doctor said it wouldn't be anything major. He assured me that once you woke up that you would be out of the woods. I've been here by your side most of the time praying you would wake up. Now my prayers have been answered!" Ann grabs a tissue from the box on the side table and pauses to dab at her eyes and gently blow her nose.

A nurse enters into the room having noticed from his monitors at the nurse's station that his heart rate had increased indicating he'd likely awakened. "Well, hello Mister Stormen! I see you are awake finally. How are you feeling?"

"Okay, thank you," He answers. "Can you take off all these tubes?"

"Not quite yet, but I believe as soon as you come back from some tests the doctor's ordered for you that we'll be able to do it then." The nurse says.

"Great can we do them now then?"

"Afraid not. I requested someone to come and get you. They'll take you for your tests and when you come back we'll remove everything."

"Well, it can't be fast enough for me. When will I be released?"

"That's up to the doctor, but I expect once he's reviewed your test results that he'll want you to stay for observation for another day or two."

"Another couple days, why?"

"Because it's standard procedure to make sure you can eat and use the restroom and stuff on your own. These are things that show that the connections in your brain are all functioning properly. You had a pretty bad conk on the head.”

“Yeah Max told the doctor he should see the car. That your head is so hard you left a dent in a perfectly good limo. Everyone laughed. You know how Max is.” Ann says smiling.

“Yeah, with friends like Max, who needs enemies?” Sam says shaking his head.

“Don’t shake your head like that Mister Stormen. We need you to remain still and not move around a lot until you are cleared after your tests.”

“Why?”

“We don’t want you to start shaking your head and causing more swelling. Behave for me because otherwise I’ll put you under again.”

“Yes ma’am. I don’t want that.” Sam says.

“I hope you mind me that easy when you get out of here.” Ann states.

“Oh he will.” His mom says entering the room. “I’ll make sure of that.”

“Mom! What are you doing here?”

“What do you mean, what am I doing here? You’re my son and you were nearly killed. Of course, I’m here. Your father is here too. He and Max are downstairs in the cafeteria. I texted them you’re awake and to get up here.”

“Until his tests, you need to limit the number of people in here.” The nurse spouts on her way out of the room.

By the time Max and Sam’s father arrive from the cafeteria, Sam’s room is empty, as he has gone for his tests. Ann fills them in and calls Mark to inform him. When he returns, most of his wires and tubes have been removed leaving only his catheter needing to be taken out. After two days, he is able to be released from the hospital. He has a thousand questions being he missed so much. A week has gone by since the crash.

He learns that Tom the driver was found dead of a bullet wound to the head in the trunk of the limo and that Silvan covered the expenses of his funeral out of respect. As for the company, there had been explosives planted in the building but had been located and removed quietly before most of the employees arrived that morning because the new security personnel Adam sent in brought in dogs who located the explosives without anyone knowing. There had been no need for Max to text Carl to put up the barrier wall when he saw the limo coming on the security monitors. Max didn't know that and although the wall wasn't needed to save Silvan, it did save each of them from being shot to death by the madman holding them hostage. The death of Almir Najya and his buddy Safar ended all involvement with the terrorists. Safar's cousin who'd hacked into Silvan was eventually caught and arrested by Adam's people when they traced things back to him.

Waiting to be released from the hospital, Ann remembers she forgot to update Sam on Jake. "Hey."

"Hey to you too my love." Sam says.

"Silly, be serious. I forgot to tell you something."

"What else could I have missed during my week long nap?"

"Lots. I'm afraid we'll be telling you as we remember I'm afraid. Anyway, I forgot to tell you about Jake."

"Oh yeah, I forgot about him. Is he out of jail?"

"Yeah, but not like you think. His sister Cindy came to see me."

"She did? Why?"

She wanted to apologize to me. She noticed Jake hadn't called her in a couple days and she couldn't reach him, so she went by his place. She didn't know he'd been arrested."

"Wow!"

"Anyway, when she let herself into his place she was horrified by what she saw. She said Jake has a long history of severe mental problems. She said his place was a pigsty, his medicines had gone untaken and unfilled. Apparently, he's been using his cell phone to take pictures of me without me knowing. He'd printed them out and they were plastered all over his walls."

"Oh my God!"

"Yeah, exactly. She said the recent photos had both of us in them and he either crossed you out of the picture or cut you out with a pair of scissors. She said it was very eerie seeing all those pictures and then with his mental issues and being off his meds, she was worried that she couldn't reach him. She said she was scared at what he might do."

"Looks like she had reason to be worried."

"I know, right? Anyway, she called the police, and reported him missing and also called his doctor and filled her in. The police came and photographed his apartment and began a missing persons', then discovered he was in lock up. His doctor reached out to the judge before his arraignment. The judge saw the pictures so he and Jake's doctor agreed that Jake wasn't fit to be released on his own recognizance and further agreed that due to the seriousness of the charges against him that he wasn't fit to aid in his own defense and ordered him committed to a mental hospital for no less than one year. At that time, they will revisit the charges against him."

"Holy cow! I knew he was unbalanced, but I guess I didn't suspect he was that far gone. How was he able to have any sort of 'normal' moments to fool people?"

"His sister said that's part of his illness. She knew he was able to fake being normal for short periods and so wanted to believe he was better that she didn't see it when she knew better. He'd even convinced his doctor until the end and stopped seeing her. Cindy is very sweet and nothing like her brother. I believe she is really sorry at what he did to us. She's taking responsibility for his actions herself."

"It's not her fault. He's deranged."

"I know. I told her we don't blame her. I think she's having a hard time forgiving herself for not watching him closer, especially in light of the events."

"Well at least he's locked up in the hospital and can't hurt anyone."

"Mr. Stormen, your ride is here." The orderly says bringing in the wheelchair that is to be the chariot for his release.

"Good, let's roll."

Arriving home at his apartment and having a steady stream of visitors, Sam can't believe everything he's learned. Late in the afternoon, all the members of the Danglebatts stop by to see him.

"Hey, good to see you guys!" Sam says seeing Chet, Dan and the other band members.

"We just stopped in to say hi and make sure you'll be able to jam with us again some time." Chet says.

"Everything's working just fine guys. I'm really looking forward to your concert next week, too."

After they leave, Max drops by and says "Guess what?"
"What Max, tell me about your week. As you know, mine has been kind of slow."

"Yeah, your nap had us all a little worried."

"I'm sorry, I'm just glad we all made it. I really thought we were all going to die. For a change, I can actually say one of your pranks has been a godsend. I never thought that would ever happen."

"Haha, yeah me too. I guess I should be re-named from King of Pranks to Max the Savior." Max smiles and gives a little bow and they both laugh heartily.

"Oh no, I think your little trick has created a monster." Sam says laughing and wincing and pain.

"No seriously, the insurance company has approved the reconstruction on my house, and it's already underway. It seems like between Jake's arrest and all the police reports of the incidents, they moved quickly to approve the claim."

"That's great Max. I'm sure you were happy to get that news."

"I'm not the only one. With all the incidents that happened and our impending death, I sort of proposed marriage to Peggy and she accepted."

"Oh my God Max! That's wonderful news, very surprising, but wonderful."

"She is waiting for you to recover before she'll set a date because she wants to be sure you can be my best man."

"I'd be happy to Max. I can't think of a better get well present."

"Great, I'll let her know."

"Max you have a habit of stepping in a pile and coming out smelling like a rose!" Sam jokes.

Finally, all the well-wishers have gone and Sam is visibly tired from the strain of moving around and trying to be social. He can see now why his visitors were limited in the hospital. To his relief, the knot in his stomach and the buzzing in his ears are gone.

Ann comes back into the room after seeing everyone out and looking at him knows he's had a long day. "Would you like me to bring you a pain pill?"

"No, it will make me sleepy and I've slept enough for now."

"Well, let me know if you change your mind. I ordered food for us and it's just been delivered. Maybe we should eat so you can take a pill and rest."

"We can eat in a bit. Come sit with me." He says as she strolls toward his bed. "I want to thank you for being here."

"Where else would I be? You scared me half to death. I was afraid you might not make it and was beside myself. You can't imagine how much I prayed sitting by your side."

"I know. Everyone said you've hardly left my side through this all, and now I hear you've practically moved into my place. I guess that proves you love me." Sam says teasingly.

"Yeah, I do. Now don't ever do that to me again, you hear?"

"Yes ma'am." He says sarcastically. "I do have a question though."

"Shoot."

"Will you move in with me?"

"I already did."

"No, I mean for real. Let's get rid of our apartments and buy a house, I'm ready to settle down. I'd ask you to marry me, except we've only been dating a few weeks."

"Yes."

"Yes to what."

"Yes, Sam. I love you. We can get a house; get married, whatever you want."

"How about a double wedding?"

Smiling, Ann shakes her head yes and leans in to kiss him. Even though Sam is stiff and sore from the gunshot wound and from lying in bed so long, he laughs with Ann. "Life is good!"

-0-

About the Author

 Living through many adventures in his life, from hurricanes to sink holes, from oak trees falling on houses to amazing rescues, has given Rob a wealth of stories to tell. He now enjoys writing adventure-mystery books that include some of his exciting life events.

Ever since he can remember, Rob wanted to write stories. Work and investment pressures prevented him from pursuing that field. He did a lot of non-fiction writing in the real estate business trying to make facts interesting, eventually writing an eBook on property management called *The Landlord Way* however; he always wanted to write fiction. He can visualize so many more adventures and interesting things happening in a good story.

His first novel *Deadly Plans* was inspired by remembering a visit to an orange bauxite lake of Jamaica. His Jamaican guide said nothing grows or lives in the lakes - a dumping place for the byproduct of Jamaica's Bauxite industry. Sometimes the littlest thing can have a lasting effect. However, the story became much more than a tale about the orange lakes. The title *Deadly Plans* evolved from the story itself. It is a tale of two friends Max and Sam who try to stop a shipment of deadly bombs. Max convinces Sam to travel to Jamaica with him. Sam, the conservative one is constantly worried about being killed. What Max inadvertently causes is a series of deadly plans.

Follow me at www.facebook.com/Author.Rob.Davis, www.authorrobdavis.com or email me at: robdavis@evershinepress.com